Death of a Glades Man

A Florida Keys Mystery

Book Three

Carl & Jane Bock

Habent Sua Fata Libelli

ABSOLUTELY AMAZING eBOOKS

Manhanset House
Shelter Island Hts., New York 11965-0342

bricktower@aol.com • tech@absolutelyamazingebooks.com
• absolutelyamazingebooks.com

Library of Congress Cataloging-in-Publication Data
Bock, Carl & Jane.
Death of a Glades Man
p. cm.

1. FICTION / Thrillers / Suspense. 2. FICTION / Mystery & Detective / Hard-Boiled. 3. FICTION / Thrillers / Crime. Fiction, I. Title.
ISBN: 978-1-1955036-44-3, Trade Paper

Author photo: Katie Ramirez

January 2023

Death of a Glades Man

A Florida Keys Mystery

Book Three

Carl & Jane Bock

Other books by Carl & Jane Bock

Dedication

To all those individuals working to restore
and save the Everglades and Florida Bay.

List of Characters

Central and Continuing Characters

Sam Sawyer, fishing guide and part-time sleuth living in Islamorada.
Katie Sawyer, forensic botanist. Married to Sam Sawyer.
George ("Snooks") Lancaster, fishing guide and bartender at Safari Lounge.
Flora Delaney, owner of Safari Lounge.

Law Enforcement

Stella Reynard, Detective, Monroe County Sheriff's Department.
Oscar Wilson, Deputy Sheriff.
Michael Spivey, Sheriff of Monroe County.
Anthony Hernandez, Monroe County Medical Examiner.
Del Blains, State's Attorney for Monroe County.
Walter Stone, Assistant State's Attorney for Monroe County.

Members of the Purple Isle Sportsman's Club

Arthur ("Whisk") Broom, retired New York City financier.
Fiona Broom, wife/widow of Art Broom.
Lou Farrelli, CEO/owner of Fantasy Cruise Lines.
Donna Farrelli, Lou's wife.
Rosalie and Tony Farrelli, Lou's grandchildren.
Johnny Krasuski, founder of national auto parts chain (retired).
Rashaan Liptan, former Miami Heat basketball star.
Julie Liptan, Rashaan's wife.

Serena and Candice Liptan, Rashaan's daughters.
Royal O'Doul, developer of Florida golf courses.
Norberto ("Norb") Padilla, Florida sugar cane grower.

Staff at the Purple Isle Sportsman's Club

Mel Campbell, fisheries manager.
Reuben Fletcher, security guard.
George ("Bud") Light, bartender.
Morrison ("Mo") Murikami, fishing guide.
Jacques Petain, cook (real name, Jason Pavlis).
Ralph Weatherbee, club manager.
Max Welty, head of security.

Miscellaneous Characters

Chet Avery, owner of a local fish market.
Marshall White, banker and one of Sam Sawyer's regular fly-fishing clients.

Chapter 1

They were little more than gray shadows moving across the flats under a pre-dawn light. But they were headed in our direction, and there were at least six of them. My client that day was Marshall White, a pint-sized bespectacled banker from Boston. He hadn't the look of a fisherman, but I knew better. He stepped up on the casting platform in order to gain all the height he could, and with one graceful cast dropped his purple and black bunny fly directly in front of the advancing school. There was a big swirl, and Marshall set the hook hard. Immediately the fish bolted for a bank of mangroves seventy yards out. We both knew if it reached the tangled mass of roots we would lose it. But Marshall put all he could into the rod, and it turned away just in time, breaking instead for open water.

The tarpon was a big one, probably better than a hundred pounds, maybe a hundred and a quarter. An hour and a half later we still weren't getting it anywhere near the boat. By now the August sun was beating down hard on the skinny waters of Florida Bay, putting glare in our eyes and sweat on our foreheads, especially Marshall's. Every time the fish jumped its big scales flashed silver in the early light.

The fish was in the middle of what we hoped might be its last run, when my cell phone chirped to life. Normally under these circumstances I would have let the call go to message, but a quick glance at the screen told me it was Stella Reynard, a detective with the Monroe County Sheriff's Department. She knew I guided fishermen for a living, and I was certain she wouldn't have bothered me if it weren't important.

"Hi Stella, what's up? I'm kinda busy right now." Just then Marshall let out a yelp. The tarpon had made a cartwheeling jump fifty yards off our bow, spraying water in all directions.

"You got a fish on?" Stella asked, almost rhetorically.

"We do. A good-sized tarpon."

"Okay, then I'll make this quick. We've got a floater over at the Purple Isle Sportsman's Club. Somebody found him face-down dead in their hogfish pond."

"Did you say hogfish *pond?*"

"That's what they're calling it. Personally, I wouldn't know a hogfish from a hedgehog. But—"

"I know what a hogfish is, Stella. But they've got 'em in ponds?"

"Apparently this place is all about the ponds. And they're salt water, not fresh. You ever been here?"

"Are you kidding? Everybody knows where the Purple Isle is, including me, but it takes an act of God to get inside the place unless you happen to be a member or one of their staff."

"Tell me about it. It's my day off and I was on the way to the grocery store in my own car when I got the call from dispatch. When I showed up at the gate they wouldn't let me in. Guess they thought I was somebody looking for work, or maybe a handout. Even after I showed them my badge, they seemed reluctant. I practically had to call out the National Guard."

"But you're in there now?"

"Uh huh, along with the medical examiner and another deputy. I finally got through to their head of security. Any chance you could get over here sometime today? There's something weird about this. Several things, actually."

"Weird how?"

At that point our conversation was interrupted by another shout from Marshall, as his tarpon jumped again, this time only twenty yards off our port side.

"Sorry Stella. Gotta go. I'll call you back as soon as we're done with this fish."

Unfortunately, it didn't take all that long. Marshall teased the tarpon in close enough to my skiff that I almost touched the leader, which we both knew would make it an "official" catch. Then suddenly it put all its energy into one final jump, and snapped off the fly.

Marshall collapsed onto the foredeck of my Hell's Bay flats boat like somebody whose legs had been knocked out from under him. He took off his cap and started wiping beads of sweat off his bald pate with a red bandana. "Damn, that was one fine fish." He shook his head.

"Oh well, it was fun while it lasted."

I was sorry to lose the fish, but at least now there was time to talk to Stella without worrying about interruptions. She'd always impressed me as somebody with a special inner calm, but just now I'd heard an unusual strain in her voice. I was curious and maybe a little bit worried.

~ ~ ~

The Purple Isle Sportsman's Club is one of the most exclusive resorts in all of the Florida Keys—maybe even in the whole southeastern United States. Technically it was inside the Village of Islamorada, but in fact they had their own little key on the bay side, connected to the rest of the village by a narrow bridge with a guard station. I'd heard lots of rumors about the place, mostly from other fishing guides. Membership was limited to thirty-five men and their immediate families. It cost a cool half a million to join, assuming you were lucky enough to get invited, and the annual dues were well up in the five-figure range.

I'd taken a few members fishing over the years, but we always met at my dock rather than at the club marina. They rarely told me their last names, and they almost always paid cash. These attempts at anonymity made me wonder if some of them had shady backgrounds. The average age of the guys I took out looked to be somewhere around eighty. I guess that's what happens when you have to wait for somebody else to die before getting asked to join the club. Maybe such an odd arrangement makes rich old men feel important.

~ ~ ~

Because Marshall White was a seasoned flats fisherman, thoroughly familiar with Florida Bay, I let him drive the boat home while I got back to Stella. Her phone went straight to voicemail, so I left a message: "Hi Stella, this is Sam Sawyer. We're on our way in. Give me a call when you get this. Bye."

She called back in less than five minutes. "Sorry, Sam. They have a rule about cell phones anywhere indoors here."

"Even for a sheriff's detective?"

After a pause: "Yeah, I know. But I'm back outside now, where things are more private anyway. How long is it going to take you to get over here?"

"We're on the south side of Palm Key, not far from Flamingo, so I'm at least an hour from my dock. Then I'll have to stow the gear and clean the boat. Oh, and probably walk the dog unless Katie got home early. Make it ninety minutes. Do you know who died?"

I heard paper rustling.

"Yeah. His name is Arthur Wellington Broom III. You ever heard of him?"

"The name sounds familiar, but I can't place the where or when of it."

"Maybe you know the man by his nickname. It's Whisk."

"As in whisk broom? You serious?"

"Yep. We learned it from the club manager."

"And the manager was the one who contacted you to report the body?"

"No. It was an anonymous call, apparently made from a landline in their main clubhouse, so it could have been anybody. All dispatch could tell me was that it sounded like a male voice."

"What did the caller say?"

"That they'd seen somebody push Broom into the water."

"I'm still not sure why you need me."

"Mostly I'd like you to take a look at the pond where they found the body. See what you think. The staff here have been reluctant to talk about it. If this turns out to be a crime scene, it was thoroughly messed-up before we even got here."

"Messed up how?"

"They have their own medical staff. A physician's assistant had the body moved to their clinic, where he began a preliminary examination."

"You're kidding."

"Wish I was. They claim it was to get a better look at the fellow and make sure he was beyond resuscitation. My guess is they were hoping to cover up this whole thing, make it look like an ordinary drowning, maybe the result of a heart attack or a stroke."

"But you think it might be something else?"

"Maybe. If the caller was right, and somebody shoved him into the water, that makes it more than an ordinary drowning, don't you think?"

"I see your point."

"Plus Anthony Hernandez, the county M. E., has taken a look at the body. He discovered some odd puncture marks on the arms and especially on the throat. None of us has ever seen anything like it."

"What was that all about?" Marshall asked, as soon as I got off the phone. "Did I hear you say somebody died?"

"Yeah. That was a detective I know with the sheriff's department. They found a body in one of the fishing ponds at the Purple Isle Sportsman's Club. She wants me to take a look at the crime scene."

"Crime scene? You mean he didn't fall into the pond by accident?"

"They're not sure." It occurred to me that Marshall might have been to the club, given his connections with the financial world. "You ever been to that place?"

"Nope. But I've heard some things about it."

"Like what? If you don't mind my asking, that is."

"Like it's way out of my price range, for one thing." Marshall stopped talking long enough to maneuver my boat through a narrow channel leading into the Rabbit Key basin, which we had to cross on the way home. "And I can't think of anything less interesting than fly fishing in a bunch of stocked ponds. That's what they have there, right?"

"Apparently. I've never been there either."

Marshall laughed.

"What?"

"I was just thinking. When I was too young to fish the real waters, my dad used to take me to one of those kiddie trout pond places. You know, where you get a cane pole and a can of worms, and you only pay if you catch something? Now I have this image of a bunch of rich old geezers doing the same thing, only with high-end fly rods."

Chapter 2

Ilive on Lower Matecumbe Key, in one of those developments where everybody is next to the water thanks to a network of man-made canals. My uncle built the house back in the 70s, and I inherited it after he died. It's a humble brown wooden structure, standing up on stilts as protection against tidal surges during hurricanes. We learned after Irma in 2017 just how important that is, and I'm grateful my uncle had the wisdom to design it that way even before it was part of the county code. The most recent hurricane, Ian, did little damage anywhere on Islamorada, including to our house.

Today our development is filling up with high-end places my uncle could not have imagined: lots of glass and concrete, swimming pools and tiki huts with built-in barbecues, and giant overpowered boats on big lifts. As a friend down the street put it recently: "Our neighborhood just isn't what it used to be, now that the billionaires are buying out the millionaires." Not that either of us comes close to qualifying for those financial categories.

But mostly it's a good place to live, with friendly neighbors and a deck that looks out on a canal alive with fish and wading birds and even the occasional crocodile. My wife Katie and I especially like sitting outside in the evening, enjoying the scenery and the wildlife along with Prince, our two-year old Welsh Corgi.

It wasn't always this way.

Seven years ago Katie and I lived in Fort Lauderdale, where we held faculty positions at the Florida Institute of Science and Technology. I was a vertebrate zoologist with a particular interest in birds. She was (and still is) a botanist with a specialty in forensic plant science—that's the use of plant evidence in criminal investigations. Then I suffered a colossal academic meltdown and ran away to the Florida Keys to become a fishing guide. Katie's career was booming, and she stayed behind. I didn't blame her. It was my midlife crisis, not hers. But it was hard living mostly apart, and we came close to splitting up several times.

Then, two years ago, Katie took a job at the Florida Keys Community College and moved down here full time. She heads up the program in forensic sciences in what has now become The College of the Florida Keys, and she stays busy with teaching and her criminal investigations. I also have put a toe into law enforcement. Mostly my cases have involved poaching or the sale of contraband wildlife, but occasionally I've gotten tangled up in more serious matters of murder and mayhem.

All of which explains the call that morning from Stella Reynard. It also marked the beginning of one of the most baffling cases Katie and I ever shared.

~ ~ ~

Katie had a class down in Key West that day, and she wasn't home when Marshall White and I got to our dock. Marshall helped me stow the gear and clean up the Hell's Bay, which was something most clients didn't do. He was flying back to Boston the next morning. He thanked me for the "almost tarpon," as he put it, and said he'd see me next time.

I leashed up Prince, took him for a short walk and fed us both an early lunch. Then I drove the short distance up the island chain to the point where a bridge connected Upper Matecumbe Key with the Purple Isle fishing club. There was a gate across the bridge, and a glassed-in guardhouse next to it. In the booth was a guy wearing a blue and white uniform that made him resemble a cop even though he wasn't. He looked familiar, but I wasn't able to place him. He was tall and heavyset, at least six-five, with a flat face, unruly blond hair, and beady blue eyes. A Monroe County sheriff's deputy named Oscar Wilson was standing in front of the gate. He was a balding man with round open face who usually worked as a desk sergeant at the Islamorada Substation. I'd met him before, and liked him.

Wilson instructed me to leave my Jeep Cherokee in a guest parking lot and ride with him. "These people are real fussy about who gets in and why," he explained.

We got in Wilson's cruiser, the guard raised the gate, and we drove onto the bridge.

A solid wall of mangroves faced us as we approached the property. There was no hint as to what lay beyond. I wondered if that was deliberate. Probably, from what I knew about the club. A two-lane blacktop continued from the end of the bridge, and after about thirty yards the mangrove hedge gave way to an immaculately groomed grassy savannah dappled with an overstory of well-spaced palms, gumbo limbos, poisonwoods, and other tropical trees. Scattered among the trees were what I later learned were called "The Cabins." They were similar in style, single story, with pale yellow stucco walls, red tile roofs, and covered porches. Gravel drives, many of them circular, led from the main road to the cabins. Signs at the end of the driveways had numbers on them, but no names. I surmised, correctly it turned out, that these were the residences of individual club members. I counted perhaps twenty of these, about half of which had vehicles parked next to them. These tended toward high-end SUVs, including Mercedes, BMWs, Cadillacs, and even a couple of Porches.

We followed the road until we came to the far side of the island, the one facing Florida Bay, where the main part of the Purple Isle Sportsman's Club sat right next to the water. It had three obvious components. First was the lodge, a long low structure of glass and concrete with a red tile roof matching the cabins. It was wrapped around a pool and patio leading down to a well-tended sandy beach. To the left of the lodge was a concrete marina. Three fishing vessels were tied up to the dock: two center-console Pathfinder bay boats of perhaps twenty-four feet, and an eighteen foot Hell's Bay flats boat similar to mine.

Beyond the fishing boats were a half dozen yachts of the ocean-going variety, another sign that I was in the land of the truly wealthy. Another component of the resort particularly caught my eye. Laying side by side down the shoreline beyond the marina was a series of rectangular ponds, each about half the size of an Olympic swimming pool, and each with a pump house at the end nearest the shoreline. Was one of these the hogfish pond Stella Reynard had mentioned? The one where Arthur "Whisk" Broom III had met his demise?

Stella was standing outside the entrance to the lodge as Oscar Wilson and I pulled to a stop. She was talking to a dark-haired young man I recognized as Anthony Hernandez, the county medical examiner. Stella had on khaki chinos and a white short-sleeved shirt. Her well-trimmed Afro sparkled in the midday sun, as did the sheriff's badge hooked to her belt.

"Hi, Sam," Stella said as I walked up to her. "Thanks for coming."

"Good afternoon, Stella. And Dr. Hernandez. Good to see you again."

We shook. "Stella, what would you like me to do here?"

She pointed toward the ponds. "The one where they found the body is marked with yellow crime scene tape. Could you go down and check it out?"

"Sure, but what would I be looking for, exactly?"

"No idea, really. But maybe your fisherman's eyes will spot something we missed."

I was halfway to what I assumed was the hogfish pond when a guy driving a golf cart came out from behind the main lodge and headed in my direction. He had red hair going to gray, with a short beard to match, and he was wearing a turquoise baseball cap with the Miami Dolphins logo on the front. When he got close I noticed a white five-gallon bucket sitting behind him in the cart.

"Afternoon," he said, as he pulled to a stop beside me. "Are you a new member? We don't normally allow fishing without staff present." Then he pointed over his shoulder. "And anyway, because of what happened this morning, you're not supposed to be here at all. Orders from that lady sheriff back there. I wouldn't be here except somebody has to feed the fish."

"No, I'm not a member. My name's Sam Sawyer, and Detective Reynard asked me to take a look at the pond where the body was found. I understand it's the one down there with the yellow tape around it."

"Oh. Well okay, then. My name's Mel Campbell, and I'm the fisheries manager for the club. Terrible thing what happened here. We're all in shock. Actually, it was me who found the body."

He leaned out of the golf cart and we shook. "Hop in and I'll give you a ride. You work for the sheriff's department?"

"Not exactly. But I know something about fish, and she thought I might see something the other people missed."

"Huh. Can't imagine what."

We pulled up beside the pond with the tape around it. I got out and walked over to the water's edge. From what I could tell the pond was around five or six feet deep, with a dark bottom. There were no signs of fish, but the water was murky and I hadn't brought my polaroids.

"You say there are hogfish in here? I'm not seeing any."

"Just wait," Campbell said. He got out of the cart carrying the white bucket. "It's feeding time."

He reached into the bucket, scooped out a handful of frozen shrimp, and tossed it into the water. In about fifteen seconds the pond came alive with fish. They came from all directions and quickly developed into a true feeding frenzy, snatching at the shrimp as they sank slowly to the bottom. It reminded me of a trout pond my dad had taken me to during a family vacation in Colorado, where they fed the fish some kind of special pellets.

I knew what hogfish looked like, of course: brick-red compact bodies, with snaggle-toothed snouts and spiky dorsal fins. Most of the fish grabbing at the sinking shrimp clearly were hogfish. But not all of them. There were others, about the same size, but multicolored with great long spines that seemed to come out all over their bodies.

Mel Campbell must have seen it too. "What the hell? Those look like *lionfish*! My god!"

"You haven't stocked them in here along with the hogfish?"

"Of course not! Those things can be lethal. Their spines are poisonous as hell! Why would we do that?"

"Good question," I said, remembering what Stella had reported about the strange puncture marks on the dead man's body. "Any chance they got in here by themselves?"

"Not unless they can walk or fly. The pumps that bring in seawater have filters to prevent that sort of thing."

Chapter 3

As anxious as I was to get back to Stella about the lionfish in the hogfish pond, I saw this as an opportunity to question Mel Campbell about what might have happened here. I also wanted to learn more about his operation in general.

"So, you discovered the body?"

"Yeah, I was out here first thing this morning working on one of the pumps when I found him. I got on my two-way and called the main office. They sent out the physician we keep on staff, and we pulled the man out of the water together."

"And you were sure he was dead?"

"That was the doc's call, not mine. But yeah, he was dead alright."

"How well did you know him? Mr. Broom, that is."

"Oh, about like all the other members, or maybe a little less since he didn't fish the ponds all that often. He preferred going out in the bay with one of our guides." Mel looked back at the pond, where the fish had eaten most of the shrimp and were beginning to sink back down into the dark water.

"Anything else you can tell me about Broom?"

"Just that he was rich as hell, like everybody else around here. Except for the help, that is." Then Mel frowned. "But say, what's with all the questions? You don't think I had anything to do—"

"No, no, nothing like that. I'm just trying to figure things out. Detective Reynard is a friend of mine, but she doesn't know much about fish." I pointed at the ponds. "As far as I know, this pond thing is pretty unusual, at least for the Keys. What varieties do you have here?"

"We have six ponds, each stocked with a different species. Right now, we have snook, redfish, pompano, hogfish, Spanish mackerel, and bonefish."

I knew that left out two important game species. "What about permit and tarpon?"

Mel shook his head. "Nope. For some reason the state fish and game people wouldn't let us stock those."

"Actually, I'm surprised they let you do this at all."

"Yeah, I was too when the club first hired me. But you gotta understand the political clout our members have. Hell, sometimes I get the impression they run the whole state."

"Where do you get the fish?"

"Mostly from the guides we keep on staff. When a member catches a good specimen, they put it in their live well and bring it back to the dock."

"Doesn't that take a lot of work?"

"Not most of the time. See we only allow fly fishing in the ponds, and it's strictly catch and release. Then, if the member wants to eat that particular fish for dinner, we get one from the local markets." He stopped to scratch at his beard. "But lately the numbers have been going down, especially in the snapper and hogfish ponds. We're not sure why."

"You think there might be some poaching going on?"

Campbell frowned. "Maybe."

"You have a restaurant in the lodge?"

"Sure do, along with a snooty French chef."

"Amazing."

"Not really, once you come to understand our members. They're used to getting whatever they want, as soon as they want it."

"And nobody ever cheats?"

"Cheats how?"

"By keeping fish from the ponds?"

"Well, like I said, our numbers have been down lately. So it's possible I suppose. Mr. Broom in particular had a thing for hogfish. Told me he liked to cook them up in some special way in his own cabin. We had an agreement that he could take one occasionally, on two conditions. So at least he was up front about it."

"What were the conditions?"

"That he pay the club an extra $100 each time, and that he always do it at night so the other club members wouldn't figure it out."

Campbell paused and scratched again at his beard. "Say, you don't suppose that had anything to do with—?"

"With somebody dumping those lionfish in here? Seems like a possibility, don't you think? Do you know if anybody had a particular grudge against Mr. Broom?"

Mel shook his head. "I wouldn't say he was the most popular guy around here, but no, nothing like that. I mean, *really*? Death by lionfish? Our members aren't like that."

"Actually, I'm looking forward to meeting some of them. But now I'd better go tell Detective Reynard what we found here. Thanks for the info."

"You need a ride back? I still gotta feed all these fish."

"No problem. I'll walk."

When I got back to the lodge, Dr. Hernandez and Deputy Wilson were in the process of loading a body bag into the back of the medical examiner's van. Stella was sitting on a stone bench writing something in a little spiral-bound notebook.

She looked up when she saw me coming. "Find anything interesting?"

"Plenty. There are lionfish in the pond where they found the dead guy."

"Is that important?"

Apparently Stella hadn't heard about lionfish.

"It sure could be. They have venomous spines that can seriously injure a person who gets stuck, or maybe even kill them. And didn't you tell me there were puncture marks on the corpse?"

"Uh huh." She jumped up and ran over to the van and knocked on the back door just as it was leaving. "Anthony! Anthony! Hold on a sec. There's something you need to hear."

The medical examiner stopped his vehicle and got out. "What is it?"

"Sam just found out there are lionfish in the pond where your body came from."

"Are you sure about that, Sam? My god, that could explain what happened here. Any idea how they got in there?"

I shook my head. "I was with a guy who identified himself as their fisheries manager. A Mel somebody or other. He claims he has no idea."

"We're gonna want a toxicology report as part of the autopsy, that's for sure," Hernandez replied.

"What do you know about their venom?" I asked.

"Lionfish venom is a neurotoxin similar to that found in cobras. The stings can be quite painful, but they rarely prove lethal in healthy individuals. Most deaths occur in adults with respiratory problems."

"Oh boy," Stella said. "I just learned from Mrs. Broom that her husband had a history of heart disease and asthma, and it had been getting worse."

"He could have fallen into that pond by accident," Anthony suggested. "And then he had an asthma attack or heart failure when he was stung."

"Maybe it was an accident," Stella replied. "And maybe it wasn't. In any event, try to get on that autopsy asap, will you Anthony? And be sure to save the stomach contents too, just in case he ate something funny."

"Of course."

After the medical examiner had driven off with the body of Arthur Broom, Stella and I sat back down on the bench.

"I guess this whole thing *could* have been an accident," Stella said. "But that doesn't explain the anonymous phone call, or how the lionfish ended up in that pond."

"Plus, the fisheries guy told me Broom had a habit of fishing in that particular pond, especially at night."

"Which means if somebody was out to get him, and they knew where he was likely to be . . ." Stella trailed off, but only for an instant. Then she slapped her thigh. "Alright, for now we're treating this like a suspicious death. I'd say a *highly* suspicious death."

"What about security cameras?" I asked.

Stella shook her head. "Naturally, that's the first thing we checked. They've got cameras all over this place, as you might expect. But guess what? The ones at the ponds weren't working last night."

"Any idea why?"

"Somebody turned them off. Their head of security, Max Welty, claims he has no idea who might have done it. They have a room in the main building with a bank of monitors showing videos from the cameras, but I guess nobody was in there last night."

"Doesn't that seem odd to you? I would think a place like this would be all about security."

Stella nodded. "I would have thought so too. But Welty said they rely instead on recorders linked to the monitors. He said the security staff includes only two other people, and the three of them take turns manning the guard house 24-7."

"Speaking of that, the guard who was at the gate when we drove in here looked familiar. Do you happen to know who he is?"

Stella consulted her notebook. "His name is Reuben Fletcher. He's the one works the day shift at the guardhouse. Been here since 2019. You know him?"

Then it clicked. I'd only seen him once, at a restaurant where my friend Snooks Lancaster and I frequently had breakfast before a day on the water. Snooks told me Fletcher was a guide who had a reputation for following other fishermen around and then horning in on their hotspots, often marking them with his GPS. This was a big time no-no among guides. We sometimes shared information, but the unwritten rule was that you never got in somebody's way while they were fishing with a client unless it was by invitation. This was especially true when it came to elusive and wary species like permit and tarpon.

"I don't know him, but I know of him. He used to be a fishing guide, and not a popular one with the rest of us. I wonder how he ended up here."

"Maybe I can find out."

"Might be worth knowing. But in any event, where do we go from here?"

"I just had a chat with the club manager." Stella stopped again to consult her little notebook. "A guy named Ralph Weatherbee. I asked him for a list of names of all the members who were present last night, along with the staff. As soon as we're done here, I'm going back inside and ask him again, only this time I'm gonna be a little less polite."

"I gather he was reluctant?"

"And then some. I get the impression he's scared of how the members might react to my bothering them. I just need to make sure he's more scared of me than he is of them. Then I'll get that list and start the interviews. Somebody's got to know something about all this."

"Anything I can do to help?"

"Nothing for right now, thanks. You did plenty finding out about those lionfish." She started to get up, then snapped her fingers. "Oh, but there is one thing. You might alert Katie that we'll likely be sending the stomach contents her way."

"Will do. I'm sure she'd be happy to help. And she might know some things about lionfish venom that we don't."

~ ~ ~

It was late afternoon by the time I got back home. A silver Prius sitting in the front yard told me Katie already was there. I went around to the back of the house and climbed the stairs to the deck. Prince the Corgi must have heard me coming, because he already was at the head of the stairs when I got there, wagging his little tail-less butt in anticipation. I gave him a scratch behind his ears, and said hi to Katie, who was sunbathing on a mat laid out on the deck.

Katie was topless as usual. She wasn't being all that daring. There was nothing but a stand of mangroves across the canal, which meant nobody could see her except me and maybe a crocodile if it happened to look up in our direction. A crocodile probably wouldn't have been all that interested, but I certainly was.

She got up and sauntered across the deck to give me a kiss. "How was your day?"

"Interesting and probably about to get better. But just so I don't forget to tell you about the interesting part, how about covering up first?"

She mustered a pout, but then got a towel and wrapped it around herself before sitting down in one of our deck chairs. "This better be good."

"They found a dead guy in a pond at the Purple Isle Sportsman's Club. He might have been stung to death by lionfish."

"What's the Purple Isle Sportsman's Club and how did you end up there? I thought you were fishing with Marshall White today."

"I was, but then Stella Reynard called and asked me to take a look at the crime scene. The club is a super-elitist fishing resort on its own little island. It's bayside off Upper Matecumbe. They have all these ponds stocked with different fish. The dead guy was a member."

"Why do you and Stella think a crime was involved?"

"Two reasons. First, there weren't supposed to be lionfish in any of the ponds. And second, the Sheriff's Department got an anonymous tip that somebody pushed the victim into the water."

"Huh. So what happens next?"

"Next comes the autopsy, including a toxicology report to check for lionfish venom."

Katie frowned. "From what I understand, that's not likely to work. Lionfish venom, like most neurotoxins, isn't very stable."

"You know something about lionfish?"

"Not really. But we had a guest lecturer in my general forensics class last semester who's a specialist on poisons and venoms. One of my students asked about lionfish in particular, because of their increasing numbers in waters off the Keys."

"Yeah, I don't think they're really all that big a threat to humans. But like so many Florida exotic species, they're taking a toll on native ones. Anyway, Stella asked if you'd be willing to take a look at the victim's stomach contents when the time comes."

"For lionfish venom? Like I said—"

"No, no, not about that. But maybe something else will turn up. Like unusual plant foods."

"Well sure then, I'd be happy to help."

Katie stood up, said "oops" as the towel fell away, and moved toward the sliding door leading to our living room. As always, it was a no-brainer to follow her inside.

Chapter 4

Two hours later Katie and I drove over to the Safari Lounge for burgers and drinks. It was our favorite local watering hole, not only because of the unique atmosphere and quality refreshments, but also because we were close friends with the couple that owned and ran the place.

George Lancaster, who went by "Snooks," was an old-time backcountry fishing guide and one of my best friends. Flora "Flo" Delaney had tended bar at the Safari Lounge for many years, until an inheritance gave her the means to buy the place. Snooks moved in with Flo after his houseboat sank during Hurricane Irma. Lately he'd been spending most of his time running the bar instead of fishing.

The Safari Lounge was a brown wooden structure built right on the shores of the Atlantic but about a half-story up on big stilts, which explains why it survived Irma with less than terminal damage. Nevertheless it had taken Flo and Snooks several months to get the place back up and running after that hurricane.

The most distinctive feature of the Safari was a collection of stuffed African wildlife hanging from the walls and vaulted ceiling. They were the reason the place was known among locals as The Dead Animal Bar, and why the t-shirts they sold were emblazoned with the motto "Where the Extinct Meet to Drink."

The bar itself dominated the room. It was a large rectangular structure with stools on all four sides, and space in the center for the bartender to walk around serving drinks and food. Peripheral to the bar on three sides were tables next to windows affording great views of the ocean. The fourth side of the room—the one farthest from the ocean—had no windows except one in a door leading back to the kitchen.

The sun was nearly to the horizon and the inky blue waters of the Atlantic were unusually calm as we pulled off the highway and took the short ride back to the Safari Lounge. I watched as a dozen brown pelicans flew by in single file, alternately gliding and then flapping their wings in unison. I've always wondered how they managed to get so coordinated.

Snooks was mixing drinks when Katie and I walked in and sat down on our favorite pair of bar stools. His thinning gray hair was tied up in its usual ponytail, and he had on a blue and yellow t-shirt advertising a local brewery. He had a quart of rum in one hand, a bottle of fruit punch in the other, and an assortment of liqueur bottles spread out in front of him. Watching Snooks in action convinced me he'd become nearly as good a bartender as he was a fisherman, which was among the best I'd ever known. He waved when he saw us, then finished serving two men their fancy rum punches before coming over to our side of the bar.

"You're getting really good at that, Snooks," I said, pointing to the drinks he'd just finished mixing. "Where did you learn how to do all that complicated stuff?"

"In my younger days I drank lots of strange concoctions, you know like sweet pink stuff, so I learned some from that. And I have this program on a computer that has all kinds of weird recipes. You ever heard of a Harvey Wallbanger?"

He didn't wait for an answer. "Well neither had I, but some guy came in here last week asking for one. And there it was on my computer. I had a sip. Not my favorite, I gotta tell you."

"What is your favorite?" I asked.

"Oh, usually just a light beer if I have anything. I learned the hard way it's not a good idea for bartenders to drink on the job. Flo helps me with that, because she quit drinking after she found out her mother had been an alcoholic."

I knew something about Flo's history because I'd been involved in solving the mystery surrounding her background. She'd been adopted as an infant and never known her biological parents. It was only through DNA testing that we figured out her mother had been a wealthy recluse living alone on a small key before she was murdered.

A half-dozen other patrons were scattered around the bar at the Safari Lounge, mostly nursing beers. A family with three young boys was seated at one of the tables, all of them working on cheeseburgers.

At the sound of our voices, Flo stuck her head out of the kitchen door. She held a spatula in her right hand, and used the other one to push aside a strand of brown hair that had fallen across one eye. "Hey guys," she said. "Good to see you. I'll be out as soon as I finish these French fries." She pointed her spatula toward the family by the window. "Got a bunch of hungry kids over there."

"What can I get ya?" Snooks asked Katie and me.

"We'll have a couple of your special margaritas, rocks and salt," Katie replied, without bothering to ask me.

"Coming up. And what's new in the world? It's been a while since you've been in."

"Same old same old," I replied. "Fishing and botanizing. But something interesting did happen today. Do you know anything about the Purple Isle Sportsman's Club?"

Snooks leaned in close and whispered: "Not much, but their staff come in here sometimes." Then he pointed back over his shoulder at the two men who'd ordered the rum punches. "Over there that's Ralph Weatherbee. He's the manager of the club. And the guy with him is their chef, a Jacques somebody or other. Come to think of it, that's funny, because it's dinner time. He must have the night off."

Weatherbee was a little guy, weak-chinned, with thick-lensed glasses that made him look like an owl. Jacques the cook was much bigger, but thin-faced and lanky, with an oversized nose and shoulder-length curly brown hair. They both were staring in our direction, and neither of them looked happy. I had no idea why.

"What happened over there?" Snooks asked, his voice still a whisper.

I gave him the short version, including the part about the lionfish because I thought he would find it interesting. Snooks did look interested, and he started to say something, but then Weatherbee waved his hand in the air and started making noises about needing to settle up. Snooks went off to deal with Weatherbee's credit card, just as Flo came out of the kitchen carrying two big platters of French fries and took them to the family still eating their cheeseburgers. Then she came back and sat down on the stool next to Katie.

Flo was a couple of inches shorter than Katie's five-eight, and a bit heavier around the middle. I'd always thought she was a very handsome woman, especially because of her alluring bright green eyes. We'd had a one-night hook-up a few years back, at a time Katie and I were having difficulties. But that was in the past.

Flo had treated me with a mild coldness when Katie first moved down to Islamorada. I'd wondered at the time if Flo had told Katie about our brief intimacy, but figured she hadn't because Katie'd never asked me about it, and believe me she would have. In any event, Flo's coldness hadn't lasted long. We now were good friends without any emotional baggage as far as I could determine.

Flo put her arm across Katie's shoulders and gave her a hug. "How you doing?"

"We're good," Katie replied, returning the hug.

Snooks put the finishing touches on our margaritas and set them on coasters in front of us. "Are you getting tangled up in this Purple Isle thing?" he asked.

"I don't think so. Why?"

"I used to work out there."

This was news to me. "Doing what?"

"I was one of their in-house fishing guides. But it didn't last long. Some of their members were way too snooty for me, especially if I had to spend a whole day in a boat with one of 'em."

"So leaving was your idea?"

Snooks pulled once on his ponytail. "I guess it was a mutual decision."

"Yeah, his and mine," Flo said. "And it's not just their members." She pointed across the bar. "See that guy sitting over there? The big one with lots of hair? He calls himself Jacques Petain, and he brags about being a French chef at the Purple Isle. But he's a phony, take my word for it."

"How do you know that?" Katie asked.

"We may be running a beer and burger place here at the Safari, but I know something about French cooking. I asked him a couple of questions once. He didn't have a clue what I was talking about."

Snooks started fiddling with the rubber band holding up his ponytail, which I knew meant he was thinking hard about something. "You want my advice, stay away from that place. Do your fishing and your crime fighting someplace else."

Chapter 5

I spent the next three days thinking about what Snooks had said concerning the Purple Isle Sportsman's Club and wondering just what he'd been trying to tell me. Was there something about the place that spooked him besides its obvious elitism? But I hadn't heard anything more from Stella, and almost decided none of it mattered. Then she called one evening after dinner and asked if she could come over, because she needed to talk with both Katie and me.

We settled on the deck with iced tea. For a while we made small talk and listened to the night birds in the mangroves across the canal. I could tell that Stella was nervous and maybe a bit reluctant to get down to business, even though our meeting had been her idea.

I wondered what was up and decided to break the ice. "Any new developments on that Purple Isle drowning?"

Stella put down her glass and ran a finger around the rim. Then she looked up, moving her eyes back and forth between the two of us. "Actually, there are. And I could use your help."

"Of course," Katie replied. "What is it you'd like us to do?"

Stella took in a breath and let it back out. "Okay. But first some update. We've heard back from Anthony Hernandez with preliminary autopsy results on Mr. Broom. He had water in his lungs, which meant he was alive when he went in the pond. And his blood alcohol was 0.12, so he was legally drunk at the time."

"Drugs?" Katie asked.

"No. Basic toxicology was pretty normal except for the alcohol. Of course we'll have to wait for the more advanced analysis. Hernandez isn't able to do that himself, so we don't know anything yet about lionfish venom. They'll be sending samples to a lab up in Miami."

"Which means you don't know what killed him?" Katie asked.

Stella shook her head. "Actually we have a pretty good idea. Hernandez found evidence of a major coronary event. And as I already told Sam, we learned from Mrs. Broom that he had a history of cardiac and respiratory problems. The man was not in good health."

"Maybe he fell into the pond drunk," Katie said. "And then had a heart attack after thrashing around for a while."

"That's possible," Stella replied. "But I'm not ready to go there just yet."

"Because of the anonymous phone call, right?" I asked.

"That, and the coincidence of falling into that particular pond. Plus there's another thing they found during the autopsy. Hernandez said the lining of his stomach and esophagus were all torn up. Said he'd never seen anything just like it."

Stella reached into her purse, brought out a small jar inside a sealed plastic bag, and set it on the table in between our drinks. "Here's a portion of the stomach contents, along with a copy of the autopsy report. Maybe he ate some toxic plant material that explains the condition of his digestive tract. Katie, I know you're an expert. Can you take a look at this and let me know what you find?"

A dead guy's stomach contents sitting right next to our iced tea kind of gave me the willies, but Katie accepted the bag and jar without even blinking, and said she'd be glad to help.

Stella had said specifically that she needed to talk to both of us, which caused me to wonder what my role in the case might be.

I didn't have to wonder very long.

"And Sam, I need a favor. It's a big one."

"Sure. What is it?"

"Would you be willing to hire on as a guide at the club?"

To say this came from out of nowhere would be an understatement, and it left me temporarily speechless. I had a well-developed work schedule for my guiding business and a large group of customers who counted on me to be available for them at certain times.

There was an awkward silence, eventually broken by Stella.

"I know this is a highly unusual request. But . . . oh shit, here's the deal. We can't—that is I can't—get anybody to give me the time of day out there, especially the members. All I get is the runaround." She stopped talking long enough to drink the last of her tea. "It's pretty obvious what's going on. I've had it before. It's because I'm African-American. The Purple Isle club is the whitest place I've ever seen, except for a few of the help."

"No minority members?" Katie asked. "Gee, that's a surprise."

"Nobody except Rashaan Liptan. And he doesn't seem to be around very much."

"The basketball player?" I asked.

"Uh huh. I guess they needed a token."

"That may be, but he's a darned good fly fisherman. I've taken him out several times. Didn't know he was a club member."

"Joined a couple of years ago, according to their list."

"What about the victim's family?" Katie asked. "Surely they'd be anxious to help."

"There's just the wife, Fiona, and she wasn't there the day he died. Apparently she was up in Palm Beach shopping. We've talked to her of course, but she didn't have much to say. I got a frosty reaction from her, just like everybody else."

Those bastards, I thought to myself, at the same time remembering what Snooks had said about the club. "Well that sucks, Stella, but what does that have to do with my working as a guide out there?"

"That's pretty obvious, Sam," Katie interrupted. "Everybody knows you have the gift of gab. You'll be taking members fishing and getting them to talk about things going on at the club, like who might have had it in for the victim."

Stella's look softened in apparent relief. "Exactly."

I remained skeptical. "But won't the people be suspicious? Some of them probably saw me out there with you the other day. And some might even have heard about my occasional involvement with law enforcement."

"That's a chance we're gonna have to take. And I've cleared it with the manager and their head fisheries guy. As it turns out, one of their guides just quit, so there's an opening."

And that was how I became a fishing guide for the rich and famous at the Purple Isle Sportsman's Club.

~ ~ ~

I met Stella at ten-thirty the next morning in her office at the Islamorada Substation of the Monroe County Sheriff's Department. She was shuffling through a stack of manila folders when I walked in and sat down on the opposite side of her battered metal desk. She was in full uniform as usual: regulation forest green pants, a crisply pressed short-sleeved white shirt with a star over the left breast pocket, and sergeant stripes on each arm.

She offered coffee, which I accepted. She went out to the bullpen where other deputies had their desks, and came back with two cups, both black.

She tipped her cup at me and took a swallow. "Thanks for agreeing to all this Sam. I think you're the right person for the job."

"Uh, . . . I haven't actually agreed to anything yet, Stella. For one thing, I've got a bunch of clients already booked over the next month. What am I supposed to do about them?"

That slowed her down, but not for long. "What about your buddy Snooks? Couldn't he handle that for you?"

"Maybe, at least for some of them. But here's another thing. We haven't talked about money. I'm supposed to be earning a living, and the guide business is pretty lucrative right now."

I hated giving Stella the runaround, but there was something about the whole idea of disguising myself as a fishing guide while playing detective that put me off.

"I understand your hesitancy here, Sam. And I'm afraid all the department can offer is five hundred a week. But that will be on top of your regular salary as a guide at the club, which I understand is pretty lucrative."

"Just how lucrative?"

"According to the club manager, that will depend on your experience. Which is considerable, right?"

"Well, I do know how to fish, and I do know how to chat up clients. But I've never been an actor, and that's what you're asking me to be, isn't it?"

Stella nodded. "I understand, Sam. Believe me. If I could think of any alternative I'd take it."

We sat, staring at each other and drinking our coffee, while I mulled over my options. Or at least I pretended to be. Stella was a good friend, and she'd done me favors in the past. "Is there anything in particular you'd like me to be watching for? It would help if I knew a little more about Mr. Broom's background, along with the other members and staff at the club."

Stella grinned. "Guess that means you're in, huh?"

"Yeah, I guess so."

With that she flipped open the topmost file folder in the stack sitting on her desk, and started reading from it. "Arthur Broom III was born in New York City in 1941, the only grandchild of his namesake, who made his money as an investment banker. Under Arthur III the company got bigger and he got richer. A whole *lot* richer from what we've been able to learn. He sold the business and moved to Palm Beach fifteen years ago. His lifelong passion was fishing, and he'd done all sorts of it, all over the world."

"What about family?" I asked.

"An ex-wife is dead, and there are no children. There may be some distant relatives around, but nobody close. He married Fiona four years ago. Before that she was his live-in caretaker after he had a heart attack."

Stella paused for another swallow of coffee and then flipped to the next page in the folder. "Here's where it gets unusual. Some time after moving to Florida, Broom developed a passionate interest in the Everglades, devoting time and especially money trying to save and restore the place. He got so interested in the subject, and had his fingers in so many pies, the press started calling him the Glades Man." She stopped reading and looked up at me. "So you have things in common with this guy, right?"

"I certainly don't have his resources and nobody's ever called me the Glades Man. But yeah, I do care about the Everglades and the future of Florida Bay."

Stella closed the folder. "So, you good with this so far?"

"Yeah, probably. I'll let you know after we talk to people at the club. But before we go, I wanted to ask you more about security over there."

"What about it?"

"Just that it seems a little lax. You'd think a place like that would be crawling with rent-a-cops. But you said there's only three on the staff, and they don't even have time to keep an eye on the monitors full-time?"

Stella nodded. "Yeah, I've wondered about that too. And from what you told me about that man Reuben Fletcher, it doesn't sound like he's had any relevant experience."

"What about the other two?"

Stella consulted her notes. "Their head guy, Max Welty, is retired from the Key West police department. The other one is Hubert Valdez. Goes by Hubie. He used to be a Monroe County Deputy Sheriff. So at least the two of them have the right background."

"You know either of them?"

"No. They retired before I moved down here."

Stella looked at her watch and stood up, obviously ready to leave.

"Actually, I have another question before we go."

"You want to know about possible suspects in the killing."

"Assuming this was a homicide, yes."

Stella sat back down. "I was gonna save this 'til later, but I guess we still have time before our appointment." She opened another folder. "First we always look at family. As I mentioned the current wife was up in Palm Beach shopping when he died."

"You sure about that?"

"Pretty sure."

"Then we have to look at the man's past, especially his business dealings. And here we may have something, because there are rumors and a couple of legal cases that suggest there were some troubles related to his investment corporation back in New York."

"What kind of troubles?"

"Like maybe a couple of shady deals fell through, and some other people lost serious money. They were the sort of people who hold grudges, if you get my drift."

"Anything recent?"

"Not that we know of."

Based on what Stella had told me so far, it wasn't clear that taking other club members fishing was going to result in much. I was about to point that out, but she didn't give me a chance.

"And that's about all we have so far. It seems likely the killer, assuming there was one, is either a club member or one of the staff. But like I said, those people are just stonewalling me."

"So, I take the members out on my boat, maybe get them to relax a bit and start talking."

"Yeah, that and get to know the other staff members, maybe over a drink or two. Sometimes that can loosen tongues."

Stella closed the folder—a fat one—and handed it to me. "This is for you. It's what I've been able to learn about Broom's fellow club members, along with the staff working there." She stood up again, this time obviously for good.

Chapter 6

Stella and I drove in her cruiser. We took time to stop at a local fast food place for fish tacos before heading on to our meeting with the manager of the Purple Isle Sportsman's Club, which was set for one-thirty.

Nobody from the Sheriff's Department was on duty when we got there. Instead it was just Reuben Fletcher in the guardhouse. Stella flashed her badge, and he raised the gate blocking the road and waved us through.

The office of Ralph Weatherbee, manager of the Purple Isle Sportsman's Club, was richly paneled and furnished in tropical woods, and overly potted with tropical plants. An oversized picture window behind his wide mahogany desk looked out on Florida Bay. The sun slanted in through the window, glinting off his bald head as we walked in.

In addition to Stella and me and Weatherbee, a fourth person in the room was Mel Campbell, the fisheries manager I'd met already. I don't know if Weatherbee recognized me from the day before at the Safari Lounge, but if so he didn't let on and instead let Stella introduce us. He stood up, reached across his desk to shake my hand, and invited us to sit. He was wearing a blue blazer with brass buttons and a light blue shirt, open at the neck.

Weatherbee plopped back down on his big leather chair and harrumphed. "I understand, Mr. Sawyer, that you are an experienced fishing guide. I have been asked by Detective Reynard if we could add you to our payroll in order that you might, uh . . . get to know some of our members, and, uh . . . help with her investigation into the recent tragic demise of Arthur Broom."

Beads of sweat had broken out on Weatherbee's upper lip, and he stopped to wipe his glasses with a handkerchief he'd pulled out of his hip pocket. "I want you to know we view this as a highly unusual request, and we would be most reluctant to do such a thing—except that we are as anxious as you are to discover what happened. Therefore, we agree to the plan with certain conditions."

Stella frowned. "I don't recall your saying anything about conditions. What are they?"

"Like all of our employees," Weatherbee replied, "Mr. Sawyer is not to socialize with club members either in their cabins or here at the main lodge, including the bar and restaurant, except at the specific invitation of a member." He paused for another harrumph. "Which I assure you will happen rarely if ever."

Stella rolled her eyes but didn't say anything.

I was beginning to understand what Snooks had meant by the place being "snooty."

"What about pay?" I asked.

"You will receive our standard weekly salary of $5,000, plus any tips your clients might wish to provide. In addition, you will have access to the cabin we reserve for guides. I will leave the remaining details to Mr. Campbell here, in his position as fisheries manager. You will report to him, and he will be responsible for arranging your trips. But please understand that you are an employee-at-will."

"Meaning you can kick me out of here whenever you feel like it, right?"

Weatherbee nodded once.

"Now just a minute, sir," Stella interrupted. "My recollection of what we discussed earlier was that Mr. Sawyer would be able to remain in this position as long as it is useful to our investigation."

"And that certainly is our intention, Detective. As I said before, we are anxious to help resolve this matter as quickly as possible. But once it is resolved, Mr. Sawyer may or may not fit into our future plans."

It was tempting to comment that there would be a snowstorm in Islamorada before I stayed around this place a minute longer than absolutely necessary. But for Stella's sake, I held my tongue.

The club manager pushed back from his desk and stood up. "And now if you will excuse me, I have to go consult with the cook about the upcoming week's menus. Mr. Campbell will show you our facilities and describe in more detail what will be expected of you, including such things as our dress code."

A dress code for fishing guides? This place was getting creepier by the minute.

"Sorry about all of that," Mel Campbell said as soon as Stella and I were back outside. "Weatherbee can be a bit formal at times. Most of our members are pretty good guys, and not bad fishermen either. I think you'll find guiding here an interesting experience."

"And this dress code?"

"Actually, it's not that big a deal. When employees are on the island, they're expected to wear chinos or Bermudas and a polo shirt like the one I have on now. When you're out fishing with a client, dress like you normally would to protect yourself from the sun. There are only two absolute rules: no jeans and no t-shirts or ball caps that advertise anything."

I was busy digesting this, and thinking about how I'd miss my hat with the Sloppy Joe's logo on it, when we all looked up at the sound of a boat approaching the marina. It was one of the Pathfinders I'd seen on my previous visit. There were two people on board, both dark and compact, but one much younger than the other. As soon as they reached the dock, the younger one jumped out of the boat and tied it up. I assumed he was the guide and the other the client, which Campbell quickly confirmed.

"That's Morrison Murikami. Goes by 'Mo.' He was out today with Mr. Padilla. Hope they did okay, or Padilla will be grousing about it for the next week."

"Is Murikami one of your regular guides?" I asked.

"Uh huh. He's *the* regular guide. Besides you that is."

"How do we decide which of us takes somebody fishing?"

"You don't. I make the schedules. There's a clipboard in the guides' cabin with your assignments for the week. Mo can show you. You're gonna be roommates. It's a nice place. I used to live there when I started here."

"Do you still live on the property?"

Mel nodded. "Yep, sure do. But I got my own place when they promoted me to fisheries manager."

I pointed toward the Pathfinder. "What can you tell me about that client?"

"Not much. Except I know his family came from Cuba, where they made lots of money in sugar before the revolution. Then they spearheaded the Florida sugar industry after they immigrated here. They own lots of land south of Lake Okeechobee."

Padilla hopped off the boat carrying a big fly rod and walked off toward the interior of the island, presumably to his cabin. He didn't tip the guide, or even shake his hand.

"Let me introduce you to Mo," Mel said, as we headed for the dock. "He drifted in here from California a couple of years ago, looking for a job. He's young, but he's damned good. You'll like him." Mel started walking, but then stopped and snapped his fingers. "Oh, and you probably shouldn't mention the weekly five grand we'll be paying you. Mo's only getting half that until he proves himself, which shouldn't take long."

I noticed Stella was frowning and looking at her watch. "Tell you what, Mr. Campbell. For obvious reasons we need to minimize Sam's connections with the sheriff's department. If he does decide to start working here, he can come back tomorrow without me, and you can introduce him to everybody then."

"Oh, sure, I understand."

Before we left, I had a question for Mel. "What can you tell me about the guy we just saw at the gate?"

Campbell's face clouded over. "You mean Reuben Fletcher? Why are you interested in him?"

"Maybe I'm not. But I know he used to be a fishing guide, so I just wonder—"

"Yep, and that's what he did here at first. Until he pissed off so many members we had to fire him. Then it turned out we needed a guard, so Mr. Weatherbee moved him over there. If it had been up to me, I'd have just kicked his ass out of here. The guy's a jerk."

~ ~ ~

Stella and I were driving back to her office when she popped the big question. "You gonna do it?"

"I need to talk it over with Katie, but yes, at least the fishing part. I'm not sure about staying in the guides' cabin on the property. I'll probably just come on the days I'm supposed to be taking somebody out."

Stella frowned. "But that way you'd miss the chance to rub elbows with members in the lodge. Remember what I suggested about chatting with folks over drinks?"

"Yeah, but don't you remember what Weatherbee said about socializing with club members being a no-no?"

"Of course I remember, Sam. But I'm also familiar with your particular charms."

That sounded like a come-on, but I knew better. In fact, Stella and I had gotten close to making it personal on a couple of occasions while Katie and I were having our difficulties. But it hadn't happened then and now it never would, not that she wasn't damned attractive.

"I'll have to think about the socializing part, Stella. I'm not sure those charms you're talking about would have any effect on rich old men deciding whether to let me sit next to them at the bar."

"They'd better have that effect, Sam Sawyer, if you expect to earn that $500 a week the department is paying."

I smiled, remembering the extra zero added on to the end of $500 that the club would be offering.

Stella noticed my grin. "What?"

"Uh, nothing. But you're telling me that staying overnight is non-negotiable?"

"Let's just say it would be my strong preference."

Chapter 7

Stella dropped me off next to my Jeep in the department's parking lot. On the drive home I wondered how Katie was going to react when I told her the new job at the club was going to involve overnights. It was going to be tricky. Our on-again off-again living arrangement had just gotten firmly back on track, and now this.

She and Prince were out on the deck when I got there, she with a glass of red wine in her right hand. She raised it up and grinned when she saw me. "Why don't you pour yourself a glass and come on out? We don't need to walk Prince for a little while."

I joined her on the couch and Prince jumped up to sit between us. She fed him one of those mini dog treats he always got at cocktail hour.

Katie grinned, then leaned over and gave me a kiss. "How was your day?"

"Uh, okay, but there's something—difficult—we need to discuss."

Her smile faded as her brow furrowed. "What?"

"You remember that possible job Stella talked about?"

"Sure. You're gonna do it, right? Sounds like she needs your help."

"Uh huh. But there's a part you don't know about. It means I need to spend nights out at the club."

Katie's eyes flicked away, as if she'd spotted something in the mangroves across the canal. But I knew that wasn't it.

"Are you happy, Sam?" she said, seemingly out of the blue.

That stopped me, but not for long. "I've never been happier in my whole life. That separated marriage deal just didn't work. We're meant to be together, and this business at the fishing club won't last all that long. Or at least I hope not." Then it occurred to me that Katie might have been asking a bigger question. Or several questions.

"Are *you* happy, Katie? I mean we're making less money than when we both taught up in Lauderdale. Is that a problem? Do you miss the action up there? Do you like your new position and our life here in the Keys? Maybe this is too small-time for you. And I would never—"

She reached out and put her hand over my mouth. "Oh hush up with that. Our income is fine. That's never entered my mind." She drained the last of her wine. "But . . . I guess I'm a little gun-shy because of what happened to you in the past, that's all. I'm worried that you're going to move out and spend most of your nights over at that fish club. And our days don't overlap much either, so it won't be all that different from our living in different places."

"But like I said, this is just a short-term arrangement to assist in a murder investigation. And I owe Stella."

I realized the mistake as soon as I said it, so I kept going before she had a chance to interrupt. "Which is less than I owe you. Believe me, I know that. But look, you said so yourself. They've frozen her out over there. Bunch of racist snobs."

That got a grin and a nod. I could feel the tension beginning to ebb.

"Most people here in the Keys aren't like that. It's one of the things I like about this place."

"You're right, Sam. And I really like the students in my classes. They're serious about it. Maybe that goes with the trade school environment in contrast to purely academic schools."

"What about your colleagues?"

"Many of them are only part-time teachers because they have 'outside' jobs and just teach about their specialties. But mostly they seem like really nice people. In my forensic program, practicing defense and prosecuting attorneys give guest talks along with some legal aides. And there's a judge who comes down for vacation each winter. She loves talking about how courts should work, and she wants to set up mock trials with the students assuming the different roles, including members of the jury."

"What do you think of that idea?"

"I love it. The part of forensic work I like least is testifying in a trial. Sometimes my expertise seems less important to judges and lawyers than things like marital status, knowledge of unrelated science, where I went to school, and stuff like that. A mock trial, if it's done right, will teach my students what to expect and how to stay on message."

"Why do you want your students to act as jury members during these mock trials?"

"I think it's absolutely crucial. That way they can learn the importance of clearly explaining the science behind a case in terms a jury member will understand."

"And speaking of cases, have you had a chance yet to look at Arthur Broom's stomach contents?"

"I have, and there's definitely something odd there."

"Odd how?"

"I recognized cells of some common foods like onions and lettuce and tomatoes. And while I'm familiar with things like tropical fruits normally available in Florida, there were plant cells in Broom's stomach I've never seen before."

"No idea what they might be?"

"Not at this point. Maybe the chef at the club could give us a list of the plant foods he recently served."

"I'll have Stella look into that."

"Thanks."

"But tell me Katie, is your life down here better than it was in Lauderdale?"

"I love it here. I think the new job suits me perfectly. Every day has surprises and nearly all the people I work with are friendly and helpful when I have troubles. I love this little house and living on the water. And you seem contented with your guide business."

I sensed a "but" coming, and I was right.

"But," she continued, "I am disappointed we don't have more time together with Prince. And I can't pretend to be happy you'll be away from home most nights, even if it is only temporary."

"I understand and I feel the same way. We just need to figure out who killed Mr. Broom. Then things can get back to normal."

I reached out to give Katie a hug, but Prince took this as a cue to muscle his way between us. Corgis are like that.

Chapter 8

Bending to Stella's wishes, and with the understanding of Katie, I agreed to start spending three or four nights a week at the Purple Isle Sportsman's Club. The guides' cabin was a modest one-room affair, with bunk beds and a minimalist kitchen that included an ancient two-burner electric range, an under-sized microwave, and a small refrigerator. My roommate and fellow guide, Morrison "Mo" Murikami, proved to be likeable as well as interesting. Being younger and more flexible than me, he generously offered to sleep in the upper bunk, and I took him up on it.

I learned that Mo had grown up on an almond orchard north of Sacramento, and had developed a passion for trout and steelhead fishing at an early age. During three years of community college he began guiding part-time, especially on the Sacramento and Feather Rivers. It became a full-time occupation after he graduated, and it expanded to fly fishing for striped bass in the San Francisco Bay Area. The move to the Florida Keys upset his parents, who'd always assumed he would take over responsibility for the orchard once he outgrew his thing about fishing. He left with the promise that it was only temporary, but confessed to me that he had little interest in a career in agriculture. The guy was hooked on fly-fishing, and I could relate. The only difference of opinion that arose during our time together was his love of sushi. Raw fish just doesn't work for me.

On our second night together I decided we'd gotten sufficiently comfortable that I could nudge the conversation toward details about the various club members we were guiding. I was working on a salad and a bowl of spaghetti that came out of a can. He was eating some kind of smelly thing I couldn't identify. I tried to make it seem casual, as if I just hoped to learn more about our clients' particular interests and abilities with a fly rod.

"First day I was here, I saw you come in with a Mr. Padilla. What can you tell me about him?"

Mo put down his chopsticks. "Not much. You been out with him yet?"

"No, but he's on my schedule for day after tomorrow, which is why I asked."

"Well, he's good with a ten-weight, and he has a thing for tarpon. Especially big ones. I think he holds the club record, a hundred-forty pounder."

"Is he easy to fish with?"

"He knows how to handle a fly rod, if that's what you mean."

"Not exactly. To me, the real test is how a client behaves on a bad day, when the fish are off and there's nothing you can do about it."

"Yeah, I know what you mean. But as for Padilla? He gets real quiet. That's when you know he's pissed." Mo paused to swallow a last chunk of greenish whatever it was. "The man doesn't like me."

"If all he does is get quiet, how do you know that?"

"Once when we got back to the dock after a bad day, I heard him say something to Mel Campbell."

"What did he say?"

Mo used a paper napkin to wipe something off his chin, and looked out the window toward the water. "He said the club should find somebody besides 'that oriental kid' to take him fishing. He thought I couldn't hear him, but I did."

I knew from the files Stella had given me that Norberto Padilla was involved in the sugarcane business on the Florida mainland, but I was anxious to hear Mo's take on the man. "And this Padilla, what do you know about his background?"

Mo turned back from the window. "He bragged once about how much land his family owns, where they grow a lot of sugarcane. Then he said something about 'those enviros' wanting to take away his water."

"Seems like an odd thing for a fly fisherman to say. Doesn't he get it about water quality in the Everglades and Florida Bay?"

"You'd think so. I haven't been here that long, and I can see what's going on. Without a steady flow of clean fresh water, this whole place is gonna be in big trouble."

"Yeah, and there's only one place that water can come from."

"Straight out of Mr. Padilla's sugarcane fields, right?"

"Mostly, you're right, Mo. Do you know what sort of a relationship Padilla had with Mr. Broom, the guy that drowned here a while back? I heard Broom was passionate about the Glades, so maybe—"

"If you don't mind my asking, why all these questions about who Padilla liked or didn't like? Just take the man fishing, okay? He's good enough at it, and you're obviously Caucasian. Shouldn't be any problem."

Apparently I'd taken a step too far. "Sorry, you're right. Forget what I said."

Mo sat silent for a while. Then he shook his head like he'd made up his mind about something. "Not good enough. I saw you standing with that cop the other day, and then you show up pretending to be a fishing guide. Since we're stuck with each other, don't you think I deserve the truth about what you actually are doing here?"

Agreeing to live at the club probably had been a dumb idea in the first place, but now it was too late. I saw no option except to take Mo into my confidence and hope he knew how to keep his mouth shut.

"You're right, Mo. So here's the thing. I really am a fishing guide, but I also do consulting work with the sheriff's department from time to time. That was Detective Stella Reynard you saw me with, and she asked me to look into the drowning of Arthur Broom because we're pretty sure he was murdered."

"Wow. How did it happen?"

"We're not sure, but we found lionfish in the pond where he died, and somebody called her department to report they'd seen him being pushed into the water."

"Good grief! Lionfish? Any idea who did the pushing?"

"Nope. We don't even know who made the call, let alone who might have done the deed. But it seems likely it was somebody staying on the property, like a member or an employee. Detective Reynard hopes I can get to know the people who were here that night, and maybe find somebody with a motive."

"While disguised as a fishing guide, right?"

"Right."

"I was here that night. How do you know it wasn't me?"

"I don't. But my gut tells me otherwise. So now I need your help. Do you have any idea who might have had a grudge against Broom?"

"Not really. But you're right. He *was* passionate about the Everglades, and very knowledgeable from what I could tell the few times I took him out. He talked a lot about how the key to saving the glades was restoring fresh water, and how agriculture and development were getting in the way. I suppose anybody around here with those interests might hold a grudge. But as a motive for murder? Doesn't seem likely, does it?"

"Maybe not. But just for the sake of argument, can you think of any club members in particular who might be threatened by Broom's activities? You have my word what you say never leaves this room."

He fidgeted a while, rearranging the chopsticks on his plate even though he'd already finished eating. Eventually he stopped fidgeting and looked straight at me.

"I liked Mr. Broom. But lots of people around here thought he was kinda nuts. You know, because of his interest in the environment. I've fished with two guys in particular who might have held the type of grudge you were asking about. One is Norberto Padilla. We've already talked about him. The other is a guy called Royal O'Doul. Weird name, huh? Anyway, you might have heard of him? He's big into developing private resorts with golf courses."

Pretty much everybody in Florida knew about O'Doul. The developer's footprints were all over the state.

"Have you fished with him?" I asked.

"Oh yeah. He thinks he's big stuff. In my opinion Royal O'Doul is a royal pain."

Chapter 9

Imet Norberto Padilla on the dock at 8 AM two days later. We shook, and he handed me his ten-weight Winston fly rod. Then he jumped into the bow of my flats boat, which I'd brought from home the night before. He already had a big olive and silver bunny fly tied on the end of his leader. It was as good a pattern as any to start with, so I checked the leader to make sure it wasn't frayed, and slid the rod into one of the storage slots built into the hull of the boat. I had a box of my favorite flies with me, in case that particular bunny wasn't what the fish were looking for.

Our goal for the day was to hunt tarpon in the backcountry. Norberto (call me "Norb") sat down on the Yeti cooler in front of the console rather than beside me at the wheel as we pulled away from the dock. As a result, there wasn't much opportunity to talk over the noise of my outboard as we made our way north and a little west across Florida Bay. It seemed like a deliberate move on his part, and I had the early impression—which turned out to be accurate—that it would be a challenge getting the man to engage in small talk.

My objective for starters was a flat just south of Palm Key, where tarpon were rumored to be actively chasing schools of mullet, one of their favorite foods. It took us about 45 minutes to get there.

We spotted several fish rolling on the surface as I cut the engine and got up on the platform to pole us out onto the flat. There was no wind, and I knew the fish would be spooky in the quiet water. I just hoped they were hungry. Tarpon are notoriously fickle fish, and some days they won't eat no matter what sorts of flies you throw at them. If this turned out to be one of those days, at least I would learn something about the man's temperament.

I poled across the still water, looking for fish chasing bait or laid up near the surface. The water was murky, like it usually was out there, but not so much we wouldn't be able to see the fish as long as they weren't hugging bottom. Padilla was up in the bow, with his back to me, but at least it was quiet now so we could talk if he chose to. The search for fish could take a while, depending on their abundance and activity level. I'd learned over the years this circumstance provided a good opportunity for a guide and a new client to get acquainted.

I began in the least personally intrusive way I could think of.

"Been fishing for tarpon long?"

"Since I was a kid. I'd go out with my dad and my brothers. But back then it was with live bait, mostly under the bridges at night. I really didn't get into fly fishing until after college."

Padilla kept looking straight ahead, scanning the water. He held the fly in his left hand and the rod in his right, ready to cast.

I was about to ask him what college—another good neutral topic—when a tarpon rolled thirty yards straight ahead of us. The early morning sun reflected bright off its big silvery scales.

"Good fish at twelve o'clock," I said.

"I see it," he replied, with enough edge in his voice to tell me I hadn't needed to point out something so obvious.

The tarpon was moving toward us, so I stopped the boat and let it come. I had yet to see the man cast, and it was going to be up to him when he thought he could reach the fish. He waited until it was twenty yards off the port bow, then made two false casts to get the line airborne, and dropped the bunny two feet in front of its nose. A near perfect cast. The fly disappeared in a big swirl, and right after that the fish went airborne in a shower of salt water. Padilla bent forward to put slack in the line, but the tarpon broke off anyway and was gone. The whole thing lasted less than five seconds.

"Damn," he said. "That was a good fish. Probably better than a hundred pounds. Best I've hooked so far this year."

It was the last fish we touched that day, in spite of having several more good shots with nearly every variety of fly I had in my box. Like I said, tarpon can be finicky.

By mid-afternoon it had grown hot and muggy, we weren't seeing any fish, and I could tell that "Norb" was about to pull the plug.

"You ever fish the ponds back at the club?" I asked.

He didn't say anything for a while, just kept scanning the water, like maybe he was making his mind up about something.

"Sure. Whenever I want to eat fish for dinner. My two favorites are mangrove snapper and hogfish. Especially the hogfish."

Now we were getting somewhere.

"Mel Campbell told me a guy drowned in the hogfish pond the other day. Did you hear about that?"

"Sure. It was Arthur Broom. Guess he was drunk again. Too bad." Then he reeled in his line and handed me the rod. "Let's get out of here. This place is dead."

We rode back to the club in silence, just like on the ride out. When we got to the dock he gave me a decent tip, said "See ya," and walked away toward the lodge.

The grand total of what I learned that day was Norberto Padilla had a dad and more than one brother, that he used to bait fish but now he fly fished and was good at it. The only thing I learned about the late Arthur Broom was that he drank too much. Maybe. If it kept on like this, there was no way I was going to earn the $500 a week that Stella had promised.

Chapter 10

My next client was an absolute chatterbox compared to Norb Padilla. Johnny Krasuski was a skinny little guy with wispy white hair and a leathery tan that told me he'd spent too many days on the water without protection. He knocked at the cabin door the night before our scheduled trip and invited himself inside. He sat down at the kitchen table with Mo and me and accepted our offer of a beer.

The first thing Johnny did was announce that he wanted to go after permit because it was "practically the only damned fish still on my bucket list." Then he explained that we were going to spin fish because he'd hurt his wrist playing senior softball six months earlier and couldn't handle a fly rod anymore.

"Hope you're okay with that. I know some of the club members look down their noses at us spin casters. Won't even consider them for membership. Lucky thing I got in before the accident. Hell, they even elected me president, so now what are they gonna do?"

I said spin fishing was fine with me, but I also cautioned him that permit were scarce and hard to catch using any kind of gear.

"Tell me about it," he said. "I've been trying for a decade to catch one of those sons-of-bitches. You got any bait? I think permit like to eat little crabs."

"You're right about that. I'll pick some up in the morning at the bait shop."

"You're gonna like that guy," Mo said after Krasuski had left. "He's a good fisherman, and not a snob. And boy does he like to talk. He might help with your other reason for being here besides fishing."

~ ~ ~

47

Mo had it right. By the time we got to the spot where permit were rumored to be cruising, I already knew that Johnny Krasuski had grown up in Columbus, Ohio, where he'd opened an auto parts outlet that eventually expanded to a chain of stores all across the eastern half of the country. He had two sons and a daughter. One of the sons went to medical school, the daughter was a Ph.D. biochemist, and the other son now ran the car parts business, from which Johnny had retired ten years earlier. He even got around to informing me that his wife had died of cancer two years previously. Then he described his fishing history.

Johnny started out as a bass fisherman, which made sense in Ohio, but quickly expanded his repertoire to include fishing in Canada for lake trout, walleye, and northern pike. Saltwater fishing had begun later when he and his wife moved to Fort Lauderdale four years ago, which is when he joined the Purple Isle Sportsman's Club. His wife had fished too, before she died.

Our objective that day was a large shallow flat west of the Arsenicker Keys, where Mo and another club member recently had taken a permit on a fly that they estimated weighed close to thirty pounds.

The sky was clear when we got there, but there was a pretty good chop on the water. I knew it would make the fish a little less spooky, which was good, but they'd also be harder to spot, which wasn't.

Permit aren't that much harder to catch than tarpon. The trick is finding one. Lots of permit trips involve poling for hours across water that turns out to be empty. We'd been at it for three hours that morning, and seen nothing except a couple of stingrays and one small lemon shark. Was it going to be another one of those days?

As far as I could see we were the only boat out there, except for a center console Mako with a blue hull that seemed to be running parallel to us, about 150 yards off to starboard. It was a little closer than I would have preferred, permit being notoriously edgy. In the three hours it hadn't gotten any nearer to us, but neither had it moved away, which seemed odd.

I'd never seen the Mako before, but I trained my binoculars on the man driving the boat to find out if he was somebody I recognized. Then I might get on the phone and politely ask him to back off a little. The man was standing at the wheel where I could see him clearly, but he was wearing one of those masks that protects the whole head from the sun, so I had no idea who he was. If there were any registration numbers on the boat they must have been black, because it wasn't possible to distinguish any against the dark blue hull. The boat didn't look all that new. The twin outboards were older model two-strokes, and the port side gunwale had scuffs on it, like it had collided with a dock on more than one occasion.

Johnny and I kept going, looking for telltale sharp dorsal fins breaking the surface. The wind had died down, but we saw no disturbances to the increasingly glassy surface that might have indicated the presence of feeding permit.

I'd been trying to figure out a way to get Johnny talking about other club members, especially Arthur Broom, when he said over his shoulder: "Were you here when that guy drowned in one of the fishponds?"

"No, but I heard about it. Terrible thing. They're saying he might have been stung to death by lionfish?"

Johnny grunted. "Yeah, so they say. I just wonder what he was doing out there in the first place. Apparently it was in the middle of the night. Maybe he was drunk or something. I've seen that guy knocking 'em back at the bar."

"Too bad he happened to fall into that particular pond. Do they regularly stock one with lionfish?"

"Oh hell no. Or at least not that I ever heard." Johnny took off his cap and scratched the back of his head. "I liked Art Broom, unlike some of the other club members."

"You mean you don't like some other members, or those other club members didn't like Broom?"

"Both I guess."

If this investigation of mine was going to get anywhere, it was time to take a chance.

"Anybody in particular?" I asked.

"Well now that's a long list. But Norb Padilla comes to mind. Guy's way too arrogant for my taste. And then there's Lou . . . holy shit look at that!"

Fishing guides, if they're any good, keep scanning the water no matter what else was going on. But I'd been concentrating so much on what Johnny Krasuski had to say about things at the club that I'd been looking at the back of his head instead of out across the flats. I lifted my eyes toward the horizon and immediately spotted two dark fins cutting through the shallow water, about 100 yards off our bow. They were moving slowly from right to left, no more than 6 feet apart. Occasionally a tail would emerge above the water, which told me they were tipping up to work the bottom. The pair obviously were on the prowl for food, which greatly increased our chances for a hook-up. My pulse quickened.

"Get ready with that crab," I said. "If they keep poking along like that, it won't take long to get you in casting range. When the time comes, try to drop it about a yard or two in front of their noses."

"Which one?" he asked.

"Your call, but the one in front looks bigger."

"I'm into bigger. Just tell me when."

Three minutes later I said "now." He made a perfect cast and the crab sank slowly down into the quiet water, right where I judged the fish would intercept it if it kept going in a straight line. Five seconds later there was a big swirl. Johnny struck hard, then held the rod high as the fish took off. We both watched and listened to the braided line screaming off his reel.

"Hot damn, my first permit!" he said. Then he let out a full-throated high pitched laugh.

At that moment I could tell without a doubt that Johnny Krasuski was my kind of fisherman.

We'd both been concentrating on the permit so hard that I was only vaguely aware of the other boat until it was almost on us. It was the blue-hulled Mako, coming fast. At first I thought the guy had just come over to watch, which was pushy enough, but at the last minute the boat veered off straight in the direction of our fish. What the hell?

"Jesus!" Johnny yelped. "Can't he see my line? What is that jerk up to?"

I cupped my hands and yelled "Hey! Can't you see we've got a fish on?"

But the Mako just kept going, zigzagging back and forth across the line, cutting it clean.

"God-damn!" Johnny said. "Who is that guy anyway?"

In all my fishing experience, I'd never seen anything like it. I grabbed my phone and took a photo of the boat, but by this time it had taken off to the south. All I could see was the stern, and it had no markings.

"You gonna chase him?" Johnny screamed. "Somebody needs to bust his ass for a stunt like that!"

It was tempting. But my 80-horse Yamaha was no match for the twin 300 Mercuries on the Mako. There was no point in even trying.

Johnny sat down hard and put his head in his hands, shaking it slowly from side to side. Who could blame him?

"Why?" he asked.

"Why indeed?" was all I said in reply. But I was thinking darker thoughts. Who was that clown, and what was his point? Was it some sort of save-the-permit patrol I'd never heard about?

Neither of us said or did anything for a while. I guess we were pretty numb from the whole bizarre experience. Finally I decided we had to make a decision about the rest of the day. "Want to keep going?" I asked.

Johnny looked up. "You mean quit and let that bastard win? Hell, no. Let's get back at it. There's lots of daylight left."

Like I said, Johnny was my kind of fisherman.

~ ~ ~

I poled for another three hours before anything happened. Johnny had gone quiet for a change, almost sullen. Not that I blamed him. As anxious as I was to pump him for more information about club members, this just didn't seem like the right time. The episode with the blue Mako had deflated both of us, I suppose. Then, just as I was about to suggest we pack it in for the day, I spotted a fin. This time there was only one, but it was headed right for us.

I pointed and yelled. "Looks like we've got another one Johnny! Get up there on the bow and get ready. Your crab still good?"

Johnny lifted his rod, pulling the crab up from where it had been dangling in the water. "Yep. Its legs are still kicking."

"Good. Try to drop it about five feet in front of the fish's nose, so it has plenty of time to sink. Crabs normally are on the bottom."

I offered a silent prayer. If we could catch this new fish, it would help relieve some of my humiliation from the previous episode. There was nothing I could have done, but the captain is still the captain, even on an eighteen-foot flats boat. Everything that happens on board is the captain's fault by definition, no matter the circumstances.

Johnny waited until the permit was about thirty feet off our bow before he cast. I might have thrown the crab a bit sooner, but it splashed about the right distance ahead of the fish, which kept coming.

My hopes rose.

It seemed like an eternity before anything happened, and at first I wondered if the fish had gone on by us. But in reality it couldn't have been more than five seconds before the line came tight and our second permit of the day took off in the direction of the setting sun.

I stowed the pole and fired up the outboard, prepared to give chase if it looked like Johnny wasn't going to be able to turn the fish in a reasonable distance. There was plenty of line on the reel, but I knew from experience that the farther a permit got from the boat, the more likely it would break off when the sagging line sawed against a piece of coral or a rock. I mouthed another silent prayer.

Apparently the fishing gods were with us that day. Johnny played the permit masterfully and I managed to keep my Hell's Bay within a hundred yards the whole time. A half-hour after the initial hook-up, and after a handful of powerful runs, we had the fish to the boat. Johnny carefully reached into the water and lifted it up, one hand under its belly, the other just ahead of its tail. I turned the boat so the sun was at my back, and took photos. Johnny's wide smile was nearly as bright as the fish's silver flank.

I hooked my Boga fish grabber onto the permit's lower lip and lifted it up. The scale read 28 pounds: not a record, but a great permit nonetheless. I felt a mixture of relief and elation. We released the fish and watched as it sank back into the dark water and disappeared.

Johnny grinned, his leathery cheeks crinkling. "Thanks. Thanks a lot. I've waited a long time for this. Can I buy you a beer?"

"You mean back at the lodge?"

"Where else? You got a better place?"

"I might. And anyway, I thought employees weren't supposed to mingle with club members on the property."

"Where did you hear that?"

"From Mr. Weatherbee."

"Well that's bullshit. I've got something to celebrate, and I'd rather not do it alone. Ralph gives you any grief, which he won't, you let me know. But don't forget the dress code. You got chinos and a polo shirt, right?" Then he pointed down at my feet. "Oh, and you might lose those old tennis shoes, maybe wear a pair without so much bait sticking to 'em."

"Don't worry, Johnny. I'll grab a shower as soon as I get back to the cabin. And I'll be so beautiful when I walk into the clubhouse, you won't even recognize me."

He let out a hearty laugh. "No need in getting carried away."

We rode in silence on the way back, until just before sunset.

"You ever seen the green flash?" Johnny asked. "The one that's supposed to happen right when the sun sinks below the horizon?"

"Yeah, a couple of times. You?"

"Nope, never. And I've been lookin' for years. But today probably isn't the day, 'cause no doubt I used up all my luck with that permit. Boy-oh-boy, what a fish."

He was right. Just like ninety-nine out of a hundred times, on this day there was no green flash.

It was nearly dark by the time we got back to the dock. We'd gone our separate ways, agreeing to meet at the bar in a half hour, when it dawned on me I'd forgotten to ask him about the club member called "Lou" that he didn't particularly like.

Chapter 11

My cell phone came to life while I was walking back to the guides' cabin. The screen showed it was Katie.

"Hi there."

"Hi there yourself. You have a good day?"

"Pretty good. Had a client caught his first permit."

Then I told her about how somebody cut the line on another fish.

"That's weird. Any idea who it was? And why would anybody do that in the first place?"

"I have no idea who, let alone why."

"Any chance you can get home tonight?"

"Uh, you know I'd love to Katie. But I'd better stick around here for the next couple of days."

There was a silence. "Why?"

"Because I'm just getting to know this place, and some of the members. Which is what Stella asked me to do." I waited for a response, but again it didn't come. "You know I'd rather be with you. Please try to be patient."

"Oh I'm good at being patient, alright." Then she hung up.

Ouch.

The guides' cabin smelled like garlic and soy sauce when I walked in. Mo Murikami looked up from a bowl of rice on the table in front of him, chopsticks poised in mid-air. "How did it go today?"

"Really good. I was with Johnny Krasuski and we hooked up two permit. His first ever. Got one to the boat."

"They can be tricky. The other one break you off on some coral?"

"Not exactly. We had a visitor. You know anybody drives an older Mako with a dark blue hull?"

He shook his head. "Can't say I do. Why?"

54

"As soon as we had the first fish on, he came over and cut Johnny's line with his boat. It was deliberate."

Mo's chopsticks stopped again in mid-delivery. "What? That's unbelievable."

"Yeah, but that's what happened."

"You get an ID on the guy or the tag on his boat?"

"Nope. He beat it out of there before I had a chance. All I know is it was a man. Anyway, Johnny's invited me for drinks at the clubhouse to celebrate the one we did land."

Mo's worried look morphed into a grin. "Wow. You do know that's a big deal, right? Employees like us don't usually get in there. I never have."

"Then I guess I'd better clean myself up." I grabbed a towel and headed for the shower. "Have you ever met a club member named Lou somebody?"

He thought for a minute. "I can only think of one. Lou Feronni. Or Farrelli, something like that. Italian name. What about him?"

"Johnny started to tell me about him today—something not good I'm guessing by the tone of his voice. But right then we got interrupted by one of his permits, and we never got back to it. So I was just wondering if you knew anything about him."

"Not much. I believe he's president or maybe CEO of a big cruise line with headquarters in Miami. Somebody told me his ships usually depart from Fort Lauderdale and cruise the Caribbean islands." Mo quit talking long enough to shovel in another mouthful of rice. He chewed and swallowed and looked back up at me. "Oh, and he's not much of an angler. He prefers fishing the ponds rather than going out in the bay, and that's a good thing because he doesn't really know how to cast." Mo thought for a minute. "That's about it, I guess. You think he might have had something to do with what happened to Broom?"

"No idea. But thanks for the info."

I made a mental note to check Stella's file on Farrelli.

~ ~ ~

Johnny and I arrived in front of the main lodge at the same time. He held the door for me, then pointed me left as soon as we were inside, toward a wing of the building with the bar and restaurant.

The bar itself was a vintage Brunswick, maybe thirty feet long, with a high mirrored back and an impressive array of bottles on shelves in front of the mirror. Pillars and scrolls at each end were carved out of mahogany and other tropical woods I didn't recognize. Johnny caught my admiring look. "That bar was manufactured in 1908. Originally it was in an old hotel in the Upper Adirondacks. Cost us a fortune to get it moved down here."

In addition to the bar there were a half dozen round tables scattered across the room, each with four chairs upholstered in red leather. The bar stools matched the chairs. A woman was sitting on one at the far end, talking to the bartender. Besides them, the place was empty.

Was it too late for cocktail hour at the Purple Isle, or was this just an off night? I saw my chances for making useful contacts shrinking, until Johnny identified the woman.

"That's Fiona Broom. First time I've seen her since the—uh—accident. I oughta go say hello. Come on and I'll introduce you."

Fiona was a strikingly handsome woman, perhaps in her late thirties or early forties, but carefully made-up so it was hard to tell. She had long blond hair tied up in a ponytail, and she was wearing lots of turquoise jewelry, including a big squash-blossom necklace perched on her ample bosom. The impression she gave from a distance was not that of a grieving widow. But I could see her eyes were red-rimmed and her right hand, which was wrapped around a glass half filled with ice and something amber, shook as she raised it up off the bar to take a swallow.

I caught Johnny by the elbow as we entered the room. "How old did you say Art Broom was?"

He whispered. "I didn't. But I know why you asked. Fiona is number two. Back home they would have called her a trophy wife. But she and Art liked each other, and she seems nice enough. Still, there have been some rumors."

"What sort of rumors?"

"Oh, you know, the usual. Younger woman married to an old geezer."

"What happened to number one?"

"I think she died."

The bartender was younger than Fiona Broom, probably early thirties, with a blond burr haircut and matching goatee. He was powerfully built, especially across the shoulders, and he was wearing an immaculate white polo shirt that was at least two sizes smaller than it needed to be.

Johnny went straight up to Fiona and gave her a big hug. "God I'm sorry about Whisk. We all are. It's just tragic what happened. Is there anything I can do?"

She pulled back from the embrace and immediately teared-up. "No, Johnny, I suppose not." She sniffed, then picked up a paper napkin and dabbed at her eyes. "But it is good to see you." She pointed at me. "And your friend here. Are you a new member?"

"My apologies," Johnny said. "Fiona Broom, I'd like you to meet Sam Sawyer. He's a new guide here, and a damned good one I might add. And Sam, this is George Light. Except we usually call him Bud. Get it? Bud Light?"

Johnny laughed while the bartender scowled. "They never get tired of that, but I am," Light said. Then he reached out and we shook. I winced from the power in his grip.

"Pleased to meet you," we both said at about the same time.

"You like gin?" Johnny asked me. "Bud makes the best dry martini in the Keys."

I've always been more of a bourbon man when it comes to hard liquor, but decided to play along. "Sure, thanks."

While "Bud" worked on our drinks, Johnny started to describe our day on the water. "It was fabulous. This guy's a real ace. Got my first permit ever, and . . . oh, hell, never mind all that." He turned back to Fiona. "Sorry. What can you tell me about Whisk's accident?"

"You mean how did he die?"

"I heard about the lionfish. But what was he doing out there in the first place? And how did he end up in the water?"

"I wasn't here, but from what the detective told me, they aren't sure it was the lionfish that actually killed him. He had a bad heart, you know."

Johnny moved beside Fiona, and put an arm around her shoulders. "How long will you be staying at the club?"

"I'll leave as soon as they let me have the . . . body."

"Drinks up, Mr. Krasuski," the bartender announced, as he set two stemmed glasses in front of us, each with a single olive and one oversized ice cube. "Just as you like 'em. Bombay Safire, with just a dash of vermouth."

The interruption was both rude and awkward, and I had the sense it was intentional. Was there something going on between the widow Broom and George Light?

"You fellas mind keeping an eye on things, while I walk Mrs. Broom back to her cabin?" Light continued. "I'll be back in a few minutes. Tell anybody who comes in to help themselves."

"Sure, no problem," Johnny replied.

"Nice to meet you Mr. Sawyer," Fiona said as she spun off her bar stool and stood up, ready to leave.

I wanted to press Johnny for details as soon as they were out the door, but right then a couple walked in from the adjoining restaurant and joined us at the bar. He was a heavyset man with a high forehead and lots of gold jewelry, wearing a Hawaiian shirt with flowers and toucans on it. She was similarly adorned, except her blouse featured palm trees and parrots.

"Mind if we join you for an after-dinner drink?" the man said to Johnny. Then he turned to me. "And you are . . . ?"

Johnny immediately came to my rescue. "This is Sam Sawyer, our new guide at the club. And Sam, I'd like you to meet Lou and Donna Farrelli."

Lou frowned briefly, but then lit up a smile that involved his lips but not his eyes. "Pleased to meet you."

We shook. His grip was weak and damp.

"Sam got me my first permit today, and we're celebrating. You should go out with this guy some time. He really knows what he's doing."

"That's great," Lou replied, sounding neither enthused nor interested. "Actually, I prefer sticking to the ponds."

"Speaking of ponds," Johnny replied. "Did you hear about Broom?"

Farrelli nodded. "I suppose he was drunk as usual, and fell in. The man just couldn't resist those mojitos Bud makes."

I knew better, but stayed quiet.

Farrelli looked around. "Speaking of Bud, where is he? Donna and I need something to wash down our dinners."

"He had to run a short errand," Johnny said. "Should be right back. He said anybody comes in should go behind the bar and pour whatever they'd like."

Donna Farrelli tugged at her husband's sleeve. "Let's just go back to the cabin, Lou. I'm tired. You've got some scotch back there anyway."

"Okay, in a minute. But before we go, Johnny, I wanted to mention something about the Broom situation. Now that he's—well you know, *gone*—we have a membership slot open, right?"

"Yeah, I suppose so. But don't you think it's a little early to—"

"And I have a suggestion. Mack Snodgrass. In fact, I intend to propose him at our next members' meeting. He's a great guy, and really into fishing. You should check him out."

The name was familiar, but I couldn't make the connection. "Who's Mack Snodgrass?" I asked Johnny as soon as the Farrellis left.

"He's a state senator, from someplace up around Tallahassee."

"Any idea why Mr. Farrelli would be interested in his being a club member?"

"No damn clue." Johnny drained the last of his martini and put down the glass. "I wonder what's keeping Bud. Usually he brings me dinner right here in the bar. But I'm starved and I'm tired of waiting. Let's go next door to the restaurant."

We did, they let me in without any hassle, and the food was excellent. Flo might have been right about Jacques Petain being a phony Frenchman, but apparently he did know how to cook. I had mangrove snapper prepared in a lemon-butter sauce with capers. Johnny had a steak.

Chapter 12

Over the next two days I fished with clients who couldn't have had anything to do with the death of Arthur Broom, or at least I couldn't imagine why. One was a nice man from southern Indiana who'd started his own insurance business that had grown into a nationwide giant. The other was an investment banker from Chicago who explained that he'd made lots money in pork futures, whatever they were.

· But on the third day I went fishing with Royal O'Doul, and that was a different deal altogether. He was pacing back and forth at the dock when I got there at 7:45 that morning. O'Doul was a robust man with a shock of black curly hair and piercing blue eyes. He was carrying a stout 12-weight Loomis fly rod. Obviously he planned on going after big prey.

As I was to learn about Royal O'Doul, everything about him involved bigness.

"You Sam Sawyer?" he asked, as I walked up. "Been expecting you. The day's not getting any younger."

"Good morning," I said.

"I've been here since seven," he replied. Then he pointed toward the ponds. "Finally gave up and went down there to make some practice casts. Now I'm all limbered up and ready to go."

"Sorry about that, Mr. O'Doul. My understanding was that 8 o'clock is the usual start time."

"Well, never mind. Let's just get going, okay?"

"Of course. What would you like to do today?"

"I heard about a book called 'Lords of the Fly,' or something like that. Haven't had time to read it myself, but I understand it's about a bunch of guys who compete to catch the biggest tarpon on a fly. So that's what I'd like to do."

I'd read the book by Monte Burke. It was a who's who of tarpon lore. "Well now that's a pretty tall order, Mr. O'Doul. We're talking about a lifetime of effort."

"Oh yeah, I understand that. So no, I don't expect to break their records. My life's way too busy for that. But they keep a log book here at the club, and I looked it up. The biggest tarpon caught by a member is 140 pounds. So that's my goal, to break that record. And Mel Campbell tells me you're just the man to help me do it. And August is still good for tarpon, right?"

"May and June usually are better, but I've been seeing lots of fish around lately."

"Great! Then let's get started. That club record was caught at someplace they call the Yellow Brick Road. You ever heard of it?"

"Uh huh. It's a stretch of water on the Atlantic side here in Lower Matecumbe. I have no idea why they named it after that place in the Wizard of Oz."

O'Doul looked blank, like he had no idea what I was talking about. "So anyway, that's where I want to go, to get that record tarpon."

I shook my head. "No, not this morning."

His mouth turned down in a little pout, like he wasn't used to anybody contradicting him, even on a subject he knew nothing about. "Why not?" he said.

"Because the tarpon over there will be moving down the coast, and we'll have the sun in our eyes, so we won't be able to see 'em coming."

"Oh. Well then do you have a better idea?"

"Yes I do. We'll start at a bank along the east side of Long Key. The tarpon will be coming out of the bay through the Channel Five Bridge and then following that bank. We'll have the morning sun at our backs, and the tide will be right. Then, if we haven't had any luck by the middle of the day, we can go on up to the Yellow Brick Road in the afternoon. Assuming you want to stay out all day, that is."

"If that's what it takes to break the record, then damn right I do."

"You do realize the odds of catching a tarpon that big are pretty slim, don't you?"

O'Doul got a smirky grin on his face. "All my life people have been telling me what I wasn't gonna be able to do. And you know what? Most of the time they've been wrong." He picked up his 12-weight and headed for my boat. "So let's get at it!"

"In my experience, a 10-weight rod is more than adequate for tarpon. Throwing a 12-weight can fatigue your arm, especially if we have the opportunity for multiple shots. I have a good 10-weight Sage back at the cabin, if you'd—"

"Nope," O'Doul replied, patting the cork handle of his Loomis. "We're going after big fish, with a big rig."

I loaded O'Doul into my Hell's Bay, along with our gear. We headed southwest out of the marina, then crossed under the Channel Five Bridge and moved out toward the Long Key bank. Two boats already were anchored in place by the time we got there.

I could hear O'Doul saying "I told you so" before he actually said it.

"Where will the tarpon be coming from?" he asked.

"Like I said, they should be moving from the bridge toward this bank, and then south along it."

"Good. Then we should go up ahead of those other boats, so the fish get to us first, right?" He had a smug smile on his face, like he'd just had a killer idea.

There was an unwritten but firmly established rule of tarpon etiquette that said you fell in behind rather than in front of somebody who already had set up. That way you didn't cut them off from the oncoming fish. I explained this to O'Doul, as I anchored about 200 yards off the stern of the second boat, and perhaps 50 yards farther out from shore.

"The tarpon will spread out by the time they get this far from the bridge, so we'll be in a good position to intercept some of them," I explained.

O'Doul grumbled but didn't say anything.

I rigged him up with a purple and black tarpon fly, and asked O'Doul to get up in the bow and be ready to cast. Then I climbed up on the poling platform to watch for oncoming fish, and the waiting game began. I hoped this would give me a chance to get O'Doul talking. Unlike Norberto Padilla a few days earlier, he didn't disappoint. In fact, the man didn't seem capable of just sitting still and waiting. He kept twitching around, fiddling with his gear, and clearing his throat.

"You play golf?" he asked, about two minutes after we started fishing.

"I used to a little, when I lived up in Fort Lauderdale. Not so much anymore."

"I love that game," he said. "You may know I own golf resorts all over the state. And I don't mind telling you it's made me a rich man. Very rich. I can get you a free membership in any of my clubs, depending on how it goes today."

I couldn't remember another time when a client tried to bribe me into fishing successfully—a completely ridiculous idea, if you think about it. Why would a guide not want to do well? But rather than point that out to O'Doul, I used the opportunity to push him about his business.

"What's your closest club to Islamorada?" I asked.

"Right now, it's in Pompano Beach. But I'm in the process of buying a beautiful piece of farmland west of Homestead. It'll be perfect for a new course, and an easy drive for you once it's finished. We're having a couple of problems putting the deal together, but I've got a team of high-priced lawyers working on it."

"What sort of problems?" I asked.

"Right now the old farmer who owns the land won't sell. Says the place has been in his family for nearly 100 years and he wants to see it passed on. But other members of the family are all for it, especially the man's son, and they'll wear him down. With my help, that is. Everybody's got their price. There's no way that senile old fart is gonna mess up my plans."

"You said there were a couple of problems?"

The briefest of frowns crossed O'Doul's brow, and I thought maybe I'd pushed too far. But his usual smug countenance quickly returned. "Oh, the usual bullshit. Those short-pants boys with the Park Service are saying I would be diverting fresh water to take care of the grass. And then the runoff could pollute the Everglades because of fertilizer and pesticides."

"Wouldn't that be the case?"

O'Doul looked back up at me. "Say, you're not one of those eco-freaks are you?"

"No, I suppose not, but I do know something about water problems affecting the Everglades, and it seems to me—"

He slammed his fly rod down on the deck. Then he folded his arms across his ample chest, and assumed the pout I was beginning to suspect was part of his usual persona. "You look here! Florida is a great place to live, now that we've got the mosquitoes under control and built amenities people expect. And I—*me*—I've been personally responsible for a whole lot of that. And that place next to Homestead? Once it's built we're gonna hire thousands of Indians to work there. Give 'em good-paying jobs."

"Thousands?"

"Well, maybe hundreds. But either way, it's more than you're gonna do." Then he shook his head and looked out toward the Channel Five Bridge, its arched concrete superstructure shining in the morning sun. "To say nothing of that sonofabitch Arthur Broom." Then, almost as an afterthought: "God rest his soul."

Now we were getting somewhere. "Was that the guy who died at the club a while back? What did he have to do with your plans?"

"He did his best to kill 'em, that's what. And he had some goddam deep pockets to try and do it. But at least now—"

O'Doul's rant was interrupted by a shout coming from the boat at the head of the line, and we both looked up to see a big tarpon clear the water in a cartwheeling leap. The guide jumped down off the poling platform, unhooked his skiff from the anchor float, and gave chase.

We both watched in silence as the fish took off in the direction of the bridge, with the client hanging on for dear life. It was an exciting thing to see, even if it did involve another guide and another fisherman, but in this instance my mind was mostly elsewhere. At one level, Royal O'Doul had just set himself up as a prime suspect in the death of Arthur Broom. But on another level, would he really have said all those things if he'd actually been responsible? It didn't seem likely. Nevertheless, I was anxious to report back to Stella Reynard. What could she learn about O'Doul's planned golf resort? And what, if anything, had Art Broom succeeded in doing about it?

The guide with the fish on disappeared under the Channel Five Bridge, so now there was only one other boat in line with us. We sat for better than an hour before anything happened, during which time I learned that O'Doul had plans to get himself elected president of the Purple Isle Club, "because there've been some bad decisions about who gets in, and that Johnny Krasuski's too wishy-washy to do anything about it."

He never clarified which members he was talking about, and I didn't ask. But it wasn't hard to guess.

Only one group of tarpon got anywhere close over the remainder of the morning. There were five of them, coming right at us until they were about 50 yards away. Then they must have seen the boat, because they veered off to their left. But they kept coming, and I knew we were going to get a shot. The second fish in the line was a good-sized one, probably better than 100 pounds. There was no way to guarantee that particular fish was the one that would eat the fly, assuming any did. I told Royal O'Doul to cast beyond and in front of the group, and then strip the fly into their oncoming path.

His timing was good, but his casting wasn't. The pod swam by my skiff about 40 feet away, but all O'Doul could muster was 30 feet. It probably wouldn't have mattered anyway, because he brought the rod way too far down on the forward cast, which caused leader to pile up at the end of the fly line with a splash that was sure to have put the fish off.

I could tell from the look on his face that O'Doul was trying to figure out why it was my fault and not his. But he didn't say anything. Instead he rummaged around in a tote bag he'd brought with him, pulled out what looked like a chicken wrap sandwich, and started munching on it. I got down off the poling platform and joined him on the deck. He took out another sandwich and offered it to me. I'd been expecting this, because it was club policy that the clients provided the food, even if they were pissed off at the guide.

We ate in silence for a while, and then I suggested it was time to move on to the Yellow Brick Road. He nodded and said "yeah," but I could tell that some of his morning enthusiasm had begun to wear off.

But then we got lucky.

The first bit of good news was that there were no other boats around when we got there. We set up in a good spot, with the sun at our backs. I climbed up on the poling platform for a better look, and immediately spotted three groups of tarpon moving down the coast in our direction. The closest one was about 200 yards away. I told O'Doul to get up in the bow and be ready to cast.

And this time it worked. He made a decent throw of about twenty feet, and the lead fish turned and ate the fly. There was a big swirl, and then a jump that almost sprayed water into our boat. O'Doul knew enough to bow down toward the fish so the line wouldn't come tight while it was in the air, and as a result he stayed hooked up.

In my experience, sometimes tarpon mostly jump, and sometimes they mostly just take off. And again in my experience, the biggest ones tend to run rather than jump.

We followed that fish for better than an hour, and I'll have to give Royal O'Doul credit. He played the fish just right, keeping a tight line the whole time, but letting it run when it wanted to. Eventually the fish tired, and he was able to bring it up next to my skiff. I put on gloves and reached down, grabbing the fish by its lower jaw, being careful not to injure its gills. This was going to be strictly catch-and-release, with the fish staying in the water the whole time, so the next step would be difficult. We needed two measurements in order to estimate its weight: length from snout to the fork in the tail, and girth just in front of the dorsal fin. From these two numbers it would be possible to calculate weight using a well-established formula. And in the world of tarpon fishing, it was the weight that mattered.

It was a big fish, probably not the record O'Doul was hoping for, but close. Because I had hold of the fish and couldn't let go, I was going to need help taking the measurements. I asked O'Doul to kneel down next to me. I laid one end of my measuring tape at the tip of the lower jaw, asked him to extend it out toward the tail, and then read the length.

"Sixty-five inches," he said.

"Okay, now wrap it around the body just in front of that top fin."

O'Doul leaned out over the water and took the measurement. "Thirty-eight inches," he said. "Is that going to be enough?"

I knew a tarpon that long and that deep was going to be close to the 140 pound record. But there was a problem. O'Doul must have thought I didn't see it, but I did. He'd cheated on both measurements. For length, he'd run the tape all the way out to the tip of the tail, instead of stopping at the fork, which the rules stipulated. And for girth, he actually had kept his forearm inside the tape.

"Maybe," I said. "We'll put those numbers into the formula when we get back."

Royal O'Doul had a self-satisfied grin on his face the whole way back to the club. Of course I knew we hadn't actually caught a 65 by 38 inch tarpon that day. But fortunately when I put those numbers into the formula, the best estimate was for a 120 pound fish. Naturally O'Doul grumped and carried on about it, but at least I was spared the problem of having to tell Ralph Weatherbee or Mel Campbell, or whoever kept the record book, that the man was a cheat.

Then it occurred to me. They probably already knew that.

As soon as I got rid of O'Doul, and finished cleaning my boat, I called Katie. She wanted to know what I'd been up to, so I told her.

"You actually fished with Royal O'Doul?" she said.

"Yep. And he's a real piece of work, let me tell you. Anyway, how about you? How was your day?"

"Not bad. Interesting, actually. Any chance you can get tomorrow off?"

"Probably. I'll have to check with the manager. But I don't think I'm booked to take anybody out. Why?"

"There have been developments in the case. I'm meeting Stella and Dr. Hernandez in my office at nine. You might want to be there."

"Is it about Broom's stomach contents?"

"Yep. Looks like he might have swallowed something really nasty."

"Huh."

It was quiet for a while, and at first I thought maybe she'd hung up. "And . . . maybe you could come over tonight? I mean as long as we're meeting Stella in the morning, and . . . oh dammit Sam, I miss you! Prince and I both miss you."

There was an edge to her voice, and I was reminded of our talk from a few nights ago. "Sure, but it'll have to be late. There's something I've gotta do at the club."

"We'll leave the light on."

"Sounds like a plan."

Chapter 13

Not only had Katie left the light on for me. She was in the living room when I walked in, and she was wearing something skimpy.

Katie nodded toward the bedroom.

"What about Prince?" I asked.

"All taken care of. He's on the deck with food and water. I told him to be on the lookout for crocodiles."

Most nights Prince ended up sleeping with us, but this wasn't going to be one of them, at least for a while.

~ ~ ~

I woke up the next morning to the sound of the Keurig hissing in the kitchen, and pretty soon Katie came padding into the bedroom with two cups of coffee. Prince tagged along behind, jumped up on the bed, and snuggled up against me. He didn't like the smell of coffee, and he turned his head away if I held the cup too close. But he did like to have his belly rubbed. It was a morning ritual I enjoyed all too infrequently, even before all this business at the Purple Isle club.

Katie sat in a chair next to the bed and took a swallow of coffee. She was beautiful as always in the early light streaming in through a window that looked out on the canal. "We gotta get moving," she said. "I let you sleep in. It's nearly eight and we need to be at my office by nine."

"What have you learned so far?"

"The man had something odd in his stomach."

"Any idea what?"

"Something I've never seen before. I'll tell you about it at the meeting."

"Okay. I probably should go straight to the club afterwards, so we should take both cars." I knew she had a faculty permit for her Prius. "But am I gonna have trouble finding a place to park the Cherokee?"

"No, that's another nice thing about this job. The place isn't all that crowded."

The traffic was light because it was August and not the tourist season. It took us only about 40 minutes to get there.

I had some misgivings about meeting in Katie's campus office, where we might be interrupted by students and colleagues. But the first thing she did was put a sign up outside her door that said "Conference in Progress; Do Not Disturb." It must have happened before.

Katie had rearranged her office since my last visit and I liked what she'd done. Her desk was at one end, and six chairs were set around an oval table at the other. There were two potted palms, one beside the desk and the other next to the table. They were the real thing, not the plastic versions lots of people favored but botanists like her usually frowned at. Her Ph.D. diploma from the University of California hung on the wall behind her desk. It wasn't something ordinary faculty usually bothered with. I knew she did it because of her dealings with lawyers and others in law enforcement to whom such credentials were important.

A door with a big window led from the far end of the office back to her laboratory. Through it I could see lab benches and another desk that, unlike the one in the office, was cluttered with papers and an elaborate computer setup.

Katie moved a MacBook computer from her office desk to the table, and plugged it in. She'd just started brewing coffee when there was a knock on the door and Stella Reynard came in, followed by the county M. E., Anthony Hernandez. We all got settled around the table. Everybody but Anthony had coffee. Stella took a small recorder out of her briefcase and set it on the table in front of her.

I assumed Katie would run the meeting since it was her idea, but instead she nodded to Stella, who quickly started things off.

"Thanks for coming, everybody," Stella said, as she turned on the recorder. "For the record, and with permission of the participants, we will be recording this meeting, which involves me, Monroe County Detective Stella Reynard, County Medical Examiner Anthony Hernandez, Dr. Katherine Sawyer, and Dr. Sam Sawyer."

Stella paused for a swallow of coffee. "When Katie called and said she wanted to get together to talk about what she found in our victim's stomach, I said of course. But then it occurred to me that we might take this opportunity to talk about the case more broadly. Anthony, I'd like to start with you. Where are we on the autopsy and causes of death?"

The M. E. cleared his throat and opened a file folder. "Unfortunately, things are still not entirely clear. We know Mr. Broom was legally drunk when he went into that pond, and it is possible he drowned. There was a small amount of water in his lungs. But death by drowning is one of the most difficult CODs to show, let alone prove, because of contributing circumstances. The most common indications of a simple drowning death are froth around the nose and mouth and greatly distended lung size due to the changes in structure as the victim struggles to breathe. There were no such indications, which leads me to suspect that death was caused by something else. And it wasn't all that hard to figure out what it was."

"So you've determined a cause of death?" Stella asked.

"I have. The autopsy revealed blood clots and a ruptured aorta. The man died of a heart attack. I was able to contact his heart doctor up in Palm Beach, and it all fits. He had advanced COPD, probably from a lifetime of smoking. Plus he had two previous heart attacks. I suspected as much when I found two stents in coronary arteries, and a grossly enlarged heart."

"Are you then prepared to rule his death as accidental?" I asked.

Hernandez shook his head, just once. "I would under normal circumstances. But for two reasons I'm prepared to leave the case open for now. First, there were those lionfish stings. And second, I found some peculiar lesions in the lining of his stomach and esophagus. It's just possible either of those could have triggered his heart attack."

"That's good," Stella said. "Those lionfish didn't end up in that pond by accident, and it's just too much of a coincidence that somebody switched off the security cameras the night Broom got pushed into the pond, assuming that's what happened. And we still need to find out what might have caused those lesions. Katie, what can you tell us about the victim's stomach contents?"

Katie punched a couple of keys on her laptop and took a swallow of coffee. "The victim clearly had eaten shortly before he died, because digestion had not progressed far. His stomach contained the sorts of plant cells you'd expect if he'd eaten a salad and probably some type of protein for his last meal. There also were copious amounts of what I suspect were human red blood cells that likely were the result of whatever traumatized the linings of the stomach and esophagus. I have made slides and photographed plant cells I was able to identify as tomato skin and pulp, onion, lettuce, pieces of bell pepper, along with spinach and potatoes. Stella, are we certain he ate at the club the night he died?"

"Yes. We have several witnesses to that fact."

"In addition to those usual foods, I found several clumps of plant cells I didn't recognize. Could be a tropical vegetable I haven't seen before. You should talk to the club chef and maybe the bartender about what was on the menu the night he died. That might give us a clue."

"I'll be sure and check. And speaking about their chef: Sam, I just learned some things about him that weren't in the file I gave you the other day. First, he calls himself Jacques Petain, but his real name is Jason Pavlis. He was born in New York City, where his father was big time in the construction business."

"And Arthur Broom owned a New York investment company that may have had some legal problems, right? Did he have any connection with Pavlis?"

Stella shook her head. "Nothing we've found yet, but we're still looking. And there's one other thing about chef Pavlis, but it probably isn't relevant to our case. It turns out he and the club manager, Ralph Weatherbee? They're married."

I remembered seeing them together at the Safari Lounge. "From what I've learned so far about the general atmosphere at the Purple Isle club, I'll bet they're real busy keeping that a secret."

Stella chuckled. "Could be. But Katie, back to those mysterious cells in the victim's stomach. What can you do to identify them?"

"I'm certain they're from a plant because of their cellulose walls. Animal cells don't have that. But so far I haven't been able to figure out what plant species, which means they must be something pretty unusual."

Stella frowned. "Obviously this could be important. I'll check with people at the club who deal with food, but what else can we do?"

"I have a botanist friend in Florida, Tom Wordsburg, who's an expert on tropical plants. He's also familiar with the flora of the Florida Keys. There's a good chance he'll be able to identify those cells. Tom directs the Rolfson Botanical Garden in Miami. You may have read about that place. It draws crowds from everywhere, and there was a nice article about it recently in the Sunday Miami *Herald*. With your permission, Stella, I'll send Tom photomicrographs of the slides I made of those strange cells."

"Absolutely. But let's keep it confidential in terms of what this is all about."

"Of course. He knows I do forensic work, but I won't give him any specifics."

"If he's been watching the news, he might guess those specifics," I said.

"Sure, but even if he does, I know he'll keep his mouth shut. As I said, he's a friend of mine. I trust him completely."

"Thanks, Katie," Stella said. Then she pointed at the recorder sitting on the desk. "I know you've already covered some of this. But just so we have it on the record, would you mind explaining exactly how you go about determining what's in a victim's stomach? And hopefully do it without an overwhelming amount of jargon?"

Katie smiled at that. "Of course, Stella. First I mix the sample of stomach contents thoroughly. Then I pipette a small amount of the mixture and place it on a microscope slide. Next I cover the sample with another small piece of glass, called a cover slip, to protect it. Then I mount the slide under my microscope, which is fitted with a camera, and systematically scan and photograph all the different types of plant cells I can find. If the slide contains material likely significant to the case, then I make it permanent by coating the cover slip in a kind of glue."

"But how can you identify these cells after they've been churned around in sombody's stomach? Aren't they all broken apart?"

"Good question. But no they aren't, and here's the deal. As I mentioned before, plant cells are encased in skeletons made of cellulose—that's what makes plant foods crunchy. The key point is that humans can't digest cellulose, so no matter how long the food has been in a victim's stomach, the cell walls remain intact. And—importantly— those walls are distinctive for each kind of plant. Over the years, other forensic botanists and I have built up a large photographic collection of known plant cells. That's why in the present case I was able to identify most of the plant foods in Mr. Broom's stomach at the time he died. All except that one, which is still a mystery."

"And what about different kinds of meat cells?" Stella asked. "Wouldn't it be helpful to learn if Broom had eaten, for example, a certain kind of fish for dinner?"

"Indeed it would. But animal cells lack cellulose walls, so they just appear as amorphous blobs after having been in the digestive system for any length of time. About the only way to identify meat cells is through DNA analysis, which is both costly and time-consuming."

"Thank you Katie, for that clear explanation," Stella said. "And next, as long as we're all here together, Sam, can you fill us in on what you've found out at the club so far? Including who might have stocked that pond with lionfish?"

I hadn't been expecting this, because I'd come to the meeting assuming it was going to be Katie's show. "Not a helluva lot, I'm afraid. I've been there less than a week."

Stella frowned, obviously not satisfied. "Sure, but who have you met so far, and what have they said about Broom?"

"I've been out fishing with several of the members, and met another one in their bar. And I have a roommate and fellow guide, Mo Murikami. I guess the general impression I have is that Mr. Broom was not particularly well-liked."

"Why not?" Stella asked.

"The one thing everybody's mentioned is his passion for saving the Everglades and Florida Bay. Apparently he's sunk a lot of his time and money into it. They even call him the Glades Man."

"But why would anybody care about that?"

"Good question. The only thing I can think of is that most of the club members are heavily invested in Florida's economic activity, and saving the glades could impact their pocketbooks."

Stella's frown came back. "Anybody in particular?"

"Three members are possibilities among those I've met so far. But please understand this is only speculation. It's not like I have actual evidence."

"Sure, I understand. But who are they?"

"The first is Norberto Padilla. His family's in the sugar cane business. Moving clean fresh water into the glades—which is about the only way to restore the place—would come at the expense of his land and his livelihood. Another is Royal O'Doul."

"The golf resort guy?"

"Uh huh. He told me he's planning to build a new course near Homestead, but he's run into opposition from people interested in protecting the Everglades."

"You mean like Arthur Broom?"

"Among other people, likely including the Park Service."

Stella rapidly was taking notes. "And the third person?"

"That would be Lou Farrelli. He owns a cruise line."

"What would be the connection there?"

"Probably none. But he said something weird when I met him at the club bar the other day. We were with Johnny Krasuski, and Farrelli said he would be proposing a new member now that there was an open slot. It would be a state senator named Snodgrass. Farrelli said he's a big time fly fisherman."

"Well now that would be a first," Stella said. "I mean killing somebody to make room for one of your buddies?"

"Yeah, like I said, it's probably nothing. But maybe you could check out this Snodgrass and see if there's any connection with Farrelli, or with Broom for that matter."

"I can do that," Stella said.

"What about family?" Hernandez asked. "Don't you always look at family in a suspicious death?"

"Sure, and that's the first thing I did," Stella replied. "It's only his current wife Fiona. His first wife is dead, and there are no children or other close relatives that we know of. I've been in contact with the attorney who's also the executor of his will. I had to push a little, but he eventually disclosed the details. Turns out he had no life insurance. His estate—which is in the ten figure range—goes two thirds to Fiona and one third to the foundation he started to save the Everglades."

"So she stands to inherit a bundle," Hernandez said.

"She certainly does, so we can't rule it out. But there are several things that argue against her as a suspect. First, we know Broom was in bad health and probably wasn't going to last much longer anyway. Second, as near as I can determine from what others have said, he treated her pretty lavishly and they got along well. And perhaps most important of all, we know she wasn't at the club the night he died."

Katie cleared her throat and put up a hand. "Sam, this Mo you were talking about—your fellow guide—sounds like a good source of information."

"Uh huh. He's a sharp guy. In fact he figured out right away that I was at the club for more than one reason."

Stella's frown, which had abated, came back stronger than before. "You mean he knows what you're up to?"

"Afraid so, Stella."

"So that means there's at least three people at the club who know about it: the manager Weatherbee, Campbell the fisheries guy, and now Mr. Murikami. Sounds like you'd better get busy before somebody blows your cover."

"That may already have happened."

Stella raised an eyebrow. "What makes you think that?"

I told them about the episode with someone cutting off Johnny Krasuski's first permit.

Nobody could believe it. Anthony Hernandez in particular seemed skeptical. "Why would anybody do that? And anyway, maybe it was just a coincidence. You don't know the guy who cut your line had anything to do with the club, do you?"

"No, I don't. And as to motive, the only thing I can think of is that somebody wants me gone, maybe by getting fired or perhaps because I'll get disgusted and leave on my own."

"Please don't do that, Sam," Stella said. She switched off the recorder, and started packing up her notes. "Thanks for coming everybody."

We were on our way out of Katie's office when Anthony Hernandez made a request.

"Katie, I was wondering. As long as I'm up here, would you mind showing me your lab? Naturally I've read some of your papers, and found them interesting. But it might help me understand just what you do if I could see some of your slides and maybe learn a little bit more about your particular methods."

"Of course," Katie replied.

Stella and I excused ourselves and walked outside to the parking lot. The asphalt was hot, as were the interiors of our vehicles. We opened doors to let things cool down a bit, and talked while we waited.

"You doing okay?" she asked. "And are you spending nights like I suggested?"

"Some. Katie doesn't like it much, and neither do I."

"I understand that, but you're pretty much my eyes and ears over there. I'm counting on you, Sam."

No pressure there.

"At this point," she went on, "what is your best guess about what might have happened to Mr. Broom?"

"Naturally, I've been thinking about that. I just can't get away from the idea that those lionfish are part of the story. Somebody had to put 'em in there, and we need to figure out who."

Stella nodded. "Sure. But then what about the damage to Broom's digestive tract? That couldn't have had anything to do with those fish, could it?"

"No way I can see."

"It's almost like somebody tried two different ways to kill the man," she said.

"Or maybe there was more than one somebody. One thing I have figured out is that Arthur Broom wasn't the most popular guy around the Purple Isle Sportsman's Club."

Stella folded her arms across her chest and stared in the direction of a flock of ibises busily picking things out of a nearby lawn. Most of the birds were pure white, but some of them wore the mottled brown plumage of juveniles. I'd seen this lots of times before. The ibises were hunting insects in the grass. Katie and I had started referring to those birds as "the lawn maintenance crew," with the younger birds apprenticing to the trade.

76

Stella was frowning again, and I could tell she was worried or puzzled about something.

"What is it?" I asked.

She stopped watching the ibises—which I don't think she really was doing anyway—and focused her dark eyes back on mine.

"There's one part of this case that makes no sense, Sam, and it's bugging the hell out of me. If somebody had it in for Arthur Broom, why fart around with lionfish or even some sort of plant poison?"

"What do you mean?"

"Why not just kill him in one of the old fashioned ways, like shooting him or hitting him over the head or something? That way, whoever tried to kill him would be lots more certain he'd actually end up dead."

"There's one obvious reason I can think of. Somebody hoped it would look like an accident, so you wouldn't conduct a murder investigation. Then the whole thing just would have gone away."

I could see a light come on in Stella's eyes. "And they might have gotten away with it if it weren't for that anonymous phone call saying they'd seen somebody pushing Broom into the pond."

"Which means the killer had to be somebody at the club that night, who would automatically look like a suspect because they had both motive and opportunity. Right Stella?"

"Right. The problem is, that doesn't eliminate any of our possible suspects except maybe Fiona Broom because she wasn't there when Arthur died."

Chapter 14

When I got to the club that afternoon, I was surprised to see that somebody had moved my boat. It was still at the marina, but several slots down from where I was sure I'd docked it after my recent trip with Royal O'Doul. Mel Campbell was doing something down at the fishing ponds, so I walked over to ask him about it. I knew he insisted on keeping keys to all the boats in his office, but I couldn't think why he would have found it necessary to move mine. Or was he even responsible?

Mel finished dumping a bucket of shrimp into one of the ponds, and was walking back to his golf cart as I approached. He waved when he saw me coming.

"Morning, Sam. How are ya?"

"I'm fine, Mel, thanks. But I'm curious about something. It looks like somebody moved my boat since I was here last. Any idea what that was about?"

"Oh yeah, that was me. Mr. Farrelli needed to bring his yacht over here to gas it up, and we needed to get all the fishing boats out of the way. Afterwards I must have put it back in a different slip. Hope that wasn't a problem."

"No, I suppose not. I was just a little surprised."

"Sure. I would have told you, or let you do it yourself, except you weren't around." Then he snapped his fingers. "Oh by the way, Mr. Liptan was asking for you this morning. I explained you were away, but you might look for him at his cabin. It's number 23."

"Thanks, I'll do that. Did he say what he wanted?"

"To go fishing I expect. What else could it be?"

Rashaan Liptan had been a regular client over the years, especially since he retired from a stellar career playing ball for the Miami Heat. He liked to fly fish, particularly for snook and baby tarpon in the backcountry.

He was a big man but a graceful one, and he threw a fly with the same precision as his storied three-pointers. He wasn't the only athlete who brought an exceptionally high level of hand-eye coordination to fly fishing. The baseball player Ted Williams was another famous athlete known for being an excellent fly fisher, especially when it came to tarpon.

Rashaan came to the door of his cabin when I knocked. His face lit up when he recognized me. His wife Julie was there too, along with their twin daughters, Candace and Serena. I'd only met Julie once before, but she greeted me with a hug and a warm smile. "Please come in, Mr. Sawyer. Would you like a cup of coffee?"

"That would be nice. And please call me Sam."

When I'd first met Rashaan, his girls were only toddlers, but by now they were young teenagers. They were busy thumbing iPhones when I walked inside, and they only had time for brief but polite "hellos" before turning back to whatever was holding their attention on the little screens.

We sat at a kitchen table that looked out on the lush tropical landscape surrounding the cabin. "I understand you've started guiding here," Rashaan said. "Mind if I ask why?"

I played it vague. "Oh, the pay's pretty darn good, and the work is regular. Thought I'd give it a try. How long have you been a member here?"

"Just over two years. It's mostly for the girls." He pointed out the window toward the marina. "Those ponds are a great place to get them started fly fishing." He paused for a glance over at his daughters, who were sitting beside each other on the living room couch. They still were on their phones and clearly oblivious to the adults in the room.

"They're both naturals, like their mother, but they don't seem all that interested."

"Just give them time, dear," Julie said.

"Oh, I'll do that." Rashaan swallowed some coffee and changed the subject. "In the meantime, Sam, what say we go fishing? I hear the baby tarpon are on the move."

"Sure. When would you like to go? I'll need to find out what they've already got on my schedule."

"How about right now?"

"Well, we only have half the day left. But I'm game if you are. Give me twenty minutes to put my things in the guides' cabin and tend to my gear. You bringing your own rod?"

"Yep. I've got a 10-weight Loomis and an 8-weight Sage. Which do you think I'll need?"

"Depends on the size of the fish we find. Assuming we find any, that is. Why not bring 'em both?"

"Will do. What about flies?"

"I've got that covered. See you at the dock."

The day had promise. I knew from my trip with Royal O'Doul that the fish were active, and my weather app said the winds would be moderate.

Mo Murikami wasn't at the guides' cabin when I went inside to get my tackle box. I was anxious to pick his brain to see if he knew anything about the relationship between Fiona and "Bud" the bartender, or about the Farrellis, so I left him a note suggesting we get together over dinner or a beer.

Rashaan was standing beside my skiff when I got back to the marina, his fly rods tucked under one arm. He easily could have hopped aboard and stowed the rods himself, and I was pleased he respected the tradition of waiting for an invitation to board from a boat's captain. He handed me his rods, and then waited until I had all the gear put away before stepping off the dock into the bow of my Hell's Bay. He chose to sit on the cooler in front of the center console instead of beside me at the wheel, most likely because there was more room there for his long legs.

"Where are we headed?" he asked, as we motored away from the dock.

"I'm thinking about the flats south of Palm Key. It's a fairly short drive, and there have been reports of tarpon feeding there."

"Sounds good," he replied, settling in for the ride.

The first part of the trip was uneventful, except there was more of a chop on the water than I expected. It wasn't until we were west of Cluett Key that I began to sense something was wrong. The boat seemed sluggish somehow, and a bit slow responding to the wheel.

Rashaan must have noticed it too. "Why are we slowing down?" he asked. "This flat seems deep enough."

I spun around and was startled to see water boiling up over the stern and filling the well in front of the outboard. I popped the shift lever into neutral and walked back to take a closer look.

"My god, Rashaan, it looks like we're sinking! What the hell?"

He jumped up and came back to join me at the stern. "It sure does!"

"Go up to the bow hold and take out a couple of lifejackets while I check the bilge pumps. This could be serious!"

"No shit, Sherlock. What are we gonna do?"

I looked over the port side and saw a steady flow of water coming out of the bilge port. That was the good news. The bad news was the pump obviously wasn't keeping up with the leak.

I had to act fast. The flat here was sufficiently shallow that we were in no real danger of drowning, but letting the boat go to the bottom way out here would be a real nightmare.

I looked around for the nearest dry land. "We'll head for Cluett Key," I said, pointing to the little island east of us. "There's an opening in the mangroves on the north side. If we can get there in time, I'll run it up on the beach. Now put on one of those life jackets and hand me the other one. Then sit tight and hope we make it!"

I put the boat in gear, and turned toward Cluett Key, which fortunately was only about 300 yards away. By now the water had come completely up over the transom and was beginning to fill the hold. It was going to be a close call.

"We gonna make it?" Rashaan asked, obviously worried.

"Yeah, I think so. I'm pushing this thing as hard as I dare."

We made it to the beach in time, and now the trick was going to be how far could I get the boat up onto the sand. The farther the better, in terms of finding the leak.

"Get back in the stern!" I yelled to Rashaan. "That'll raise the bow up and get us farther out of the water when we reach the sand. Then hang on. I'm gonna gun this sucker!"

We hit the beach hard, and the Hell's Bay lurched to a sudden stop. In spite of my warning, Rashaan pitched forward and sprawled on the deck.

"You okay?"

He sat up, examining his knees for damage. "Yeah, yeah, I'm fine. Just lost my balance. What happens next?"

"Why don't you grab the cooler and go ashore? There's bottles of water and some snacks inside. And there's mosquito repellent, which I expect we're gonna need. First thing I gotta do is shut off the bilge pump so we don't run the battery down. Then I'll take a look at the hull and see if I can find the leak."

I got out and walked all around the boat, which was about halfway out of the water. There were no obvious cracks or splits in the visible part of the hull, but the stern of the boat was still in the water and it was possible the leak was down where I couldn't see it. I knelt behind the stern, reached my hand under the hull, and immediately found the problem. The drain plug was gone.

It's common practice to remove the bilge plug from underneath a boat when you take it out of the water, in order to drain any moisture that may have accumulated inside the hull. And most of us have learned the hard way about the absolute necessity of screwing it back in before you re-launch.

There is no more certain way to sink a boat than to forget to put in the drain plug. But that is exactly why the present circumstance had me flummoxed. If someone had removed the plug back at the dock, we wouldn't have gotten as far as we had, even with the bilge pump working full-time. And I almost certainly would have noticed the boat riding low in the water, if not under it, before we even left the dock.

Rashaan had been sitting in the shade of a coconut palm, sipping on a bottle of water. "Find anything?" he asked, from his perch on my cooler.

"Yep. The drain plug is gone."

"What? Then how could we—"

"Only one way I can think of. Somebody didn't shove it all the way in, or maybe forgot to flip down the lever that expands the rubber seal. Then it vibrated out the rest of the way as we went along. It was a bouncy ride part of the time."

"Were you that somebody?"

"No."

"Which means somebody else did it."

"Had to be. The question is who and was it an accident or on purpose?"

"Huh."

I thought about Mel Campbell, who most likely was the last person who handled my boat. Was he responsible? I couldn't think why.

I walked up the beach, and sat down next to Rashaan. A flock of laughing gulls were circling around, probably expecting that he and I were going to have a picnic and there might be snacks to share. Their eerie calls added a sense of unworldly madness to the whole scene.

"What happens next?" Rashaan asked. "You have any ideas how to plug that hole? Or are you gonna call somebody? Can we even get a signal way out here?"

I checked my phone. Just one bar, but with luck it would work.

"I might be able to carve a makeshift plug out of a lead sinker. But then if we started back and it fell out while we were in deeper water, uh . . . I think I'll try the phone first."

"You gonna call Mel Campbell? After all, if he's the one who did this—"

I shook my head. "There's a couple of other options I'd rather go with. We're inside Everglades National Park here, and their head ranger is a friend of mine. So he's a possibility. But first I'm gonna try my fishing buddy, Snooks Lancaster. He owes me a favor or two."

"Sure, I know Snooks. He went out with me and the kids last year. He has an amazing knowledge of basketball statistics."

"Yeah, he loves the game. I think he and his brother played together on their high school team. When you fished with him, was he working for the Purple Isle Club?"

"Uh huh. But I haven't seen him around lately. Guess he quit."

"Yeah, he did."

"Any idea why?"

I pretty much knew why Snooks had quit, but decided to keep it vague. "Not really, but he doesn't fish much anymore. He and his lady friend run a food and drink place together, the Safari Lounge. You ever been there?"

"Nope."

"You should try it. Anyway, I gotta make that call now."

I glanced down at my phone. There still was only one bar, and even it kept fading in and out. "Gonna look for a better spot, Rashaan. You sit tight, and I'll be back."

I stood up and walked toward the interior of the island, looking for a place where the signal might get better. At one point it jumped up to two bars. The mosquitoes were wicked, and I regretted not taking the time to lather up with repellent. But I made the call, and Snooks answered on the first ring.

"Hey Sam, what's up?"

I waved futilely at the cloud of mosquitoes and told him what happened and where we were.

"Good grief! Really?"

"Yeah, really. Any chance you could bring me a spare drain plug?"

"Sure. You say you're on the beach at Cluett Key, right? And your drain is one-inch I assume?"

"Uh huh." Then I had another thought. "And maybe bring an extra battery. There's no way to tell how long my bilge pump was running before we figured out what was happening."

"Will do. I'm at the Safari right now. I gotta go home and see if I have a spare plug. If not, I may need to stop by West Marine and pick up one. And then I need to splash my boat, which has been out of the water for a couple of weeks. I'll see you in—say—an hour and a half to two hours depending?"

"Thank you, Snooks. Rashaan Liptan and I really appreciate this."

"He's your client today? I'm hurrying."

If there were a silver lining to this whole mess, it was that the wait would give me a chance to pick Rashaan's brain about things at the Purple Isle club. I joined him back under the palm tree and cracked open a bottle of water.

"My friend Snooks will get here as soon as he can."

"You think I should call Julie and tell her what's going on?"

"No need to worry her yet. If this all goes right, we shouldn't be much later than if this were an ordinary fishing trip."

"Yeah, I suppose you're right. She is used to my being gone and out of cell phone range." Then, as an afterthought: "Though it may not be happening all that much longer, at least from the club. Think I'm gonna quit that place."

This was news. "You mind if I ask why?"

He sat silent for a while. "The Heat people were good to me, so it's not as if I can't afford the dues. Julie and I have no financial worries. But some of those people at the club . . . on the surface they're polite and everything . . ."

He trailed off, but I could hear a "but" coming.

"But they never let you forget who you are and who they are."

"I know what you mean, Rashaan."

"No, Sam, you *don't* know. You *can't* know, believe me."

"Yeah, sorry."

"That's okay," he said. "And anyway, the only reason I joined the club in the first place was that Art Broom invited me. And now that he's gone—"

"Yeah, I heard about that. So you knew him?"

"Knew him well. We first met because he was a big Heat fan. Had season tickets, courtside. He was friends with the owners, and even bought the team fancy new uniforms one year for the playoffs. And we both belonged to the same Rotary Club. But our relationship grew into something more important."

"What was that?"

"He had this passion about trying to restore the Everglades and Florida Bay, and he set up a foundation dedicated to that cause."

"What did he call it?"

"He called it the Everglades Rescue Foundation."

"And you were involved?"

"He asked me to be on their board of directors, and I agreed. We make an annual contribution, though probably not at his level." Rashaan swatted at a mosquito that had landed just under his left ear.

"Did you lather up with DEET like I suggested?"

"Yeah, but I must have missed a spot. Too bad about Art Broom. I really liked the guy. You know they called him 'Whisk' around the club? He hated that."

"I understand he drowned in one of the fishponds."

"Maybe. Or maybe it was something else."

"What do you mean?"

"There's talk around the club that maybe it wasn't an accident."

"You mean somebody killed him?"

"I told you we were friends, and sometimes friends tell each other things. That man had some enemies."

"Who?"

"No idea, except that it had to do with his earlier life in the New York area. Something about shady business dealings. I never knew any of the details. One thing I do know about Art, and it's about his only negative as far as I'm concerned. He was kinda' paranoid."

"Paranoid about what?"

"Mostly about money. He was always worried somebody was after his money."

"But not that his life might be in danger?"

"Yeah, maybe that too, now that you mention it."

Rashaan stopped to slap at another mosquito, and frowned. "But why are you so interested, Sam? Did you know Art?"

"Nope. Never met him. There's something I need to tell you, but please keep this absolutely confidential."

"Sure. What is it?"

"The reason I'm working at the club is to help a deputy sheriff friend of mine try to figure out if somebody did kill Mr. Broom and if so, why. In addition to being a fishing guide, I've sometimes helped law enforcement in cases where my knowledge of wildlife has been useful."

Rashaan raised an eyebrow. "Why is it useful in this case?"

"When Stella—that's the deputy sheriff I was talking about—found out Broom had fallen into one of the fishing ponds, she asked me to take a look. That was when we found out somebody dumped lionfish into it. He may have gotten stung to death, though we haven't figured that out yet."

"Huh. I saw a deputy outside the main lodge the other day, who happened to be a black woman. Is that who you're talking about?"

"Yeah, that's Stella. And one of the reasons she asked for my help is that most of the staff and club members have been giving her the runaround on this Broom thing."

"Not surprised, Sam. I told you Julie and I are about done with that place. But in the meantime, if I think of anything else that might be useful about Art Broom, I'll be sure and let you know."

"I appreciate that."

Rashaan was quiet for several seconds, then cleared his throat and spoke softly. "Art Broom nominated me for membership, but he had a little help getting it accepted, from what I understand. Another member also belongs to the Augusta National Golf Club. You know, the one where they play the Masters? Anyway, he backed Art by saying Augusta had admitted some African American men into membership and the golf had improved as well. I am no stranger to being a token member of things because of basketball, and it doesn't bother me unless members of my family are not welcomed. Is your deputy friend a token?"

"No, I don't think so. She's very good at her job."

"I'd like for my daughters to meet her, if that's possible. Julie and I are always looking for female role models with interesting and unusual careers."

Just then I heard the sound of an approaching outboard, and half a minute later a familiar Dolphin flats boat came around the corner.

Snooks Lancaster to the rescue.

Chapter 15

Snooks cut his motor, drifted onto the sand beside my Hell's Bay, and dropped his power pole anchor. Then he hopped out into a foot and a half of water, and waded ashore with a toolbox in one hand and a 12-volt battery in the other.

I walked down to join him on the beach. "Boy am I glad to see you."

"No problem. But how did this happen?"

"Good question, Snooks. Somebody must have loosened the plug and then it fell out while we were crossing the bay."

Snooks fiddled with his ponytail, which was sticking out from under a faded Florida Marlins baseball cap. "Any idea who that somebody might have been?"

"Nope, except it had to be somebody at the club, 'cause my boat hasn't been anywhere else."

Snooks turned his back to where Rashaan still sat under a palm tree, and whispered. "I told you not to get involved in that damn place."

"Yeah, yeah. And it's okay to talk in front of Rashaan. He knows what I'm doing there. Now give me that plug, and let's get on with this. We need to be out of here before the sun goes down."

The plug fit, and there appeared to be plenty of charge left in my battery to pump most of the water out of the bilge.

We walked up and joined Rashaan under his palm tree, while we waited for the bilge to empty. The two of them shook, after which Snooks lathered up with mosquito dope.

"Any new records to report?" Rashaan asked Snooks.

"You mean fishing records?"

"No, I mean basketball records."

Snooks shook his head. "No, not really, Mr. Liptan. And if you're talking about your record for the most three-pointers in the first quarter, it still stands as far as I know."

Rashaan grinned. "Please call me Rashaan."

I knew Snooks was into basketball, but as an NBA numbers freak? This was something I hadn't expected. I thought about posing a couple more trivia questions just to see how good he really was, when I noticed that the pump flow had slowed to a trickle, either because the battery was dying or because the bilge was nearly empty.

Fortunately it was the latter, because when I got to the boat I could hear the pump still running strong. I waved back at Snooks and Rashaan. "Looks like we're good to go. Wanna help me push this thing back out into the water and see if it floats?"

The tide had dropped some since I'd first beached the boat, but the three of us had no trouble pushing it back off the sand. I got in, fired up the outboard, and invited Rashaan to hop aboard. We were ready to go.

~ ~ ~

Snooks followed us in his Dolphin all the way back to Islamorada, "just in case there's any more trouble."

There wasn't any.

We were about 100 yards from the Purple Isle marina when Snooks sped up and passed me, and then stopped. I pulled up beside him, suspecting what was going on.

"Thanks again, my friend. I owe you one."

He shook his head. "You don't owe me anything. But if it's all the same to you I think I'll go on home now. I'm sure you can make it from here." He pointed toward the shore. "That place still gives me the creeps."

"Sure, no problem. See you soon."

"Yeah, why don't you and Katie come by the Safari tonight and have a beer and a burger? And you too, Rashaan, whenever you can make it. Flo would love to meet your family."

With that, Snooks put his outboard in gear and headed off down the bay.

"This place Snooks owns. Does it have good food?" Rashaan asked.

"Yeah, darn good for what it is."

"Where is it?"

"Right here in Islamorada. Formally, it's the Safari Longue. But we locals call it the Dead Animal Bar because it has this assortment of stuffed big game animals hanging on the walls and from the ceiling. It's a popular spot for fishing guides and their clients."

"I'd like to go there, especially if Snooks is doing the cooking."

"Mostly he tends bar. His lady friend Flo actually owns the place, and she does the cooking."

"When is it open?"

"Seven days a week, 10 AM to closing. And they're thinking about starting a breakfast catering to fishermen who want an early start. But that hasn't happened yet."

"Could I bring my wife and daughters there for lunch? That might be better than mixing them with the happy hour crowd."

"Of course. The kids can't sit at the bar, but there are lots of tables with great views of the beach and the ocean. Flo and Snooks both love children."

"We'll go there for sure. Now let's get on back before Julie starts to worry."

I left Rashaan at the dock, with the promise that we'd try fishing again soon, this time hopefully without any unexpected interruptions. I secured the Hell's Bay, ran the bilge pump one more time just to make sure all the water was out, and then set out to find Mel Campbell. He and I needed to have a talk.

Mel wasn't hard to find. As soon as I got out of the boat and looked around, I spotted him down at one of the fishponds, doing something with Mo Murikami.

When I got closer, I could see that most of the water was gone from the hogfish pond, and Mo was wading around in it with a long-handled dip net. Mel was standing beside the pond with two white buckets. Both men were wearing hip waders and heavy rubber gloves that came up to their elbows.

Mel waved when he saw me coming. "Me and Mo are trying to get the last of the lionfish out of here. Only way to do it is to drain the pond. How did it go with Mr. Liptan?"

"It didn't."

"What?"

"We never got fishing. My boat started to sink and we had to put ashore on Cluett Key. Lucky we were close enough to get on the beach before she went to the bottom."

"You're kidding. How did it happen?"

"Actually, we need to talk about that. You got a minute?"

Mel frowned. "Sure. I think we're about done here."

"What are you doing with those fish?"

"We dumped the hogfish into the next pond over. They get along okay with the snappers." He pointed at the buckets. "These are full of lionfish. Mo, can you finish up while I go talk to Sam?"

Just then Mo lifted up the net. I could see at least one fish flopping around inside, but I was too far away to tell what it was. "This could be the last one, but I'll keep looking."

Mel peeled off his gloves and walked in my direction. "Can't be too careful with those lionfish. Their spines are nasty buggers."

We kept walking toward each other. "So tell me again what happened?" Mel said, as soon as we got close.

"The bilge plug fell out."

"Huh. How did you get back?"

"My friend Snooks Lancaster brought out a new one. You know him?"

"A little. He used to work here, but he left right after I started." Mel stopped and scratched at his beard. "How do you suppose that plug came out?"

"Good question. And I guess I have to ask this. As far as I know, you were the last person on my boat, when you moved it out of the way of that man's yacht. You didn't say whether you had to take it out of the water, or whether you had the plug out."

"Hell no, I didn't! All I did was move it down to the other end of the marina, and then bring it back. I know boats, Sam. I woulda' noticed if it was floating low. So don't go accusing me of something I didn't do."

"I'm not accusing you of anything, Mel. Just trying to figure out what the hell happened. The only thing that makes sense is that somebody loosened that plug, but not all the way. And then it fell out somewhere between here and Cluett. Did you see anybody messing with my boat between when you moved it and when Rashaan and I left the dock?"

"Nope. But Mo and I got busy with the lionfish about then, so I might not have noticed."

I liked Mel Campbell, or had up until now. The whole thing made me suspicious, but I couldn't think of any reason he would have had to sabotage my Hell's Bay, or any more questions to ask him about it, at least not for now.

"What are you gonna do with those lionfish?"

Mel sighed, obviously relieved that I'd changed the subject. "We give 'em to the chef. He'll put lionfish on the week's menu. They're good eating, and he serves them pretty regularly."

"I've heard the filets are light and tasty. But aren't they tricky to prepare?"

"Not really. I mean the spines are full of venom, and you gotta know where they are because some of 'em are shorter than others and harder to spot. But once you get past that, the meat isn't poisonous or anything. And it's good for conservation if we kill as many as possible. They're an exotic species introduced from the western Pacific, and they're killing off our native fish and crustaceans. If we can develop a market for lionfish, it's bound to help." Mel stopped and shook his head. "Not that we're ever gonna get rid of 'em."

From what I knew about the subject, Mel was spot on about all of it. "Speaking of markets, when they don't come from your pond back there, where does the chef get his lionfish?"

Mel shrugged. "I don't know. Lots of places around here sell 'em. You'd have to ask him. Why? You want to try some?" Then he snapped his fingers. "Oh I get it. You're thinking maybe he's the one who put them in with the hogfish. But why would he do that?"

"I have no idea. But somebody did."

At this point it was nothing but speculation, and in any event I wasn't about to share with Mel the possible New York connection Stella had unearthed between the chef's family and Arthur Broom.

"You know, Katie has been talking about trying some lionfish. I think I'll go ask your chef if he might share a recipe or two. Do you think he'd mind?"

"Who are you kidding, son?" Mel said. "But sure. Knock yourself out. I'm as anxious as you are to figure out what happened. Just don't mention my name when you talk to our precious French chef, okay? He can be as prickly as a lionfish."

"No problem. You got anything for me tomorrow? I'm gonna spend the night at home."

"Yeah. Mr. Farrelli's grandkids are here on vacation, and they'd like a fly fishing lesson. I'd recommend the snook pond. They'll be expecting you around nine."

"How old are they?"

"Not sure. Early teens I think. Why?"

"No particular reason. It's just that teenagers sometimes have different ideas about what to do on a vacation than their parents or grandparents."

Chapter 16

Katie and I had made a date for dinner that night at the Safari Lounge, but I decided to pop into the Purple Isle restaurant before heading home. I walked into the lodge and took the second door to the left, glancing at the bar as I walked by. Fiona Broom was at the far end, chatting with George the bartender, just like before. I decided it must be her regular routine. I waved and they both waved back, but they didn't miss a beat in whatever they were talking about.

The restaurant was one big rectangular room laid out with tables but not booths. Each table was set with linen and silver. The place was empty except for two couples I didn't recognize. The far end of the room was all glass, affording a good view of coconut palms spaced along the beach like somebody had planted them there. Knowing how things worked at the club, it probably was true. The sun was a red-orange globe, low on the horizon across Florida Bay. The water was dark, and there weren't any waves to pick up the last of the sun's rays. That much calm water was rare off the Keys, on either the ocean or the bay side.

There were double swinging doors halfway down the wall to my right, each with a window into the kitchen. I walked down, nodded to the people eating fish filets, and looked through the first window. An impressive array of pots and pans hung from the ceiling over a large wood-topped center island. The wall beyond included a large gas range and two ovens. I knocked and then pushed open the doors without waiting for a response. Two men were standing shoulder to shoulder at the island, huddled over some papers. They had their backs to me, but they whirled around and quickly backed away from each other as I walked into the kitchen. One was the chef who called himself Jacques Petain, and the other was the club manager, Ralph Weatherbee.

"Sorry to disturb you, gentlemen," I said.

"Yes? What is it?" said Weatherbee, who did not look happy to see me. "As you can see, we're busy here. Working on the week's menus."

"Actually, I was hoping to ask, . . . uh, Mr. Petain is it? Would he perhaps be willing to share a recipe?"

"Absolutely not!" said the chef, whose scowl closely matched that of Weatherbee's.

"I know it's an unusual request, and I wouldn't normally do such a thing, Mr. Petain. But this is about lionfish, and I can't seem to find a recipe for them anywhere else. I understand you serve them here, and my wife and I are interested in trying them for dinner."

"We don't normally do that, even for members, let alone staff," Weatherbee said.

I couldn't help but catch the tone in his voice when he said "staff," like we were some sort of lesser beings. But he turned to the chef, nodded once, and said "Get the man what he wants, Jacques." Then back at me: "But don't make this a habit. Mr. Sawyer, please."

At least he said mister. And please.

"Jacques" reached down and pulled a ring binder off a shelf built into one end of the kitchen island. He slammed it down on top of the island, sighing conspicuously in the process. Then he opened it up, leafed noisily through some pages, and began scribbling notes on a blank piece of paper, which he handed it to me. "This is a good one. It calls for lemon butter and capers. I'm sure you'll like it."

"And now if you don't mind, we need to get back to work," Weatherbee said.

"Of course. But I do have one more question. I've never seen lionfish in a market around here. Could you tell me where you get yours?"

The two men exchanged glances, and once again the chef let Weatherbee do the talking. "We get most of our fish from a market on Conch Key. It's called Avery's I think. Isn't that right, Jacques? That they do occasionally have lionfish for sale?"

"That's right. Occasionally."

~ ~ ~

By the time I got home it was nearly seven. I went upstairs and out onto the deck, where Katie and Prince were taking in the evening air. Mangroves cast long shadows across the canal, and a red-bellied woodpecker was perched at the very top of one of them, his red crown catching the last of the sun. Katie was working on a glass of white wine, and relaxing in one of a pair of old Adirondack chairs I'd found at a garage sale. Prince was barking and growling at a trio of pelicans that were begging food scraps from a neighbor who was cleaning fish and tossing their entrails into the water. Prince had a thing about pelicans and was so busy worrying about them he didn't notice me until I said hi to Katie. Then he came bounding over to lick my hand and ask for a scratch behind the ears, which I obliged.

"Sorry it got late," I said to Katie, while taking the chair next to hers. "I had a busy day, and a strange one."

"Strange how?"

I told her about the incident with my boat. As I was describing what happened, what started as a frown on Katie's face morphed into unmistakable wide-eyed fear. Not that I blamed her.

"My god, Sam," she said after I finished my story. "But you're okay? And your boat's okay?"

"Uh huh. It could have been a whole lot worse if we hadn't been close to a small key."

She sipped some wine and looked out into the spreading darkness. Then reached over and put her hand on my arm. "Between that incident with the permit, and now your boat . . ." She trailed off. "You need to get away from that place. Now."

I knew this was coming, and a part of me felt the same way.

"Just can't do it. At least not yet."

Even in the failing light I caught a flare in her eyes. "Why the hell not? And please don't give me any of that 'a man's gotta do what a man's gotta do' nonsense."

"We've been around on this before. I promised to help Stella." I put my hands up. "And—I know—she's not as important to me as you are. But surely you can understand. I've seen what happens when you get involved in a case you care about. You sink your teeth into it and won't let go until it's solved."

"Sure, but usually my life's not in danger." Katie gulped down the last of her wine, and twirled the empty glass by its stem. "Come on, Sam!"

Clearly, it was time to change the subject. "And speaking of your involvement, any progress since this morning in identifying those strange plant cells in Broom's stomach?"

"A little. I spoke with my friend this afternoon, and he's anxious to help. I'm not sure I ever told you, but I first met Tom Wordsburg when we were in graduate school together at Cal Berkeley. I sent him photographs of the cells last night."

"And you're optimistic he can figure it out? I mean you're an expert in forensic botany, and you had no idea what they were."

"Tom has some special skills and experiences that may help. He runs that botanical garden in Miami now, but before that he was at Yale, where he was regarded as the leading US plant anatomist. He says these days his job in Florida mostly involves raising money and attending social events. He still has tenure at New Haven, so he could go back. He's told me he misses academic research, but he and his family like Florida way better than those dreary Connecticut winters, so I don't think they're going anywhere."

"I get that. I suppose it's too early for you to have heard back from him about the cells?"

"Actually, Tom just emailed me that he'd taken a preliminary first look. He didn't recognize the cells specifically, except to say that they resemble some he's seen from various plants in the family Euphorbiaceae."

"Is that important?"

"Could be. The family is known to include things that are poisonous, like castor beans."

"Huh." I scooted my chair back and got ready to stand up. "Anyway, are you still up for the Safari Lounge? We probably should get going."

"You bet," Katie said. "I haven't done anything about dinner, and it was your night anyway."

We did have such an arrangement, me on Tuesdays and Thursdays, which were the days she had a late class. Of course that had pretty much gone out the window, now that I was spending at least some nights at the club.

"Okay, let's go. You wanna take Prince?"

Prince had been asleep next to my chair. At the sound of his name he immediately perked up, ears forward, nose quivering.

"Of course," she said. "Flo and her cats are expecting him."

Chapter 17

Both Monroe County and the Village of Islamorada had all kinds of regulations about dogs in restaurants, except the service kind, and Prince clearly didn't fall in that category. But Snooks had built a room in the basement below the Safari kitchen where they kept their two cats when he and Flo were at work. They'd given Prince the okay to join them down there. There had been the usual dog versus cat difficulties at first, with lots of hissing and back bristling on the part of Mocha, a Siamese, and the white tomcat Snooks had acquired, named Gringo. But by now Prince and Gringo seemed to have become actual friends, while Mocha just ignored both of them.

Prince always was excited when we got to the restaurant, and strained to get with the cats as soon as possible. It didn't hurt that Flo enticed him downstairs with dog biscuits. Snooks had run a duct from the air conditioner down to the "cat house," as he put it, so at least the canine and feline arguments didn't get overheated.

Prince sat on my lap as Katie drove the short distance down to the Safari Lounge.

"You know he's crazy about you,' she said. "He's not happy when you're gone. When you're home he pretty much sleeps the night through at the foot of our bed. But when you're gone he keeps wandering around."

"Hopefully it won't be too much longer. You know I love that dog almost as much as I love you."

Katie drove in silence for a while. I could tell she was thinking about something.

"Is that enough?" she eventually asked.

I was pretty sure where this was going. It was something we'd talked about before, but not often and not recently. For some reason today I wasn't in the mood to hear about ticking biological clocks.

"Yes, it's enough," I said. "Until you decide it isn't."

Katie sighed, and when I looked over there was a single tear running down her cheek. Fortunately or otherwise, just then we arrived at the parking lot next to the Safari Lounge. It was getting dark over the Atlantic, but I could still see the Tennessee Reef Lighthouse at the edge of the continental shelf out beyond Long Key. Its outline was faint against the graying sky, and you had to know just where to look.

"That's not fair," she said with a sniff.

And I knew it wasn't. We'd talked about someday starting a family, but our careers had always gotten in the way, even before I'd run off by myself to the Keys. But now that we were back together, maybe it was time to revisit the topic.

"Yeah, sorry. It's just that I don't see how it could work, unless—"

"I know. Unless one of us took time off until the kid was ready for daycare."

"As far as I know, there's no such thing as paternity leave for fishing guides."

"We need to talk more about this," she said. "The college does have maternity leave, but I probably should wait until my programs and classes are fully developed enough for somebody else to take over for a while." Then she shook her head. "But this is making it sound so mechanical, like pushing a button."

"You've always pushed my buttons," I said, hoping it would lighten things up.

"Haven't you thought about being a dad?" she asked, without a hint of a smile on her face.

"Sure. But—"

At that point Prince, who had been waiting patiently, started to whine and paw at the door. He knew where we were, and he knew what was waiting inside. The last of the light caught Katie's eyes. They weren't sad eyes, but they weren't happy either. Just sort of wistful.

There were lots of things I wanted to say, but by now Prince had completely lost it. "We'd better get inside. But let's promise each other we'll get back to this once the Purple Isle business is over, okay?"

"Deal," she said.

I put Prince on a leash before we went inside, because I didn't want him dashing around trying to beg food from the customers and otherwise making a nuisance of himself. He tugged all the way up the stairs, and then headed straight for the kitchen. A handful of drinkers at the bar looked up as we walked by. A couple of them smiled. Corgis often get that reaction.

Snooks was delivering a pitcher of margaritas to a couple sitting at a table on the ocean side as we came in. I waved and he waved back, as we made our way toward the kitchen. Flo was busy flipping burgers at the grill when we got there, but she put down her spatula and bent over to rub Prince behind the ears as he came running up to her.

"The kitties are waiting downstairs," she said to Prince, as she opened the door and threw down a handful of dog treats. As Prince disappeared downstairs, Flo wiped her hands on a greasy apron, and then pulled Katie into a full embrace. At the same time she caught my eye and frowned. "Snooks told me what happened today. What the hell was that all about?"

"I don't know exactly. Somebody must have loosened my bilge plug. We darn near sank."

"Any idea who it was?" she asked.

"Not for certain."

"Huh." She pulled back to look at Katie and then over at me. "Anyway, what are you guys eating?"

"This 'guy' will have one of your tuna melts on rye," Katie said. Lumping her as a "guy" was one of her pet peeves, but if Flo caught it she gave no clue.

"Make mine a grouper Reuben sandwich," I said.

We excused ourselves while Flo went back to her grill.

"Let's grab a table by the window tonight," Katie said as we walked out into the bar.

There wasn't much view left in the fading light, and I wondered why she'd chosen a table instead of our usual stools at the bar, which were empty and which happened to be right next to the spot where Snooks mixed drinks and where we could chat with him as he worked.

Snooks saw where we were headed and got a puzzled look on his face. But then he asked what we'd like as if it wasn't that big of a deal.

I asked for a Maker's Mark on the rocks, while Katie requested a gin and tonic.

"Any particular gin?" Snooks said.

"What's your house brand?" she asked.

Snooks looked down below the bar where he kept the rows of bottles. "Today, it's Gilbey's."

"That'll do fine," Katie said. "With a twist of lime."

We sat down and looked out the window toward the ocean, but by now there was nothing to see except our own reflections looking back at us.

"Why are we sitting way over here instead of at the bar?" I asked, though not without some hesitation. Did she want to talk about the family thing again?

But that wasn't it.

"We need to talk about your choice of careers."

"I know you worry sometimes when I'm out fishing and you can't get me on your cell. But it seems to be getting better, like they're building more towers or something."

"That's not it."

"We're back to the cop thing again? I told you I owe it to Stella. One way or the other, I don't think it'll be that much longer."

"And then what about the next time?"

I was about to answer when Snooks walked up with our drinks, which he set on little red and white coasters that said "Dead Animal Bar, Where the Extinct Meet to Drink." Then he pulled out a chair and sat down across from us.

"You heard what happened today?" he asked Katie.

Talk about bad timing.

"Damn straight," Katie said. Then she looked down and pretended to be interested in the slice of lime floating around in her gin and tonic.

Snooks apparently realized he'd stuck his nose in where it wasn't welcome, because he stood up and started to leave. But then he must have changed his mind and sat back down.

"I told you not to get involved in that place," he said to me. "And that was before what happened today."

"It turned out alright," I said.

"That's bullshit and you know it, Sam. There's bad stuff going on at the good old Purple Isle. It's pretty obvious somebody has it in for you. Any idea who?"

"Not really." Then something occurred to me. "Actually, you might be able to help with that."

"You mean besides rescuing your ass off Cluett Key? What, then?"

I told him the story about somebody cutting off Johnny Krasuski's permit by driving his boat over Johnny's line, and that it was a man driving a Mako center console with a dark blue hull.

Snooks barked a short laugh. "That's the strangest thing I ever heard of."

"You know anybody drives a boat like that?" I asked.

Snooks thought about it for a little while. Then he snapped his fingers. "Now that you mention it, I do. A fishing guide named Reuben Fletcher. Or at least he used to be a guide. And you know what? He's just the kind of sonofabitch who would do something like that."

"What do you mean?"

"Back when I was guiding a lot, he had a reputation for horning in on your spot. Had no respect for another fisherman's space. We all hated to see him coming. I never heard of him driving over another guy's line, but maybe he's started taking it to another level. Maybe you were butting in on his favorite spot for permit."

"There could be more to it than that."

"What?"

"Fletcher's working at the Purple Isle club."

Snooks raised an eyebrow. "As a guide?"

"Used to. But now he's a security guard."

"Huh. Fletcher comes in here sometimes. Next time I see him I'm gonna ask him about all this. I'm telling you, Sam—"

I put up a hand. "I'd rather you not do that, Snooks."

"And why not?"

It was a good question. "Let's just say I don't want to spook the guy. At least not yet. If he's got it in for me, we need to find out why."

"This 'we' you're talking about?"

"Me and Stella Reynard. The Deputy Sheriff I'm working with on the murder out there. But you say Reuben Fletcher drinks here at your bar? Have you ever seen him with anybody else?"

"Usually he's alone, but the last couple of times he was with Chet Avery. They got pretty drunk together. You know him?"

"No, but I think I'm about to."

"And now I suppose you want me to nose around the next time the two of them are in here? Maybe listen in on their conversation?"

I thought about that for a minute. "Yeah, I suppose so, if you can do it without letting on."

Snooks smiled. "I'm a bartender, Sam. I'm good at hearing things and acting all innocent about it." Then his smile faded. "But in the meantime, Katie, see if you can talk some sense into this husband of yours before he gets himself killed, okay?"

Snooks pushed back his chair with a loud scrape, stood up, and huffed himself back toward the bar.

Katie didn't say anything at first, but I was pretty sure it wouldn't last. She took a sip of her gin and tonic, and watched Snooks walking away, presumably until he was out of earshot.

"You haven't answered my question," she said.

I could have pretended I didn't remember what it was, but she deserved better than that. Before I could think of a good answer, she asked another one.

"You make a good living as a fishing guide, don't you?"

"Yeah, I guess so."

"We both know it's true, Sam. And with my salary from the college, we're doing fine financially. Which means—"

"But that's not all—"

"Don't interrupt. Which means this law enforcement sideline of yours isn't about the money."

I stuck a finger down into the glass of Makers Mark, and twirled the remaining ice cubes. "No, I suppose not."

"Then what is it? An ego trip? Or the thrill of cracking a case?"

"Something like that, I suppose."

Katie banged her glass down on the table. It was so loud some the patrons at the bar glanced over in our direction. "Hey, as long as we're just 'supposing,' suppose I asked you to stop. Could you do it? *Would* you do it?"

I sat silent for a while, and this time Katie let me just sit there, stewing in my own juice. I pretended to look out the window at something, but just like before the only thing visible out there was me looking back.

"If you asked, I'd quit. But are you?"

Now it was her time to stare out the window. After what seemed like an eternity, but probably wasn't more than half a minute, she spun her chair sideways and locked her eyes on mine.

"No," she finally said. "Not if it's that important to you."

"It is that important, Katie. And it's not just an ego trip, or at least I don't think so. Instead it—this is hard to explain—it fills a gap in my life that's been there since I quit the university."

"I'm not sure I understand."

"Guiding fishermen is fun, or at least usually it is, and it can be rewarding in ways beyond just financial. But what I miss about the university is the feeling that I'm doing good. That teaching and doing research is good for the world and not just for myself. I'm guessing you can understand that, with the work you do."

"Maybe you could get a teaching job at the college, even part time. Maybe we could do forensic investigations together. Would that work?"

I had to admit it might. "Hadn't thought of that," I said.

We were so locked in conversation that neither of us heard Flo coming with our sandwiches.

"Hope you guys are hungry," she said. Then she must have caught something, some look that said food might not have been foremost in our minds.

"Are you okay?" she asked, as she laid the sandwiches down in front of us.

"Yeah, we're okay," Katie replied. "Just having a little chat."

Flo raised an eyebrow. "Well chat away, then. But don't let these get cold." She looked back toward the bar. "Snooks is settling up with the last of his customers, so I'm gonna let Prince back upstairs. Maybe he can help you eat these, so we can close up and go home. Looks like we're done for the night."

Chapter 18

The first couple of times I'd driven myself onto club property, Reuben Fletcher had made a big deal out of stopping me at the gate to check my ID. But lately he hadn't even bothered to look up from whatever he was doing on his phone. He just pushed a button, the gate went up, and he waved me on through. Therefore I was surprised the next morning when I arrived, because when he saw me coming he heaved his substantial self off the stool in the guardhouse, waddled outside, and put his hand up to stop me.

I rolled down the window on the Cherokee. "Morning Reuben. Is there a problem?"

"Not with me," he grunted. "But I heard what happened to you yesterday. Not good."

I was reminded of the old adage about bad news traveling fast. I also remembered that Snooks had a history with Reuben, back when they both were guiding, and I wasn't about to share details of my rescue with the man.

"Yeah, my bilge plug fell out. It was a close call, but in the end it all worked out."

Reuben squinted against the morning sun, and at the same time managed to raise an eyebrow. "Those things don't usually fall out by themselves. Aren't you suspicious?"

"Maybe a little." I pointed to the gate blocking the entrance to the property. "And now if you don't mind, I have clients waiting."

He went on as if he hadn't heard me. "That happened to me once, and it wasn't an accident. Me and another guide got into a turf battle over what he thought was his exclusive tarpon hotspot. Which was bullshit, since nobody owns the ocean. But the next day when I got to the dock, somebody'd taken out my bilge plug, and my boat had sunk. I knew it was that son of a bitch, but I never could prove it."

This confirmed what Snooks had told me about Fletcher's habit of horning in on other guides. Was Reuben trying to tell me something?

Eventually Reuben went back inside the guardhouse, and raised the gate.

"Just be careful out there," he said, as I drove across the bridge.

Having gotten past Reuben Fletcher, I went to the guides cabin and picked up an eight-weight Sage, a nine-weight Loomis, and an assortment of flies I knew worked for snook. There was no sign of Mo Murikami, except for an empty sushi carton in the sink. I checked the clipboard, but there was nothing on it to tell me where he might have gone. Apparently Mel Campbell had forgotten to make out the week's schedule.

By the time I'd collected my gear and walked to the ponds, Lou Farrelli was already there waiting, with an impatient look on his face. He was alone and he was fidgety, looking at his watch like he was late for something. We shook and exchanged good-mornings.

"Grandkids will be along," he said. "They're just finishing breakfast. I told them to be ready early, but you know how it is with kids. I think they were up half the night on their phones or their laptops or something."

"Have they fished before?" I asked.

"Yeah, deep sea with me and their dad a couple of times, but not fly fishing. I understand from Mr. Campbell that you're an expert, so I'm hoping you can give them a lesson."

"Happy to," I said, while not actually feeling that way. The fact that they were late only added to my earlier suspicion that maybe this whole thing was more their grandfather's idea than it was theirs.

Five minutes later two young people came walking across the lawn. The girl had long dark hair tied up in a ponytail. She looked to be in her early teens, maybe fourteen or fifteen, but tall for her age. Her younger brother, who lagged behind, had one of those haircuts that was much shorter on the sides than on top. Neither was especially tan, which was unusual in Florida in the summer. I wondered where they were from and, wherever it was, whether they spent much time outdoors.

Lou introduced me to Rosalie and Tony. "I'll leave you kids to it," he said. "Your grandma and I are going down to Key West, but we expect to be back by the middle of the afternoon. There's sandwiches in the refrigerator when you get hungry."

I realized it was going to be a long day.

"So you haven't fly-fished before?" I asked as soon as Lou had left.

The both shook their heads. "But I really want to learn," Rosalie said.

I told them we'd be starting on the lawn rather than in the pond, because it was important to learn the basics of fly casting without actually being distracted by the fish. Tony frowned but Rosalie nodded like she got it. I started by having them watch me cast, explaining and demonstrating the differences between casting a fly and other sorts of fishing. Next I gave each of them a rod and let them try. It took Tony longer than Rosalie to get the basics, but after a half hour I decided they both were ready to move to the snook pond.

Like any wild game fish, snook are naturally wary of anything bigger than they are. But these snook clearly were no longer wild. When we walked up to the edge of the pond, instead of bolting off for deeper water, they swam right toward us. Did they think I was Mel Campbell and were they expecting him to throw in a handful of shrimp? Giving snook or any other fish credit for "thinking" and "expecting" may have been a bit generous, but it was hard coming to any other conclusion. At the very least, snook obviously were trainable.

Given the behavior of these fish, probably anything dragged through the water was going to work. Nevertheless, I attached 9-foot 3x leaders to both fly lines, and then tied on my favorite snook fly: the chartreuse and white Clouser minnow. Might as well let these kids have the best shot possible.

Tony's first cast barely cleared the edge of the pond, probably because the sight of all those snook circling around caused him to forget everything we'd been practicing on the lawn. Rosalie did much better—surprisingly well in fact—and her fly landed gently on the water a good twenty feet out. She'd barely begun her retrieve when there was a big swirl and she was hooked up.

"What do I do now?" she shrieked, as the fish tore off across the pond.

I realized that while I'd been concentrating on teaching them how to cast, I hadn't told them what to do afterwards if a fish happened to eat the fly.

"Hold the rod up high, and let it pull line off the reel. Then, once the fish slows down or turns, start cranking the reel. But be ready to let the fish run again, because it probably will. If you hold on too tightly it could break the line."

Rosalie did as she was told, and a couple of minutes later I helped her slide a nice thirty-inch snook up on the grass, its silver-green flank glistening in the sun.

"Can we keep it?" she asked. "Are they good to eat?"

"They are, but we practice catch-and-release here, so we need to let it go."

"Can we get a picture first?"

"Yes, as long as we're careful not to keep it out of the water too long."

I unhooked the fly, then picked the fish up and held it out toward Rosalie so she could admire it one last time. "Can I let it go?" she asked.

"Of course, just wet your hands before you take hold of it. These fish are tough, but they're not used to getting dried off even a little bit."

Rosalie gently cradled the snook in both hands, and I took a photo with my phone. Then she knelt down at the edge of the pond and let it go. We both watched as the fished turned slowly out into the deeper water and disappeared.

In the meantime, Tony had managed to gather up his fly line from where it was piled at his feet, and make another cast. This time it went better, perhaps fifteen feet from shore, and almost immediately he too was hooked up. His fish was smaller than Rosalie's, but just as energetic.

It went on like that for a better part of the next hour, both kids hooking, then landing or sometimes losing three more snook apiece.

"I'm hungry," Tony announced, after his third fish. "Can we go back to the cabin?"

I could tell the last thing Rosalie wanted was a sandwich. "Okay Tony. Just one more cast and we'll go."

Spoken like a true angler.

We agreed to meet in an hour back at the ponds. I suggested we might try a different one after lunch, maybe for redfish or snapper. Then we headed off to our respective cabins.

Mo Murikami was there when I got back to the guides' quarters. He had his back to me, and he was looking at the clipboard that held our weekly schedules. "You seen Mel Campbell?" he asked, over his shoulder.

"No, not since yesterday. Why?"

"I was supposed to take Mr. Farrelli and a guest fishing this morning, but he never showed up. I thought maybe there was a change of plans, and Campbell might have something else for me. I looked all over but couldn't find him anywhere. I saw you at the ponds with those kids. Who are they?"

"They're Lou Farrelli's grandson and granddaughter. Farrelli told me he was going down to Key West."

"That's pretty weird. He could at least have let me know. Did he say why he was going there?"

"Nope. Just said he expected to be back later this afternoon."

Mo frowned. "Strange," he said.

"You said Farrelli was bringing a guest. Do you know who it was?"

"Not exactly. But Campbell told me it was some big shot politician."

When I'd first met Farrelli at the bar, he was touting a state senator for club membership, but I couldn't remember his name. It seemed likely the senator and the supposed guest fisherman were the same person, but I couldn't be sure. And why had Farrelli changed his plans and not told anybody about it?

Mo went over to the refrigerator and pulled out a package of hot dogs. "Want one?" he asked.

"Sure, but what happened to your sushi?"

"Hey, I'm an Asian-American, not just an Asian. What's more American than hotdogs?" He held up the package. "And what could be more American than these. They're Ball Parks."

Mo wrapped a pair of hot dogs in paper towels and nuked them in the microwave for 90 seconds, while I poured us some iced tea.

"You a baseball fan?"

"You bet. Me and my dad used to go down to the Bay Area to catch the Giants or the A's. If we timed it right, we'd get to see both teams. I have a cousin who lives in Berkeley, and we'd spend the night with him."

We chewed on our hotdogs and talked baseball while we ate. He took a last bite, then wiped ketchup off his chin and drank some tea. He pushed back from the table and changed the subject. "How's the detective work coming along? You any closer to figuring out what happened to Mr. Broom?"

"Maybe a little bit. But the Medical Examiner and the Sheriff's Department still haven't figured out exactly what killed him."

"You mean it wasn't those lionfish?"

"It could have been. We're still not sure."

"Huh. Anyway, how's it going otherwise?"

I told Mo what had happened with Johnny Krasuski's permit, and about my boat nearly sinking. He was shocked.

"You know anybody drives a Mako center console with a dark blue hull?" I asked.

Mo shrugged. "I might have seen one around."

"You mean around the club?"

"No, it was somewhere else. If it comes to me, I'll let you know. But about your bilge plug. You think somebody was tampering with it?"

"Seems likely. The last person dealing with my boat, before Rashaan and I got in it yesterday, was Mel Campbell. But I can't imagine it was him."

"Me neither." Mo stopped to stare out the window, back toward the main lodge. "Sure wish I could find that guy. It'd be nice to know what I'm supposed to be doing over the next week. What are your plans?"

"I guess I'm in the same boat. But I'll be spending the night here with you. Maybe we can work something out. Or maybe Mel Campbell will have shown up by then and we'll get a schedule."

"Hope so," Mo said. "Even though we get paid for doing nothing around here if nobody wants to go fishing, I'd rather be busy than just sitting around."

I'd learned over the years guiding that there were two broad categories of fishermen among those who've gone out with me: those who merely like it and those who've become obsessed by it. When I got back to the ponds that afternoon, I had a pretty good idea which Farrelli youngster was falling into which category. Rosalie was standing next to the redfish pond, staring down into the water, but there was no sign of Tony.

She waved as I walked up, then nodded back toward the cabins. "Tony was asleep when I left. I think he'll watch a Star Wars movie when he wakes up. Can we still fish?"

We could and we did. Before the afternoon was over, she caught redfish and mangrove snapper, before ending up back at the snook pond. "They're the most fun," she explained.

Lou Farrelli had long since come and gone before she was ready to quit. I thought about asking him why he'd stiffed Mo, but decided against it. I could just hear Ralph Weatherbee getting on my case about being too personal with the members.

Before Rosalie and I split up, I asked if she'd like to go fishing some day in my skiff, out in the bay. At first her face lit up, but then she hesitated.

"Maybe."

"Is there a problem? From what you showed me today, you're more than ready."

"I guess there's no problem. It's just that, . . . uh, I may not be around here much longer."

I waited for an explanation, not wanting to stick my nose in where it didn't belong.

"Grandpa says he may have to quit the club if some things don't happen."

"What things?" I asked, no longer able to contain myself.

"It's about his cruise line. Like it might go out of business or something. I don't know the details, but I can tell he's really worried. I heard him talking to my dad about it. They thought I couldn't hear them, but I did."

"Did you hear him say why it might go out of business?"

"Not exactly. Something about ports, or docking rights, or something."

Chapter 19

Mindful of Stella's admonition to be spending more nights at the club, I had decided this was going to be one of them. But there still was enough of the day left for me to drive down to Conch Key and check out Avery's fish market. If the place was full of lionfish, and especially if some of them were alive, it could be a clue as to the source of those that had ended up stinging Arthur Broom. Had it been this man Avery himself, or perhaps his supplier? Could that supplier have been Reuben Fletcher? It didn't seem likely, assuming his job at the Purple Isle club was a full-time one.

The afternoon traffic was moderate, this being summer, and it only took me about a half hour to drive from the club down to Conch Key on US-1. The island was populated mostly by modest one-story houses, some on stilts but most old enough to pre-date the zoning requirement that they be built up to better survive hurricanes. There also was an assortment of commercial fishing operations, and a couple of smaller marinas. The little key had a comfortable old-time feel to it, having so far escaped the invasions of fancy homes, plush resorts, and expensive restaurants that were changing much of the Florida Keys.

Avery's fish market was a ramshackle white clapboard place right on the water at the northwest point of the island. I pulled into a small gravel parking lot, got out of the Cherokee, and crunched around taking a look at things. A white Ford 150 pickup with a camper shell was parked next to the building, and a small lobster boat was tied up to an old wooden dock out behind. The dock was badly warped, and both the boat and the pickup needed paint.

A scrawled note on the front door said "back in fifteen minutes," but there was no way to tell how long it had been up there.

I knocked, but there was no response. I peered in through a window next to the door. Display cases across the back wall were packed with ice, but I could see only a handful of fish. I went back to the door and knocked again. Eventually a voice behind me said "Can I help you?" I turned to see a man coming out of a small stucco house painted a bright lime-green. There were hurricane shutters on all the windows, but they were cracked open.

The man looked to be in his mid-fifties, a bit on the pudgy side, with a ruddy complexion and a full head of curly brown hair. He was busy tying a white apron around his waist. "Are you Mr. Avery?" I asked, as he walked across the street.

"I'm Chet Avery," he said. "What can I do for you? We don't have many fish left."

This was going to be tricky, because I didn't want to come right out and tell him my real reason for being here. "I have a special request, and maybe you can help me."

Avery frowned and kept coming. He unlocked the door and invited me to follow him inside. The interior of Avery's fish market was dank, poorly illuminated by weak overhead fluorescent lights, and smelled like fish. A trio of yellow-tailed snapper lay side by side in one of the two display cases, while two undersized Spanish mackerel were in the other. A tank on the wall to my left held about a half-dozen live lobsters. But these were not what got my attention. Instead it was a 50-gallon aquarium on the right-hand wall that had lionfish swimming around inside it. Their vertically-striped bodies and long spines shown burnt-orange and white, even though the aquarium had no light. My hopes rose.

"As you can see," Avery repeated, "there's not much left of today's catch. But I can recommend the yellow-tails. They're pretty good eating. Or would you like some lobsters? Brought them in just this morning."

This explained the boat tied up behind the shop, and told me that Avery was a fisherman as well as a proprietor, which was unusual.

"What about the mackerel?" I said, trying not to stare at the lionfish.

Avery rotated his right palm back and forth in a "not so much" gesture. "They're okay if you smoke 'em. Make pretty good fish dip."

I looked to my right and pretended to see the aquarium for the first time. "Are those lionfish?" I asked. "I've heard about them."

"What have you heard?" he asked.

"That they're dangerous."

"They can be if you don't know what you're doing. But they're pretty good eating, actually."

"Huh. You know my wife, she's a pretty serious aquarist. We've got tanks all over the house, most of them salt water. I'll bet she'd love one of those."

Avery shook his head. "Those are already sold."

"But can you get me a couple?"

"Sure, I can do that. But it might take me a day or two. They're hard to catch. I have to use a special trap. You'd want 'em live, right?"

"Yeah, but I'll have to check with my wife first and make sure she'd like one. I'll get back to you. Oh, and what would you charge?"

"Fifty dollars for one that's alive. The price would go down if you wanted more."

"You sell many live lionfish?" I asked, trying to sound casual.

"Not that many. Most people want 'em to eat."

"But you do sell some alive?"

"Yeah, sometimes. In fact, there was a guy came in here a couple of weeks ago, said he'd take as many live ones as I could get. He ended up with more than a dozen."

"Was his name Jacques?"

Avery shrugged. "Didn't tell me his name, and I didn't ask. He paid cash. Why do you want to know?"

"Was he a tall man, kind of lanky, with a lot of hair?"

"No, that doesn't sound right. But what's this all about anyway? Why do you give a damn about some other guy? What's going on here?"

I had to think fast.

"I, . . . uh, thought he might be a friend of my wife and me. He has a big aquarium operation up in Homestead. Thought maybe he'd sell me one for less than fifty dollars, which is pretty steep."

Avery raised an eyebrow, like he didn't believe me. "Well I don't know anything about this Jacques guy. Now I got things to do on my boat, if all you came in here for was to talk."

"Actually, I'll take four of those lobsters. Can I just have the tails? We'll be eating them tonight."

"Sure, I can do that," Avery said.

I paid for the lobsters, got back in the Cherokee, and thought about what had just happened. The good news was I'd probably just found the source of the lionfish that somebody had dumped into the hogfish pond at the Purple Isle Sportsman's Club. The bad news was, I was no closer to finding out who it was, except it probably wasn't their phony French chef. I'd been tempted to push Chet Avery for a better description of the "ordinary looking" man who'd bought his lionfish. Was it Reuben Fletcher? That didn't seem likely, since he was a fisherman himself. In any event, Avery had grown suspicious enough as it was, and I decided it would be up to Stella what steps we ought to take next.

I called her as I was leaving Conch Key, but it went straight to message. I left one telling her what I'd found, and then headed back for the club. One good thing: Mo and I were going to have lobster for dinner. I stopped at a little country market on the way back and picked up some essential go-withs.

Mo was in middle of his supper when I walked into the guides' cabin, his chopsticks poised over a little rice cake with a piece of salmon on top.

"You might want to save room for these," I said, holding up two plastic bags, including one with the lobster tails inside. "You ever had 'em barbecued?"

Mo dropped his chopsticks. "I've never had 'em period."

"Well then, let's get at it. There's a grill back over toward the members' cabins."

"What's in the other bag?" he asked.

"I got coleslaw for a side dish, plus there's aluminum foil, butter, and a couple of lemons. All we have to do is split the tails open, load in butter and lemon juice, and wrap them in the foil. Then five or seven minutes on the grill, depending on the heat, and we're ready to go. We got any beer left?"

"Uh huh."

"You have a good day?" I asked, as we were getting things organized.

"It was okay. I went out with Johnny Krasuski. We got into a school of good-sized jacks, and they're always fun. He even tried fly fishing. Said his wrist was feeling better." Mo finished slicing up the lemons, and then wiped his hands on a towel over the sink. "When we got back Weatherbee was at the dock."

"What did he want?"

"He wanted to know if I'd seen Mel Campbell."

"Had you?"

"Nope. Apparently nobody's seen him since yesterday."

"Maybe there was a family emergency or something."

"Sure, but you'd think he would have told somebody what he was doing. Plus Weatherbee said his car is still parked beside his cabin. Said he knocked, then used his pass key to get inside when nobody came to the door."

"Did he find anything unusual inside?"

"He didn't say, so I guess not."

"That does seem pretty weird."

Fifteen minutes later Mo and I were enjoying the sweet flavor of barbecued lobster tail, washed down with ice-cold Landshark lagers, when we heard a scream. It was high-pitched and loud, like it had come from a woman or a child who wasn't that far away. We looked at each other and simultaneously bolted for the door. As soon as we got outside a second scream gave us a direction to follow: beyond the fishponds someplace, and not in the direction of any of the cabins.

We ran toward the second scream, and almost collided with a young woman running out of the woods. It was Serena Liptan, one of Rashaan's twin daughters.

"What's back there?" I asked, pointing in the direction from which she'd come. "Is somebody hurt?"

She managed to squeeze out a single "no" in between gasps for breath.

"It's okay," I said. "Take it easy, and try to tell us what happened."

"It's . . . I think he's dead!"

As tempting as it was to ask who might be dead, instinct told me not to do it. "Would you like to go back to your cabin?" I asked.

"Yes," she sobbed. "Yes!"

"Serena, this is Mr. Murikami. He'll take you back to your parents. But please, if you can, point me in the right direction and tell me how far away."

"It's . . . back there," she said, pointing toward the interior of the island. "I don't know how far. Really."

I left Serena with Mo, took a best guess where to walk, and headed off. Whatever Serena had seen, I knew if I couldn't find it on my own we'd need to get her back out there. Hopefully that wouldn't be necessary.

Needless to say, I hadn't taken time to put on any bug spray. As I worked my way farther into the dense vegetation bordering the island, the worse the mosquitoes and noseeums became. But I knew if I went back to the guides' cabin to lather-up, there was little chance I'd be able to pick up Serena's trail again. So I just kept going.

It only took about another 100 yards. There was a body lying face-down at the base of a big gumbo limbo tree near the far southern tip of the island. I got close enough to recognize the red hair streaked with gray, and the familiar t-shirt and Bermudas. It was Mel Campbell. The back of his head was matted with blood, and he didn't appear to be breathing. Even with limited forensic training, I knew enough not to disturb what looked like an obvious crime scene. Nevertheless it did seem important to determine if he actually was dead. I picked up a branch lying nearby, reached out with it, and gave Mel a prod. He didn't move. I pulled a red bandana out of my hip pocket and tied it to the gumbo limbo as a marker, and then beat it back to the cabin where I'd left my phone. It was time to call Stella.

Chapter 20

It was nearly dark by the time Stella made it to the Purple Isle, and she wasn't alone. Penny McMasters, the head of the department's crime scene unit, was with her, and she'd thought to bring along not only portable lamps but also a generator. Anthony Hernandez, the M.E., also was there, along with Deputy Oscar Wilson. Stella, Wilson, and I stood back while Penny and Anthony set to work.

Word must have spread around the resort, because after a short while both Ralph Weatherbee and Max Welty, their head of security, came crashing through the woods, each carrying a flashlight. Stella saw them coming, and put up both hands to stop them from coming any closer.

"What's going on here?" Weatherbee said, flailing at the swarm of mosquitoes that had gathered around his head.

"Please stay back," Stella replied. "We have a body here."

"Who?" Welty asked.

"We believe it's Mel Campbell."

"My god," Weatherbee said. "What happened?"

"We're not certain," Stella said, even though it was pretty obvious. "But here's what I want you to do. I want you to go back to the lodge, then get hold of all the members and staff however you do that, and have them wait there for me. Don't let anybody come out here, and don't let anybody leave the island. You got that?"

"But I'm not certain—"

"And to make sure it happens exactly like I said, I'm sending Deputy Wilson with you."

Stella didn't say "Now git," but she might as well have.

Once Welty and Weatherbee had left in the company of Oscar Wilson, Stella turned back to the crime scene. "What have we got?" she asked.

"There's an obvious blow to the head," Hernandez replied. "We'll have to wait for a full autopsy to be sure, but that certainly looks like the cause of death."

"Any sign of a possible weapon?" Stella asked.

"Nothing so far," Penny McMasters said. "We'll have to wait for first light to do a more thorough search."

"What about blood on the ground?" Stella asked.

"Not all that much," Penny replied. "Plus there's drag marks in the dirt. Looks like the killer moved the body from over there by the ponds. We should be able to trace it back, but again I'd prefer to wait until morning."

"Okay," Stella said. "I'll leave you to it. Sam, please come back to the lodge with me. I'd like you to be a witness when I break the news to the members."

Stella looked off toward the fishponds as we made our way back out of the woods. Even in the dim glow cast by her flashlight, I could tell by the frown on her face that something was bothering her, and I guessed it was more than just the body lying back there.

"I know what you're thinking Stella. There goes our whole case on Broom."

"Uh huh. This is a real nightmare, Sam. I mean all those suspects with possible motives to kill Broom, why would any of them give a damn about Mel Campbell? What possible connection could there be?"

I laughed and immediately regretted it.

"What?" she said, obviously not amused.

"Yeah, sorry. I was just thinking. If Campbell died from a blow to the head, at least we can be sure it actually was murder. Like what you said the other day about killing somebody the old fashioned way?"

If any of this amused Stella, she gave no sign. "You say one of Liptan's daughters found the body?"

"Yep."

"My god, that must have been awful. Did she say how she happened to be out there?"

"No."

"We'll need to talk to her for sure," Stella said. "She might have seen something."

"You gonna do that now?"

"First thing is to talk to the assembled group. They need to know what happened, and they need to hear it directly from me, not filtered through Weatherbee."

By the time we got back to the lodge, Weatherbee had most of the staff and residents rounded up in the lobby area. He'd moved chairs over from the dining room, so everybody had a place to sit. I stayed in back with Oscar Wilson while Stella walked up in front of the assembled group.

I recognized all the staff, including Mo, Weatherbee, various housekeeping and maintenance people, George the bartender, Jacques the cook, and the security guys. Most of my recent clients were there, including Johnny Krasuski, Rashaan Liptan, Royal O'Doul, and Lou Farrelli along with his wife Donna. Krasuski and Liptan looked worried, and the Farrellis both looked puzzled. O'Doul had his arms folded across his chest and he was pouting, as if this was a big intrusion into his important life. Conspicuously absent was Norberto Padilla, the big sugar guy.

"Thanks for coming everybody," Stella said. "As some of you may have heard, we recently discovered the body of Mel Campbell, your fisheries manager. And I'm very sorry to tell you his death most likely wasn't an accident."

"You mean somebody killed him?" Johnny Krasuski asked. "My god, that's awful. Was it a shooting?"

"The medical examiner is out there now, and we'll know more when he and the crime scene crew have finished their work. But in the meantime, I need to ask if any of you have seen something that might help us determine just what happened and when."

Stella waited, but nobody said anything. "Alright, then, what I'd like to do next is interview each one of you separately."

"Now wait just a second," Lou Farrelli said. "It's already getting late. Can't this wait until tomorrow?"

This brought a chorus of responses, mostly from fellow club members, all at about the same time. The clear opinion that filtered through the din was that Farrelli had it right.

Bock

Stella looked at her watch. "I suppose we could wait until morning," she said. "But on two conditions. First, nobody is to leave the property overnight for any reason. And second, I'm gonna ask Deputy Wilson here to start a sign-up sheet where you'll put down your contact information and choose a time for your interview."

Royal O'Doul stuck up a hand. "Can we go after that? I've got an important meeting up in Homestead tomorrow afternoon."

"Unless something comes up during your interview, you can leave as soon as it's over, Mr. O'Doul. Just be sure your contact information is up to date and complete, in case we have more questions."

"Questions about what, exactly?" O'Doul said loudly. "You think we're all suspects or something?"

"At this point we have no reason to suspect any of you in particular. But because Mr. Campbell may well have been killed by somebody on the property, none of you is exonerated either." Stella paused to let that sink in. "Look, I know this is difficult, and we appreciate your cooperation."

"Maybe some of us would feel more like cooperating if we weren't being spied on," O'Doul said.

"What do you mean?"

"You know damn well what I mean, lady." O'Doul pointed directly at me. "That guy, Sam Sawyer. He's not really a fishing guide, is he? He's working for you! Tell me I'm wrong!"

I had never seen Stella Reynard flummoxed before. She clearly was this time, but it didn't take long for her to recover. "Mr. Sawyer actually is a fishing guide, as you know very well. But it also is true that he occasionally helps me on matters of law enforcement. The department has engaged him to look into the matter of Arthur Broom, because of his familiarity with lionfish, among other things."

"Lionfish my ass," O'Doul said. "What he's been doing is snooping into our private lives because you think one of us might have had something to do with what happened to Broom."

Stella hesitated, like she was making up her mind about something. "Dr. Sawyer is not a snoop, Mr. O'Doul. He's a paid consultant with the Sheriff's Department. And a trusted colleague, I might add. This had been a very difficult case, partly because some of you have been reluctant to talk to me personally about it. That is why I asked Sam for help."

At this point Johnny Krasuski, bless his heart, came to the rescue. "I for one am damned glad you did, and not just because of my permit." This got a couple of chuckles, but O'Doul wasn't among the chucklers, and neither, I noticed, was Lou Farrelli.

"Some of us liked Art Broom," Krasuski continued. "We appreciated what he was trying to do for the Bay and for the Glades, and we're awful sorry about what happened. If Sam Sawyer can help you get to the bottom of this, then more power to him."

This brought a few murmurs from the group, but it was hard to tell whether they were in agreement with Krasuski or otherwise.

Stella clearly had decided it was time to bring the meeting to an end. "Once again, thank you all for coming. And be sure to sign up with Deputy Wilson for your interviews tomorrow. I'd like about thirty minutes from each of you."

I started to follow Stella outside, when somebody came up from behind me and put a hand on my arm. I turned, and saw that it was Fiona Broom.

"Do you have a minute?" she asked.

"Of course."

She got her face up close to mine—in my experience closer than normal for two people only casually acquainted. "I didn't want to say anything back there," she said. "But I'm glad you're helping the Detective. And I'm hoping you can do me a favor."

"What is it?"

"Could you persuade her or the Medical Examiner, or whoever is holding things up, to please let me have Art's body?"

"I'm not sure I can do that."

"He's supposed to go in the family plot back up in New York, and I'm being pressured about it by some relatives."

"Close relatives?"

"Oh no, just some distant cousins. But they're getting pushy and it's making me uncomfortable." She stopped to brush away a stray lock of hair that had fallen over one eye. "And, frankly, I'm getting tired of waiting myself."

"I can understand that, Mrs. Broom. But as you may know there are uncertainties about just what caused your husband's death, and until that gets resolved our hands are pretty much tied."

Fiona got her big blue eyes even closer to mine. "But can't you understand? Can't you help?" A single tear had started to make its way down her cheek. "Please?"

"I'll talk to Detective Reynard. But I'm sure she's doing all she can."

Stella was waiting for me when I got outside. "What was that about?"

"You mean with Mrs. Broom?"

"Uh huh."

"She was pressing me about Broom's body. Any idea when Hernandez might let it go?"

"Probably not until we figure out what was in his stomach, and whether it might have killed him. Speaking of which, how is Katie coming with her work on that?"

"I guess she's making some progress, but she still doesn't know for sure."

"Well maybe you can help. Now that your cover here is thoroughly blown, I don't think there's much point in your hanging around the club. And in fact it could be dangerous."

"I don't know about the danger part, but it will be nice moving back in with Katie full time."

"I'd still like to keep you on the payroll. With this second killing, I've really got my hands full. And I'd like you to sit in on the interviews tomorrow. By now you know most of these people better than me. Maybe you'll hear something that doesn't add up."

"The way Royal O'Doul feels about it, and maybe some others, are you sure that would be productive?"

"I can't see how it would hurt, Sam." She shook her head. "Hell, they don't like me any better than they like you. Maybe less."

I could hear a generator running, and there were lights visible through the trees. Hernandez and the crime scene crew were still at it.

"This whole thing is a total damned cluster fuck," Stella said.

I'd never heard her use that word, or sound so bitter. I tried to come up with some constructive next steps.

"Let's assume for the moment that the two cases are related. What did Broom and Campbell have in common?"

Stella shrugged. "That's just it. I can't think of anything."

"Maybe Campbell found out something about how Broom died and who was responsible, and that person went after him."

"Sure, I suppose that's possible, but then why hadn't Campbell already come to me with it? Or to you?"

I couldn't think of an answer for that. "Alright then, let's assume for the moment the two cases aren't related. I can think of at least two things we ought to be doing regardless, in addition to Katie's work on the mystery plant."

"And they are?"

"First, you got my message about the fish market down on Conch Key?"

"Yeah. It sounds like you may have discovered the source of the lionfish, right?"

"Right. And a possible connection to the club."

"Who's that?"

"Reuben Fletcher, the security guard. Seems like he's pals with the owner of the market, Chet Avery. At least Snooks tells me they've been drinking together at the Safari Lounge."

Stella thought about that for a minute. "I think I'll go down there tomorrow, as soon as we've finished the interviews. Maybe throw my weight around a little."

"Good idea."

"You said there were two things?"

"Yeah. The other has to do with what Mel Campbell told me when I first got here. I asked him if they had trouble keeping the fishing ponds stocked up. He said usually they didn't because it was all catch and release. But then he said something that didn't seem important at the time, but now it could be. He told me that fish had been disappearing from some of the ponds lately, especially the snappers and the hogfish."

"Like maybe somebody was poaching?"

"Exactly."

"And you're thinking maybe Campbell figured out who it was and they had a confrontation?"

"I know it's all speculation, Stella."

"Yeah, well, all we've got at this point is speculation."

We walked together out to where Anthony Hernandez and the crime scene crew appeared to be wrapping things up, at least for the night. He and Penny had Campbell in a body bag, and were carrying him out toward the van they had parked near the marina.

"You find anything more out there?" Stella asked.

Hernandez shook his head. "As I said before, there's not much doubt he died from a heavy blow to the back of the head. I'll do an autopsy just to be sure there wasn't anything else going on. But I think you can count on it."

"Any idea what sort of weapon?"

"Not really. Something big and blunt."

"What about time of death?"

Hernandez scratched at a bristle of hair above his left ear. "Can't say for sure, but based on the rigor and condition of the wound, I'd guess no more than two days ago."

"Any sign of the possible murder weapon?" Stella asked Penny McMasters.

"Nope. But we did find one interesting thing. There was blood on the front of his shirt. A lot of it actually. Anthony and I agree it's hard to imagine how it got there from the wound on the back of his head."

"You're thinking it might be somebody else's blood?" Stella said.

"Exactly," Hernandez replied. "I'll type the blood as soon as we get back to the morgue, and then we'll do DNA of course."

Hernandez and McMasters loaded the body into the van and drove away.

"Do you know anything about Campbell's family?" Stella asked, as soon as we were alone.

"Nope. Sorry. I know he lived by himself in one of the cabins on the property, but I never saw him with anybody else and he never mentioned family."

"Ralph Weatherbee likely knows something. I'll ask him about it tomorrow. But first there's somebody else we need to talk to."

"Who's that?"

"Max Welty, their head of security. I know they have at least two cameras at the fishing ponds. Maybe they picked up something."

The good news was we found Welty in the lodge. But he wasn't in the little room with the security monitors. Instead he was drinking in the bar.

Stella was polite at first. "Could I see you out in the lobby Mr. Welty? We may be able to use your help."

Welty reluctantly put down his beer and followed us out of the bar. He had a long narrow face that reminded me of a horse. "What is it?" he asked.

"My forensics team believes Mr. Campbell was killed beside one of the fishing ponds, where I believe you have security cameras. We need to take a look at your recordings."

"Sure. When do you think it happened?"

"Most likely it was some time yesterday, so that would be a good place to start."

We followed Welty into the room with a bank of monitors. There were six of them altogether, and I could see that two of the six showed images of the ponds. He sat down in a plastic swivel chair and began typing on the console in front of him. Pretty soon two of the screens—the ones showing the ponds—turned to snow.

Welty kept fiddling, but nothing was happening.

"That's funny," he finally said. "It looks like there was something wrong with those cameras yesterday. There's nothing there. Sorry about that."

I could almost see the steam coming out of Stella's ears. "You've got to be kidding! What about the day before?"

Welty fiddled some more, and eventually images of the ponds came back on the screens.

"Is that live?" Stella asked.

"No, those are the recordings from three days ago. You want me to fast forward and see if anything shows up?"

"You bet."

We watched and waited as the recordings played out. It must have taken a half hour before anything happened. Then a man driving a golf cart came into view on one of the screens. Welty hit a button and the recording went back to normal speed. The man got out with a bucket and dumped something into the pond. Then he got back into the cart and drove off.

"That's Mel Campbell, feeding the fish," Welty said. "But it looks like he was alone, and he left before anything happened."

"That's because it was the day before he was killed. Can't you figure that out?" Stella paused and shook her head. "Sorry about that. Alright, Mr. Welty. Here's what we're gonna do. You're gonna give me those tapes. Not tomorrow. Now. I'll be taking them to our forensics lab down in Key West. Maybe they can find something you missed. You've got other tapes you can load up in the meantime, right?"

"Right. But Mr. Weatherbee isn't going to like you running off with all our recent recordings."

"You let me deal with Weatherbee. We'll get the tapes back to you as quickly as possible. Oh, and one other thing. No matter what you hear from Weatherbee or anybody else, Sam Sawyer is still on the case. He's to have free access to club property at all times. Make sure your people at the guardhouse know it, okay?"

Stella spun on her heels and stomped out, not giving Welty a chance to respond.

"Can you believe that?" she said, once we were back outside. "We've got two killings here, both in the same place, and on both occasions the security cameras just happened not to be working?"

"Or somebody erased the recordings afterwards," I said. "In which case, one or both killings could have been spontaneous and not planned in advance."

"Either way, Sam, that's just too much of a coincidence for me. The same person had to be responsible."

"It looks that way."

Stella stared off into the night sky. "I'm beat, Sam. I'll see you in the morning when we talk to everybody. Maybe they'll get us somewhere."

"You still think that's a good idea, my being here for the interviews?"

"I do."

Stella walked back toward the parking lot, while I headed for the guides' cabin. It was time to pack out and head for home.

Mo was in the shower when I got there. He came out wrapped in a towel and drying his hair with another one. He watched as I started collecting up my things.

"You leaving tonight?" he asked.

"Yeah, might as well. Now that my cover is blown, Detective Reynard and I agree there's not much point in my staying here."

"You have any idea how that O'Doul guy found you out?"

"Nope. But I'm sure it's gonna come up when we interview him tomorrow."

"So you'll be in on those interviews along with the Detective? I'd like to be a fly on the wall for that one."

"Why?"

"Oh, no particular reason I suppose, except it'd be fun to watch him squirm. That guy's a real jerk."

I finished zipping up my travel bag and headed for the door. Mo came over and we shook. "It's been good," he said. "I'll miss having you around."

"You're not done with me yet, Mo. I won't be spending nights at the cabin, but Stella has asked me to stay on the job until we get this case solved."

"You mean cases plural, right?"

"Uh, yeah, I suppose it is cases plural. Unless we find out whoever shoved Art Broom into that pond is the same person who killed Mel Campbell."

"You think that's likely, Sam?"

"No idea at this point. But as long as we're on the subject, are you aware of any particular links between Broom and Campbell?"

Mo shook his head. "They were both good guys, in my book. And as far as I knew they liked each other. But besides that, nothing I can think of."

Chapter 21

I met Stella in the lodge at 7:30 the next morning. There was coffee available in the lobby. We each grabbed a cup and she pointed to a leather couch sitting against one wall. A big mounted tarpon hung on the wall. Actually, I was pretty sure it was a plastic reproduction, because nobody kept the actual fish anymore. They just took pictures and measurements and had somebody craft a replica.

"Let's sit," she said. "There's a couple of things I want to go over before we get started. I checked out Mel Campbell last night. He grew up in the Tampa area, where he began working as a fishing guide just out of high school. He got married, had a couple kids, but it didn't last. He's spent most of his life working in or around the fishing business."

"So nothing special that might be related to his murder?"

"Not that I could find."

"Which leaves us with no obvious connections between Broom and Campbell, right?"

"Right."

Stella took a big swallow of coffee and stood up, looking at her watch. "Rashaan Liptan asked if we could meet with him and his family first thing this morning, and could we do it at his cabin. Apparently his daughters are pretty stressed out, which is understandable. Oscar Wilson put the Liptans first on our list of interviews."

Rashaan answered the door when Stella knocked, and he immediately stepped outside rather than inviting us in. "The girls are really upset, especially Serena. She's the one who found the body. Are you sure you need to do this? I can tell you what she told me, which isn't much."

"I'm sorry Mr. Liptan, but I really do need to talk with her. This shouldn't take long."

The twins were sitting at the kitchen table when we walked in, working on the last of their scrambled eggs, toast, and bacon. Julie hovered in the background, not looking happy.

Rashaan introduced Stella to Serena and Candace.

"Good morning," Stella said to the girls. "My name is Detective Reynard and this is Dr. Sawyer. I'm guessing you're named after two famous athletic stars, right?"

Both girls looked at Rashaan, who grinned.

"And which one of you is Serena?" Stella asked.

"That's me," said one of the girls. Then, in a hurry: "And my sister Candace didn't see anything, so you don't need to bother her."

"Why don't we all go into the living room?" Stella suggested, ignoring the hint.

Julie sat between her daughters on a leather couch, and Rashaan in a big recliner adjacent. We took chairs opposite.

"I'm sorry that I have to ask you these questions," Stella said. "But we're very anxious to find out who did this terrible thing to Mr. Campbell, and we hope you can help."

Serena looked out the window instead of at Stella or me. "I don't see how. All I did was find the—uh—the body. It's not like I know how it happened or anything."

"Of course, I understand. But how did you happen to be out there in the first place? So far from the cabin, I mean."

"I was trying to catch the kitty," Serena replied, finally making eye contact with Stella.

"The kitty?"

"There's been a cat around," Julie explained. "We've been feeding her on the patio, but she's too shy to let us touch her."

"We don't think it's a she, Mom," Candace interrupted. "We named him Ruggles because Serena and I decided he's a boy."

"Anyway, you were chasing this cat when you came upon the body?" Stella asked, obviously less interested in the sex of the cat than in matters relevant to the case.

"I already told you that," Serena replied, with a sideways glance at her mother.

"What else did you see?" Stella asked.

"What do you mean?" Serena said.

"I mean was there anything besides the body?"

"Like what?"

"Like anything that you wouldn't normally find out in the woods?"

Serena glanced over at her father. "No."

"What about other people? Did you see anybody else out there?"

"Nobody."

"What about the cat?"

"I never found her. I mean as soon as I saw the body, I ran back out of there. I guess I kinda forgot about Ruggles."

"After Mr. Murikami walked you back to the cabin, what did you do?"

"I told my Mom and Dad what I'd found. Then I went to bed."

I couldn't help but notice how calm—almost casual, really—Serena was about this whole thing compared to her condition when Mo and I had found her the day before. Was it a show for her parents or her sister, or just the passage of time?

Stella folded shut a notebook she'd been holding and clicked off her ballpoint pen. I knew her well enough to recognize a look of disappointment. "Thank you for talking with us, Serena."

"Are you gonna catch who did this? I mean I know I wasn't much help."

"Not at all, Serena. You were very brave and you've been a big help. If it hadn't been for you, we might not have found Mr. Campbell for several more days. So thank you."

For the first time, the hint of a grin appeared on Serena's face. "Actually, you ought to be thanking Ruggles."

Stella grinned back. "I would if I could."

Rashaan, who had been sitting silently in his recliner the whole time, rocked forward and put his hands on his knees. "Now why don't you girls go into your room and start packing? We'll be heading home as soon as we've done the dishes."

Once the twins were gone, Stella turned to Rashaan. "Thanks for letting us do that, sir. I know it was tough."

"Doesn't sound like Serena was much help, though."

"Maybe not, but we had to ask those questions. And speaking of questions, before you go I need to ask you and Mrs. Liptan a couple that we will be asking all members of the club."

"Shoot."

Stella re-opened her notebook and pulled out one of the two gold ballpoints she always carried in her shirt pocket. "First, did you see or hear anything that could be related to the murder of Mel Campbell? And second, are you aware of any connections between Arthur Broom and Mr. Campbell, beyond the obvious ones here at the club?"

Rashaan and Julie looked at each other and simultaneously shook their heads.

~ ~ ~

Deputy Wilson had a list ready for the interviews, which were due to start at 9:30. Except for a lunch break, Stella and I spent the rest of the day asking club members and staff if they knew anything about the murder of Mel Campbell, and about possible relationships between him and Arthur Broom. For the most part, it was a waste of time. Nobody had seen or heard anything, or at least they all claimed they hadn't. And nobody could think of a connection between Broom and Campbell.

The day might have been a complete loss, except for three of the interviews. It wasn't because any of those individuals was especially willing to talk. It was because Stella had done her homework.

We met with Jacques Petain in the morning, just before he had to rush off to cook lunch. We sat in comfortable chairs around a low coffee table at one end of Ralph Weatherbee's spacious office, under the spreading fronds of a big plastic palm tree. Stella wasted no time, once Petain finished claiming he didn't know anything about either murder.

"Why did you change your name?" she asked.

The cook harrumphed. "Who told you that, and what business is that of yours anyway?"

Stella could have harrumphed back, but instead she just smiled. "Do you deny that you were born in New York City, and that your name back then was Jason Pavlis?"

"I, uh . . . no I don't deny that. But I still don't see what that has to do with anything."

"And is it not true that your father was in the construction business, and that your brother still manages the company?"

Jacques/Jason brushed a straggle of curly hair off his forehead. "Uh, yes, that is true. He works hard. It's an honest business. Our clients are very pleased. Always have been."

"And isn't it true that he did business with an investment firm owned by Arthur Broom? And wasn't there an investigation a decade ago into possible illegal financial dealings between your company and Mr. Broom's?"

By now the cook had begun sweating hard, and his normally ruddy complexion had turned even darker than usual. "Nothing ever came of that, which you undoubtedly know since you've done such a thorough job of snooping into my private life."

"Then I'll ask you one more time. Why did you change your name?"

"I always wanted to be a French chef. Having a French name seemed like a good idea."

His answer had come so fast that I wondered if it might actually be the truth. Or was it just very well rehearsed? Was Stella wondering the same thing?

"And for the record, Mr. Petain, did you have anything to do with what happened to Mr. Campbell or Mr. Broom?"

"Absolutely not! How can you ask such a thing?"

"Because it's my job, Mr. Petain. Before we let you go, I need to ask you one more thing. Dr. Sawyer here tells me you occasionally buy lionfish from a market down on Conch Key, which you then serve in the club restaurant. Is that right?"

"Yes. They're quite good using my personal recipe."

"He also tells me you buy them from a man called Chet Avery, who owns the market. Is that right?"

"That may be right. I wouldn't know."

"So you don't go down to Conch Key and buy them yourself?"

"No. They're delivered."

"Are they alive when you get them?"

"Oh hell no. But I still have to be careful when I filet 'em. Those spines can be nasty, even on a dead fish."

"Who brings them to you?"

Petain faltered. "I, uh . . . I'm not sure."

"How can you not be sure Mr. Petain? Don't you see who's delivering them? After all, it's your kitchen."

"Yes. But I don't always pay that much attention to who's bringing us what."

"I find that surprising. In fact isn't it Reuben Fletcher who brings you the lionfish?"

This time Petain seemed genuinely confused. "Who's Reuben Fletcher?"

"He works for the club as a security guard. We understand he's acquainted with Chet Avery."

"I wouldn't know anything about that." Petain fidgeted and made standing-up motions. "And now if that's all, I need to get back to the kitchen. There's a lunch to be served."

The second interview of any consequence was with Reuben Fletcher. He came into the office wearing his usual blue and white rent-a-cop outfit.

"Thank you for seeing us, Mr. Fletcher," Stella said. "Dr. Sawyer here has a couple of questions he'd like to ask."

I'd known this was coming, because Stella and I had talked about it beforehand.

"The other day I took a club member, Johnny Krasuski, out fishing. We were after permit. He'd just hooked up to one when a man driving a blue Mako came along and drove over his line, breaking off the fish."

"What about it?"

"I understand you own such a boat. Was it you out there that day?"

Fletcher blinked. "I have an old Mako with a blue hull, yes. But it wasn't me that cut your line. Why in hell would I do something like that?"

"So it wasn't you?"

"Damn right it wasn't me. I already told you that."

"Well now that's funny, Mr. Fletcher, because I was watching with my binoculars, and the man at the wheel looked just like you. Plus I got a partial on your boat's license, and it matches yours."

It was a total bluff, of course, and wasn't something we could ever use in court. But there was little or nothing to lose.

Reuben Fletcher was one of those people who tapped his feet all the time, and his right heel had been bouncing up and down ever since he'd sat down. Now it went into overdrive.

"I, uh . . ." He stopped and glanced at Stella. "Okay, . . . yeah, that was me. But I didn't mean to drive over his line. Honest. It was just an accident. You gotta believe me."

"It sure didn't look like an accident, Mr. Fletcher," I said. "Your boat came in fast—way too fast—and left the same way. You must have seen we had a fish on. Why did you do that?"

"There'd been talk about permit being around, and I was curious to see what you had."

"Maybe. But then why did you run off like that?"

"I, . . . uh . . . I got scared is all."

I was pretty sure he was lying, but there didn't seem to be any way to prove it. So I changed the subject.

"A couple days after the incident with Mr. Krasuski's permit, I took Rashaan Liptan out fishing, and we damn near sank because somebody had loosened my bilge plug. Was it you?"

Fletcher slammed his hand down on the table in front of us and jumped up out of his chair. "Alright, that's it! Detective—Reynard is it?—I thought this was supposed to be about what happened to Arthur Broom and Mel Campbell. What in hell do Sam Sawyer's fishing and boating adventures have to do with it?"

With that he whirled around and rushed out of the room.

"A bit touchy, isn't he?" Stella said, with a twinkle in her eye.

Our last interview of the day was with Royal O'Doul, the developer of golf courses and would-be grand champion tarpon fisherman. He came stomping in, refused to sit down, and quickly volunteered that he knew nothing of any possible use to our investigations.

"Please sit down anyway, Mr. O'Doul," Stella said. "This shouldn't take long."

O'Doul lowered his substantial bulk down into a chair. He did so carefully and slowly, like his back must have been hurting. Maybe it was from fighting that big tarpon a few days earlier. Not that it was as big as he'd made out.

Once again Stella was all business. "Please tell me what you know about Mel Campbell, Mr. O'Doul."

He frowned, causing his already low forehead to get even closer to his eyebrows. "Don't know anything about him, except he runs the fishing program here, I think. Why?"

Ignoring his question, Stella fired off her next one. "And what about Arthur Broom?"

This time a hint of worry might have flashed across O'Doul's face, but it disappeared so quickly I couldn't be sure. "What about him?"

"What was your relationship with him?"

"I didn't have one."

Stella rustled some papers, but I was pretty sure she hadn't actually needed to consult anything. "Then perhaps you can explain why you opposed his membership in the Purple Isle club when it was first proposed?"

O'Doul shrugged. "I dunno. Maybe I just didn't like the guy."

"So it had nothing to do with the fact that his firm denied your loan application ten years ago back in New York?"

Color rose in O'Doul's cheeks. "I have no idea what you're talking about."

"Then perhaps I can refresh your memory." Stella shuffled more papers. "Would you like to see copies of your application and Broom's written response?"

Royal O'Doul rose quickly from his chair, and folded his arms across his chest: by now a familiar pose. "What's with you, lady?" he blurted out. "Everybody but you and maybe Mr. Sawyer knows that Art Broom was drunk that night and fell into the pond, where he died from a heart attack. This whole investigation of yours is nothing but a witch hunt!"

O'Doul scowled and stared at the ceiling. Then he walked out of the room, slamming the door behind him.

Stella and I exchanged glances.

"Well that was interesting," she said.

Chapter 22

Stella and I were sitting alone in Ralph Weatherbee's office, having finished the day's interviews.

"When did you find time to look into Royal O'Doul's background?" I asked.

"Actually, I didn't. Weatherbee told me how he'd opposed Art Broom's application for club membership. But the part about the loan was mostly a bluff. I learned he'd done business with Broom's company, but I had no idea there was any trouble." Stella grinned, obviously pleased with herself. "And my bluff worked, didn't it?"

"From the way he got all excited, I'd say so. And now you'll dig deeper, right?"

"Damn straight I will. Though I suspect the guy's pretty good at covering his trail."

I was about to remind Stella that in addition to any possible dealings back in New York, Broom might also have been getting in the way of O'Doul's plans for a golf course near Homestead. But just then Ralph Weatherbee came bursting into the room. He shut the door behind him with a flourish, and stomped over to his desk. I could tell he was hot, both literally and figuratively, from the scowl on his face and the sweat glistening on his bald pate.

Weatherbee sat down in the big leather swivel chair behind his desk. "We need to talk," he said, pivoting in our direction. He waggled his right index finger at the two empty chairs on the opposite side of the desk. "Are we gonna do it by shouting across the room, or are you gonna come over here?"

Stella shot me a look, and then made a point of taking time to carefully gather up her notes. "Be right with you," she said.

We'd barely had time to sit down when Weatherbee started in. "How *dare* you treat Jacques like that! It's none of your damned business why he decided to change his name. And besides, what could that have to do with what happened to Arthur Broom or Mel Campbell?"

Weatherbee stopped talking and drummed his fingers on the big mahogany desktop, clearly expecting answers.

Once again, Stella took her time. "As you are well aware, there have now been two murders at *your* club, neither of which has been solved. Mr. Petain is no more and no less a suspect than anybody else around here, including you. Now if you'll excuse us, we need to get on with our job. Which, by the way, will be conducted as I see fit."

Stella started to get up, but Weatherbee raised a hand. "You may have the right and the duty to do that job, Detective. And I hope you start making some progress, because you obviously haven't accomplished much of anything so far. But let me tell you two things. First, you have my word that Jacques had nothing to do with any of this. And second, wherever your investigation takes you, from now on you'll be doing it without your partner here." Weatherbee glared right at me. "Mr. Sawyer, you're fired!"

I was about to make a smart-ass comment about jumping before being pushed, but Stella squeezed my arm. "I fully intend to keep Mr. Sawyer engaged in this investigation, Mr. Weatherbee. As it happens, I've already decided that his working here as a fishing guide is no longer in our best interests. He won't be working for you, but he will for me, okay?"

With that Stella rose, pivoted, and walked out of the office, with me trailing along behind.

As soon as we got outside, Stella pointed toward a bench down at the marina. "Let's go sit a minute while I clear my head. Then we're gonna make some plans."

It was early evening. The sun was a fading red globe fast approaching the horizon. A mild breeze had come up out of the north. The rippled gulf waters sparkled with angled light. We sat, and I waited for her to begin.

Things didn't start off as I expected, because usually Stella was all business.

"As soon as the sun hits the water, watch out for the steam," she said, with a dry chuckle.

"And the green flash," I said.

"What? I know the old 'steam' joke. But the green flash is a new one on me."

"Actually, it's not a joke. I'm surprised you haven't heard of it. Sometimes, right after the sun disappears below the water, the sky lights up with a green flash. It's brief and it's rare, but it happens. Maybe only once in a hundred sunsets, but it happens."

"Huh. Do they know what causes it?"

"Something about the earth's atmosphere bending the sun's rays like a prism. I read somewhere that Jules Verne—the sci-fi writer—first used the term. Some people think seeing a green flash is a lucky omen."

"Have you ever seen it?" she asked.

"Three times. Twice I was with Katie out in my boat, but she missed it on both occasions. She claims I was just making it up. But she must have blinked or something, because I really did see it."

Stella looked out at the sun, which was about to disappear. "Here's hoping for the green flash. If there's one thing we could use right now, it's a little luck."

We watched and we waited. But as on most evenings, there was no green flash. Instead the sky gradually faded from orange to lavender and finally to blue-gray.

"Oh well," Stella said. Then she shook her head as if to claw her way back to the business at hand. "You know, Sam, we probably interviewed at least one murderer today. But it was pretty much a total bust. Petain is a phony, O'Doul is a liar, and probably so is Fletcher, but I think we knew that already. And all the others? We basically got nothing."

"We especially got nothing from Norb Padilla, because he didn't show up."

"Yeah, I noticed that," Stella replied. "I asked Weatherbee about it, but all he said was that club members were free to come and go as they pleased. And Padilla had left before I got everybody together last night after we found Campbell's body. So it might not mean anything."

"Still, are you gonna talk to him?"

"Oh you bet. Meanwhile we have a more urgent problem. Anthony Hernandez still hasn't made a determination about whether Broom's death was from natural causes or a homicide."

I knew where she was headed.

"And that's likely to depend on whether that mystery plant Katie found in Broom's stomach could have killed him, right?"

"Exactly. Which is why, now that you're no longer guiding here at the club, I want you to help Katie figure this out."

"There's no way I can identify that plant. That's Katie's department. I'm no botanist."

"No, but you're a bulldog, Sam, and you've got great instincts. If nothing else, I know Katie can use another pair of eyes and ears, and maybe even a nose. I mean where did that plant come from? And how did it get in his stomach? Things like that."

I wasn't completely comfortable with what Stella was asking. My involvement in the plant aspect could make Katie feel like neither Stella nor I had confidence in her ability to solve this aspect of the case. I almost said something to Stella about it, but then had second thoughts. This was a subject to be discussed with Katie, not Stella.

"Okay, I'll help Katie. And there's one other thing I'd like to try."

"What's that?"

"It has to do with the Campbell murder. I have a hunch it had something to do with poaching in the fishing ponds over there."

"You mean Campbell might have caught somebody poaching and confronted them?"

"Yeah."

"What do you propose doing?" Stella asked.

"I want to run a stakeout. At night."

"If Welty and his crew do their job with the security cameras, it shouldn't be necessary."

"Yeah, but that could turn out to be a case of the fox guarding the henhouse. I have my suspicions about that guy Fletcher."

"So do I," Stella said. "But what if he's at the guardhouse when you show up for your stakeouts? Wouldn't that blow your cover?"

"I've thought about that, but there's another way of getting into this place."

"By boat, right?"

"Yep. And if it's late at night, which it will be, nobody should see me."

From the frown on her face I could tell Stella remained skeptical. "But isn't it likely that Fletcher—or whoever did this—wouldn't they quit poaching in light of what's happened?"

"Can't rule it out. But what have we got to lose?"

"You could lose a bunch of nights with Katie, that's what. I can just imagine how thrilled she's gonna be when you take off in your boat in the middle of the night."

"My problem, not yours."

Chapter 23

That night marked the point where my life with Katie entered a new chapter. It wasn't that I wouldn't be staying overnight at the Purple Isle club, which pleased her. And it wasn't that I was going to stake out the place in the wee hours, which didn't please her at all. Instead, it had to do with my becoming a forensic botanist. Or, more accurately, an apprentice forensic botanist, partnered with one of the best.

We were out on the deck enjoying an after-dinner decaf, when I brought it up.

"Stella suggested I start working with you to figure out what plant might have poisoned Arthur Broom. I told her I was no kind of botanical expert, but she insisted. Are you okay with that?"

A bolt of lightning followed by a clap of thunder got in the way of our conversation, but it also lit up Katie's face enough I caught a flicker of a frown. The thunder had long since rolled away as I sat waiting for her to say something.

"Better question is, are *you* okay with that?"

"What do you mean?"

"I mean I love you to bits, Sam. But sometimes I get the impression you make a better leader than a follower."

"Depends on who I'm following. In your case the view makes it all worthwhile."

Lightning flashed again, and this time I saw her smile.

"Would you be willing to follow me—or lead me or whatever—to the Rolfson Botanic Garden in Miami? Tom Wordsburg thinks he's identified our mystery plant. In fact, they have some growing on their grounds."

"Wow! What's it called?"

"It's a small tree called manchineel. He looked through the early history of the garden and found a reference to a highly toxic, illegal plant and its location. Then he went to that spot in the garden and found it, tightly surrounded by a clump of bigger trees. The manchineel was in fruit, so he collected some and made slides. And guess what? It matches the images I sent him of Broom's stomach contents. The cells are identical. So we've got it nailed!"

"That's terrific news Katie. Have you told Stella?"

"Not yet. I just found out myself. Tom suggested I come up to the garden and get a look at the tree itself, so we'll know what we're looking for in the Keys, including around the crime scene. This might be the perfect opportunity for you to get involved. Want to come along?"

"Wouldn't miss it. When?"

"Tomorrow. Tom has it all set up."

A tarpon broke the surface somewhere down the canal. More lightning and thunder followed on the heels of the splash, and then it began to rain.

Squalls usually don't last all that long in the Keys. Katie and I debated riding it out under the big umbrella attached to the table on our deck. But then the wind came up, driving rain sideways off the Gulf. Prince let out a couple of substantive woofs, telling us he'd had enough. Then he headed for the sliding door and scratched at the glass. We followed close behind, as the wind drove sheets of rainwater up the canal behind our house.

~ ~ ~

We weren't due at the garden until noon, and it wouldn't take us more than two hours to get there from Islamorada as long as the traffic was okay. This meant we could have a leisurely morning in bed, something that was all too rare in our lives. The only family member unhappy with the arrangement was Prince, because he got booted out the back door a little before eight. We wouldn't have done it, but it was the only way to prevent a threesome.

Debris from the previous night's storm littered the highway, which slowed things down but probably not enough to make us late. But then the Snake Creek drawbridge was up when we came to it, and it stayed that way long enough to let two sailboats and a big blue water charter boat go through. By the time that was over, and the bridge had inched its way back down and the traffic had unsnarled itself, I was starting to get worried whether we'd make it on time. Katie called the garden and told the receptionist we probably would be a bit late. Apparently it wasn't going to be a problem.

We proceeded on to the mainland without incident, and then turned east on US-1 toward Biscayne Bay, arriving at the Rolfson Botanic Garden by a quarter past twelve. The guard at the gate found our names on a list and directed us to headquarters.

For some reason I had expected the grounds to be formally landscaped, with paths winding through well-tended gardens of individual plants, each with an identifying label. Some of it was like that, but even more consisted of natural woods and wetlands. It must have been what all of coastal south Florida looked like before most of it succumbed to urban sprawl.

"This is an impressive place," I said to Katie, as we followed a road toward Biscayne Bay. "How many acres do they have?"

"I'm not certain. Close to a hundred I think. Most of which is left in its natural state."

"Is that where your friend found the manchineel?"

"I think so. We're about to find out."

Tom Wordsburg was standing on the front steps of garden headquarters when we pulled up. It was a long low building with lots of glass. Two large greenhouses stood off to the left. Tom pointed to where we should park our car and walked over to meet us. He opened Katie's door and helped her out. Tom matched my six feet, but he was thinner, with a shock of sandy hair. I was surprised when he gave Katie a kiss on the mouth. Had they been an item when they were in school together?

Katie introduced us, and we shook. "Let's go inside," Tom said. "We'll have lunch in my office while I tell you what I've found."

The director's office was spacious, with a big mahogany desk and multiple chairs. One wall was all books, and another was all glass. The glass wall looked out on a palm-lined walk leading down to the bay. We ordered sandwiches from his secretary.

"Tom, please tell us what you've found out about a candidate for our plant," Katie said.

"My discovery happened by accident. I was reading old archives, preparing a talk about the history of the garden. Some early directors kept personal notes on matters that interested them. I found a note about the location of a dangerous native tree called manchineel, or false guava. It got me wondering if this might be your plant. This was way before the days of GPS, but from the description I had a pretty good idea where to start looking. And sure enough, I found it."

"Just one?" Katie asked.

"That's all I've found so far. There could be more."

"And you know for certain it's the species that was in the victim's stomach?"

"Yep. The tree was in fruit. I picked some and made slides. It's a perfect match for what you sent me."

"Can't wait to see it!" Katie said. "Can we go now?"

Tom shook his head. "Let's have lunch first, and I'll tell you what I've learned about the plant. It's interesting and—frankly—pretty scary. As soon as we're done eating, I'll take you out there."

There was a knock on the door, and Tom's secretary came in with our sandwiches and iced tea. We ate and drank while Tom filled us in on the life history of manchineel.

"The scientific name of manchineel is *Hippomane manchinella*," he began. "It's a Linnean species in the family Euphorbiaceae. I think it was first collected on Jamaica. It grows in brackish water, ranging from subtropical areas of the US and Mexico, down through Central and perhaps northern South America, as well as throughout the Caribbean."

"What does it look like?" I asked.

"The plant has gray bark, and it grows as a shrub or short tree up to 12 meters tall. All parts of the plant are poisonous, including the leaves, trunk, branches, roots, and especially the fruits. It's dangerous to the touch. Even a person standing under a tree in the rain can be severely blistered."

"Wow," I said. "That sounds nasty."

"Which is why we need to be careful when we go out there," Tom replied. He took a bite of his tuna salad sandwich, and continued. "Pieces of the plant likely were used by indigenous people as fish poisons and weapons against enemies. The descriptions of modern human exposure are alarming."

"In what ways?" I asked.

"Temporary blindness, blisters, lesions that won't heal resulting in staph infections. Things like that."

"Yipes."

We munched on our sandwiches for a while, while Tom and Katie caught up a bit on their respective careers since graduate school. Then Tom pointed to a table on the other side of his office. "I've put out three herbarium sheets over there. Let's go take a look."

The specimens were attached to stout cardboard and covered with clear plastic, an obvious precaution against accidentally touching them. The leaves on the specimens were shiny green, varying from five to perhaps ten inches in length, with fine teeth along the edges. Fruits attached to some of the branches looked to me like little green apples, about two inches in diameter.

Katie pulled out her phone. "Mind if I take some pictures?"

"Of course not," Tom replied. "And you'll want to photograph the living tree as well, I'm sure."

We sat back down, finished eating our sandwiches and drinking our tea, and then followed Tom outside. He led us down a gravel path, following signs with arrows pointing to "The Everglades" section of the garden. At one point we stepped off the path and worked our way into a dense stand of mangroves and other trees and shrubs I didn't recognize. It was hot and humid, there being little or no air movement under the canopy.

"Be careful in here," Tom said. "I found only one manchineel, but there could be more."

We walked for another fifteen minutes, with Tom in the lead, until he stopped and pointed to a tree directly in front of us. "That's it there," he said.

The manchineel was about twenty feet tall and tent-shaped, with long side branches reaching all the way to the ground. We walked closer, and I saw a couple of apple-shaped fruits lying beneath it. Katie and I both took pictures with our phones, being careful not to touch any part of the tree, or even to get too close.

"Are you going to leave it there?" Katie asked, as we made our way back to headquarters.

"Good question," Tom said. "I'll be asking our Board of Directors about that. We might want to take it out along with any others we find, given their potential danger to the visiting public. On the other hand, we might want to leave at least one—carefully marked and roped off naturally—for educational purposes."

We went back to Tom's office and thanked him for lunch and the field trip. He gave Katie the slides he had prepared of the manchineel fruit cells, along with photographs showing details of leaves, bark, and whole fruits.

"What about flowers?" Katie asked. "There weren't any on the tree we just saw."

"I couldn't find any either," Tom replied. "I'll keep checking in case it eventually blooms. In the meantime, if you need me as an expert witness on this I'd be glad to help. But with these slides for comparison, I doubt you'll have any trouble convincing people what your victim had in his stomach."

"Or what probably killed him," Katie replied.

Tom and I shook hands and he kissed Katie on the mouth again. Now I really was beginning to wonder about their past relationship. But . . . none of my business I suppose.

As we drove back down to the Keys we talked about what we'd just learned.

"That manchineel in Broom's stomach makes his death look really sinister, doesn't it?" Katie said.

"And it raises some serious questions, though. Who knew enough about manchineel to use it as a poison? And where had they found it?"

"What's next?" I asked as we approached Key Largo.

"First thing we need to do is call Stella and tell her what we've learned. In fact, I'll do that right now," she said, pulling her phone out of her purse.

Katie punched in the number, and waited. I could tell from her first words that the call had gone to message. She left one describing what we'd seen at the botanic garden. Then she asked Stella to call back if she had any questions, and clicked off.

"I expect Stella's going to want us to start looking for manchineel trees, ideally those with fruits, don't you think?" Katie said.

"Yeah, but the Keys include a lot of the right kind of habitat, and yet the trees aren't all that common. Aren't we looking for a needle in a haystack?"

"I can think of one way to make it a smaller haystack."

"How's that?" I asked.

"Let's start with the Purple Isle. Maybe there's one right outside Arthur Broom's back door."

"That would help," I replied. "So would finding those fruits in somebody's refrigerator."

"Now wouldn't *that* be exciting!" Katie said.

Chapter 24

I waited that night and the next day, expecting to hear from Stella. But all I got was a brief text message thanking us for the information about the manchineel. It wasn't like her, and I wondered what was up. In the meantime, I decided to initiate my nightly stakeout at the Purple Isle fishing ponds.

I untied my skiff from our dock just before dark and took the short boat ride over to the Purple Isle marina. It was hot and humid and the air was dead calm—what Snooks called tarpon weather. Katie had sent me off with a thermos of coffee, a batch of oatmeal cookies she'd somehow found time to bake, and a world class frown. She tried but failed to persuade me take the sidearm I was licensed to carry but rarely used. I'd argued that poaching fish was scarcely a capital offense, especially if they were being caught out of a stocked pond. Whatever might happen, even if I did catch somebody in the act, it couldn't be all that dangerous. Or could it?

I guided my skiff into a slip at the marina as quietly as possible, got out with my coffee and cookies, and made my way into a clump of trees midway along the row of fishing ponds. A pair of sodium vapor lamps provided sufficient illumination that I wouldn't need the flashlight I was carrying to identify anybody who showed up. I wondered if the security cameras were operating, given their recent history.

I drank two cups of coffee and ate four cookies over the next three hours, during which nothing happened. There was a good-sized gumbo limbo tree against which I could rest my back. It made things comfortable—perhaps too comfortable—and at some point I must have dozed off despite the caffeine.

When I woke up it was because of a noise. Even half-awake I knew it was the noise that had roused me, but I was still too groggy to determine just what sort of noise it had been, or where it had come from.

I stood up for a better look around, heard the noise again, and then everything went black. The next thing I remember I was lying on my back, looking up into a blinding light. "Are you okay?" came a familiar voice.

"I, . . . uh, . . . I think so. Who are you?"

The light went off. "Sorry about the light, Sam. It's Mo Murikami."

I attempted to sit up, wincing at a sharp pain at the back of my head. I instinctively put a hand there, and it came back wet. Even in the distorted amber light I was sure it was blood.

"Looks like somebody clipped you," Mo said. "What were you doing out here anyway?"

"Trying to catch a poacher. He must have found me first. Did you see anybody?"

"I saw a man running toward the lodge."

"Could you tell who it was?"

"No. It was too dark, and he had his back to me. Lucky thing I came along. I probably scared him off before he had a chance to do even more damage."

"You sure it was a man?"

"Pretty sure, yeah."

I shook my head to clear the fog and attempted to stand. The only reason I made it was that Mo put his arm around my waist and helped me up.

"You look pretty woozy," he said. "And you've got a nasty welt at the base of your skull. We need to get you to the infirmary. You think we can make it just the two of us, or should I go get more help?"

"No . . . uh . . . I'm fine. Just get me back to my boat and I'll—"

"No chance, my friend," Mo interrupted, as he led me gently but firmly in the direction of the lodge. "Your boat isn't going anywhere, at least not tonight."

The Purple Isle infirmary was a small windowless room down a hallway to the right of the manager's office. It held the usual equipment and furnishings, including an examination table where Mo helped me lie down before he went off hunting for the doctor.

It seemed like forever, and I even thought about sneaking out and heading for home, when Mo came back with a young man in tow. He had a stethoscope around his neck and a name badge that said "Aubrey" pinned to his shirt pocket. I wondered if that was his first name or his last but didn't bother to ask.

Aubrey introduced himself as a physician's assistant. He asked me to sit up so he could take a look at the back of my head. He poked and prodded for a bit, and then asked if I'd experienced any dizziness.

"A little woozy when I first stood up, but not since."

"Can you tell me what happened?"

I described it as best I could, while he came around and shined a light in my eyes.

"Well," he said, followed by enough of a pause to make that one word seem profound. "You've obviously had a pretty sharp blow to the back of your head. The good news is your pupils are the same size and they're responding appropriately to light, so there's no sign of concussion, at least not yet."

I tentatively fingered the wound, and winced in pain. "How bad is it?" I asked.

"Bad enough. I recommend a couple of stitches. Would you like me to do that, or would you prefer going to emergency?"

"You'll do fine, thanks," I said.

A half hour later, armed with painkillers and extra gauze bandages, I was in Mo's pickup, headed home. I called Katie on my cell and gave her an abridged version of what had happened. She pushed for details, but I put her off.

"Mo Murikami is giving me a ride," I said. "See you in a bit." Then I turned to Mo. "How did you happen to be out there by the ponds?"

"One of the saltwater pumps has been acting up, and I wanted to check on it. In case you haven't heard, I'm the new fisheries manager now that Mel's gone."

That gave me an idea. "Could you keep an eye out for whoever's poaching fish out of the ponds? That's less likely to raise anybody's suspicions, compared to my doing it."

"I can do that," he said. "After all, if somebody's stealing our fish, that's now officially my responsibility."

"Good," I said. "But watch your step, and I do have a request."

"You want me to keep it to myself, except for you?"

"Yep. Just me or Stella, okay?"

"Sure. But let me ask you something. Why are you so interested in somebody that might be poaching our fish?"

"I wouldn't be Mo, except that same person likely is the one who killed Mel Campbell."

"Because he caught them in the act," Mo said. "Sure, that makes sense. But what about the security cameras? Have you checked the tapes? I know they have at least two trained on the ponds."

"They were shut off the night Mel was killed."

"Which means your bad guy could be somebody with access to the security system, who would know enough to turn off the cameras on a poaching night. Now I understand why you snuck in here in your boat."

No fleas on Mo Murikami.

Katie was waiting in the living room when we got home, looking understandably anxious and less than happy. She didn't say "I told you so" when we came in, but I could read it on her face.

Prince, who held no grudges, grinned when he saw me, and then went around to sniff the back of my head when I bent down to give him a scratch behind the ears.

I introduced Katie to Mo and explained how he'd come to my rescue.

"Thank you for that," she said. "And you have no idea who did this to Sam?"

"No, ma'am," he replied. "But I'll be keeping an eye out."

"Mo's the new fisheries manager at the club," I explained to Katie. "And he knows what's going on."

"I wish I did," Katie replied. Then she found her manners. "Would you like something to eat or drink? Coffee? Cookies?"

Mo shook his head. "No thank you, ma'am. I'd better get back. Sam, what do you want to do about your boat? I could drive it over in the morning."

"No, that's not necessary. You've already done enough. We'll come over and pick it up. Probably some time tomorrow."

"Just be sure and do it when the sun's up, okay? I don't think I'm up for another late-night rescue."

"Seems like a nice young man," Katie said after Mo had left.

"Nice, and also plenty smart. He could be a big help in our search for whoever killed Art Broom and Mel Campbell. Already has been, in fact."

"Apparently not enough," Katie replied, her bitterness returning. "You know Sam, I was there when Snooks warned you not to get involved with that place."

"Yeah, and I told you why I felt I had to. Look, my head hurts and I'm tired. Let's talk about this in the morning, okay?"

Her look softened as she reached out and gently touched the side of my head. "I'm sorry," she said. "That wasn't fair. It's just that I worry about you."

"You should. After all, now that I'm your apprentice forensic botanist, you'd be in real trouble without me, right?"

Katie grinned, which was very good to see. "Oh I'd be in trouble without you all right, but not because of your skills as a plant guy, which are pretty darned minimal."

Chapter 25

I waited until a decent hour the next morning to call Stella and tell her what had happened. Just as I was about to punch in her number, my phone lit up and it was her.

"Good to hear from you," I said. "I was about to call you, because Katie and I were wondering why you didn't return our earlier call."

"Sorry about that." There was a pause. "We need to meet. There have been—uh—*developments* you need to hear about."

"What developments?"

"I'll tell you when you get here. You and Katie, if she's available. Anthony Hernandez, the M. E., will be coming too. My office. Nine o'clock?"

"Of course. But first you need to hear about what happened to me last night."

"I hope it was something positive. I could use some happy news right now."

"I wouldn't say it's happy, but it could be interesting. Eventually, that is."

I told Stella about my encounter at the fishponds.

"Holy crap!" she said.

Before we left for Stella's office, I called Snooks to see if he would be available that afternoon to help me get my boat back from the Purple Isle marina. He answered on the first ring, and I explained what was going on.

"I told you not to get involved with that place," he said.

Where had I heard that before?

"Yeah, so anyway, can you help? Katie doesn't want me to drive the boat alone because of the bump on my head, even though I told her I'm feeling fine. She can drive us over there."

"Glad to help, but I've got a better idea. Why don't the four of us—you, me, Flo, and Katie—drive over there in my skiff, and then the girls can follow us back. That way, if somebody's messed with your boat again, we won't be stuck out in the bay, or sunk or something."

It seemed like a remote possibility, but between Katie and Snooks I'd had my quota for the day of being nagged about the supposed perils of the Purple Isle Sportsman's Club.

"Deal," I said, reluctantly. "We've got a meeting with Stella Reynard this morning. Shouldn't last much past noon. I'll call you when we get out."

~ ~ ~

As soon as we walked into Stella's office, I could tell from the look on her face that things were not good. Hernandez already was there, staring down at his coffee cup and not making eye contact with Katie or with me. Stella pointed at the coffee machine without saying a word, and sat down in a swivel chair behind her desk. The three of us crammed ourselves into armless wooden chairs on the opposite side of the desk. We did not engage in casual chatter.

Stella ran the fingers of her right hand back through her hair and cleared her throat. "First off, let me apologize for being out of touch. Anthony and I have been in meetings with the Sheriff and with the State's Attorney for Monroe County for the last couple of days, and we didn't want to bother you until certain issues got resolved. Now that they have, more or less, you need to know what's going on." Stella did the hair thing again. "We have some interesting news. The blood on the front of Mel Campbell's shirt wasn't his. Anthony put a rush on the DNA, and we just got the results back."

"Have you tried for a match?" Katie asked.

"Tried, yes." the M.E. replied. "A match? No, but we'll keep looking. The databases are in a lot of different places, which makes any search expensive. It could take a while. I'll keep you posted."

"What about the security recordings from the club? Did your techs find anything interesting?" I asked.

Stella shook her head. "Nope. Our people came up empty, just like Welty did the other night. But anyway, armed with the blood evidence

156

and the identity of the fruit from Broom's stomach, I asked the powers-that-be to authorize three things: swabbing everybody at the club for their DNA, taking blood samples, obtaining a search warrant to look for manchineel fruits."

"Including club members and their cabins?" I asked. "How did that work out?"

"It pretty much didn't. The State's Attorney suggested I was on a 'fishing expedition' as he put it, after which he actually cracked up at his own joke."

"So you got nothing?" Katie asked.

"We got nowhere on the DNA or blood typing, which actually didn't surprise me. We did get permission to search for manchineel in the main lodge, plus anywhere on the grounds, and in staff quarters. Just not in the members' cabins. It was then I figured out what was going on."

"Somebody at the club has been putting pressure on the State's Attorney's office and the Sheriff's Department," Katie said. "Somebody with political clout."

Stella nodded.

"Any idea who that somebody was?" I asked.

"Nope. As we talked it became clear the Sheriff and the State's Attorney really want us to concentrate on the Campbell murder and bury the Broom case."

For the first time since we'd walked into the office, Anthony Hernandez looked up from his coffee cup. "That's not going to happen. I finished writing my medical examiner's report yesterday. Broom officially died a suspicious death, and the case stays open."

"And we thank you for that," Stella replied. "I know you're putting your career on the line here."

"Don't you think we both might be facing that possibility?"

"Maybe, and maybe not. Either way, it's time to plan our next steps in both murder investigations."

"I think we need to start looking for manchineel trees and their fruits," Katie said. "And the logical place to start is at the club."

"My thinking exactly," Stella replied. "Even if we can't go inside members' cabins, at least we can look everyplace else. You and Sam want to handle that?"

Katie and I looked at each other, and then back to Stella. "We'd be glad to," Katie said.

"Good," Stella replied. "You know what the thing looks like. I'll head over to the club right after we've finished here and serve Weatherbee with the search warrant. I'll tell him you'll be doing the actual looking, starting tomorrow. How early can you make it?"

"The earlier the better in this heat," Katie said. "It's gonna be a tough job. You'd better tell Mr. Weatherbee to expect us at dawn."

"There may be a problem getting into the lodge and staff quarters that early."

"We'll start by searching the grounds. That's gonna be the nasty part anyway, and it'll be good to get it over with before the sun gets too high."

"I really appreciate your doing this, Katie. And you too Sam."

Up to this point I'd let Stella and Katie do the talking and the planning, but now I had a question. "I understand why we're looking for the manchineel fruits. We find them in somebody's refrigerator or wherever, and we've got a likely suspect. But why are we looking for the tree? Even if we find one, how does that get us closer to finding the killer?"

From the way the two women looked at each other, I could tell they were surprised I hadn't figured that out.

"Because of the security cameras," Stella said. "Maybe there's one trained on the tree, if there is a tree, and maybe somebody forgot to turn it off while they were picking the fruits."

"That's a lot of ifs and maybes."

"Granted," Stella said. "But I think it's worth the effort, don't you?"

Without waiting for an answer, Stella started shuffling some papers on her desk. "Now as to the Campbell case. If whoever conked you on the head last night is the same person who killed Mel Campbell—which seems likely—then your stakeout isn't going to work anymore, is it Sam?"

"Unless by 'work' you mean getting him hurt again, or maybe even killed," Katie interjected, a bitter edge to her voice.

"Actually, there is a way to keep that going without involving me," I said, hoping to spare Stella the necessity of explaining that the stakeout was my idea and not hers.

"What's that?" Stella asked.

I told them about Mo Murikami: that he'd just been appointed fisheries manager, and that one of his duties was keeping an eye on the ponds. "He'll report to us—and only to us—if he sees anybody poaching or poking around."

"Good," Stella said. "Now before we go, Sam recently asked me to look into a couple of matters and I wanted to bring you up to speed on what I've found. The first has to do with a man named Chet Avery, who owns a fish market on Conch Key that may have been the source of the lionfish. I paid him a little visit yesterday, in an official capacity. He seemed nervous as hell, but he couldn't—or at least wouldn't—give me a name or even describe for me the man who bought live lionfish."

"Doesn't that make you suspicious?" I asked.

"Sure it does," she said. "And I'll keep after him."

"You know it's possible the man who bought the lionfish, or perhaps even Avery himself, was the person Mo saw running away last night at the ponds after I got hit on the head. Which means he could be our poacher."

"Then we'd better hope Mo sees him again," Stella replied. "Another thing I did was look into a possible relationship between club member Lou Farrelli and a State Senator named Mack Snodgrass. It wasn't hard to figure out. Snodgrass is chair of the senate's transportation committee, which has the power to grant docking rights to cruise ships. From what I understand, Farrelli's cruise line may be teetering on the brink unless he can get some new places to land his boats. One of which, as it happens, is Key West."

"The quid quo pro seems pretty obvious," Hernandez said. "I put you up for club membership, and you save my cruise line. But how does the Broom murder fit in?"

"Good question," Stella replied. "It probably doesn't, except that Sam heard Farrelli suggest Snodgrass as a replacement for Broom now that he was dead. Apparently club membership is capped, and the only way for a new member to be admitted is for somebody else to leave. Dead or alive."

"Still seems like a stretch," Hernandez said. "But I suppose a desperate circumstance could lead to a desperate act."

"What about Norb Padilla?" I asked Stella. "Did you ever figure out why he was a no-show for our interviews?"

"I did. Got him on his cell. He said he had to leave because there was a problem at one of his sugarcane plantations. I asked him if he knew Mel Campbell was dead. He said he didn't but he sure was sorry. That was about it."

"Do you know when he left the club?" I asked.

"Yeah, I checked on that. They keep a log at the guardhouse of all the members' comings and goings. He drove out early in the morning on the day we found Campbell's body."

"So he was there the night he died."

"Yep."

"If you ask me, Padilla's motive for killing Broom is a lot stronger than Farrelli's. Arthur Broom's Everglades Rescue Foundation had drawn a direct bead on the sugarcane business."

~ ~ ~

Contrary to Snooks' expectations, nobody had sabotaged my skiff overnight, and the boat ride back from the Purple Isle was uneventful except for a moderate chop that made for a bouncier ride than usual. The real turbulence came later at the Safari Lounge.

Flo and Snooks had invited us for a beer and burgers after we'd gotten my boat safely back home. We'd brought Prince, had him stowed in the basement with the cats, and were waiting on our food, when Reuben Fletcher and Chet Avery walked in.

Snooks, who had been busy mixing Margaritas for another couple, noticed them right away. Like all good bartenders, he'd learned to keep an eye out for who was coming and going. He turned so only we could see his face and mouthed something like "oh great."

"What'll it be boys?" Snooks called out over his shoulder.

"Make it a Bud Light," Fletcher said.

"Me too," Avery said.

I had an idea, and motioned Snooks closer. "Any chance you could serve their beer in glasses instead of in your usual plastic cups?"

Snooks looked puzzled. "Sure, but why would I want to do that?"

"And keep track of who drinks out of which glass, and then give them to me afterwards?"

This time he got it. "Yeah, I can do that, Sam. You working on an idea about one of them?"

"Or maybe both. But it's just a hunch, so keep this under your hat, okay?"

Snooks nodded and went about delivering beer to two of the people I thought might—just might—have something to do with poaching at the Purple Isle fishing ponds, or maybe worse.

I noticed that Fletcher in particular had been staring fixedly in our direction since the two had come through the door and chosen a pair of stools on the opposite side of the bar. He didn't even break eye contact when Snooks walked over with their beers.

Snooks was about halfway back to where he always stood while mixing drinks, when Reuben said in a loud voice: "I always kinda liked this place Chet, but that was before they started letting cops drink here."

Chet looked at Reuben like he didn't know what the hell he was talking about.

"You didn't know about that Chet? Well I didn't either, until the other day when Sam there helps out a lady sheriff while she grills all of us about a dead guy at the club."

Up until this point, Chet Avery hadn't been paying much attention to me or to Katie. But now he did, and right away I caught the look of recognition in the guy's eyes. Recalling my visit to his fish market, where I'd passed myself off as something distinctly not cop-like, it wasn't hard to interpret the look. It fell way short of friendly.

I decided this was an occasion where honesty might prove productive in addition to being the best policy. Instead of sitting there having a staring contest, I got up—shrugged off Katie's tug on my elbow—and walked around to where the two men were seated.

"Evening gentlemen," I said. Then to Avery: "I have to apologize for the other day. All those questions about lionfish? Deputy Sheriff Reynard asked me to look for places that might have lionfish for sale, because somebody deliberately dumped a bunch in a fishing pond at the Purple Isle, and they might have killed a man who fell into it."

"And you thought I had something to do with that?" Avery asked.

"No, not necessarily. But when I found out you sometimes have lionfish available, I thought you might remember who'd bought some, somebody who specifically asked that they be alive."

Avery drank some beer and put his glass back down on the bar. (That's one of two, I thought to myself.) Then he pushed back from the bar, at the same time wiping some foam off his chin. "As you will recall, I told you at the time I had no idea who that was. He paid cash, he didn't give his name, and he looked—unremarkable." Then, as an afterthought: "Which is just what I told your pal the lady sheriff. Who at least was honest about who she actually was, unlike you." Avery spun on his bar stool. "You ready to go, Reuben?"

Much to my relief, Fletcher took two big swallows of beer before he left.

Snooks walked over to where I was standing as the two men went out the door. By good fortune, they were the only customers in the place besides us, which meant we could deal with the beer glasses without drawing anybody's attention. "What do you want me to do with these?" Snooks asked, pointing to the two half-full glasses of Bud Light sitting on the bar.

I looked back over to Katie, who knew a lot more about handling evidence than I did.

"We need to put them in something that will pass for chain-of-custody," she said. "Snooks, do you have some rubber gloves around here?"

"I think Flo has some in the kitchen."

"Good. Go put on a pair, then bring the glasses over here and carefully pour the remains down the sink. Then get two paper bags, some tape, and a pen. Label one bag "Reuben Fletcher" and the other one—what was his name, Sam?"

"Chet Avery."

"Be sure to put the right glass in the right bag, then sign and date each one and tape them shut. Sam and I will sign as witnesses."

Once all that was done, Katie took her cell phone out of the shoulder bag she always carried. "Those signed paper bags and their contents should hold up as evidence in court, but just in case I'll take photos of each one, with you—Snooks—in the background. You might be called as a witness if this comes to anything."

Katie took her photos, and then turned to me. "You're thinking those glasses might have recoverable DNA on them, and that it might match the blood on Mr. Campbell's shirt?"

"Just a hunch. There's something going on with Fletcher, but I'm not exactly sure what it is. He claims cutting off Johnny Krasuski's permit was an accident, and he denies having anything to do with trying to sink my boat."

"And what about Avery?" Snooks asked. "Has he got it in for you too?"

"Not that I know of. And anyway, Snooks, I'm not saying this is personal."

Snooks laughed. "You sure about that?"

Just then Flo popped out of the kitchen carrying a big platter with four burgers and a heap of fries in the middle. "I heard all the excitement," she said. "Did it make anybody hungry?"

"In my experience, Sam's always hungry," Snooks said.

We ate and drank in silence for a while, but Flo only nibbled at her burger and I could tell she was fidgety about something. Finally, she spoke up. I thought it was going to be about the case, or cases, but I was wrong.

"Snooks and I have a problem, or he says it's my problem, not his. I want to discuss this with you. Okay?"

Katie nodded.

"When my mother died, her estate was in limbo until we found out I was her only close relative. Her money came to me, and I used it to purchase and modernize the Safari Lounge. As you know, Snooks has been involved in every step of this as much or more than I've been. He did most of the carpentry and deals daily with the customers. I couldn't manage the place without him."

"Don't get carried away, Flo," Snooks said. "I only work here."

"That's just the problem," Flo replied. "I want him to own half of the bar with me so when I die, he would inherit it all. Don't you agree that's the right thing to do?"

Katie glanced back and forth between the two of them, while I stayed out of it. This was a hot topic that Snooks and I had discussed before when we were alone. I knew he was nuts about Flo, but he just didn't feel right about taking over half ownership of the Safari Lounge.

"You know there's another way to solve this problem, don't you?" Katie said. "You two should get married and then whoever lives longest gets the whole thing. That would work, wouldn't it?"

Snooks started fiddling with the rubber band that held up his ponytail. He did this a lot. This time he did it a lot more.

"Marriage?" he said. "Did I just hear the word marriage?"

Chapter 26

We began the next day by dropping off the (hopefully) DNA-rich beer glasses at the sheriff's substation where Stella worked. It was 5:30 in the morning, and the night clerk was still on duty. We stressed the importance of giving the samples to Stella as soon as she arrived, and signed off on a chain-of-custody form before leaving for the Purple Isle. After that came the start of what Katie dubbed the "Hunt for the Great Manchineel."

I assumed we would drive directly from the sheriff's office to the Purple Isle Club, but Katie had other ideas. "We need to come by boat. Manchineel grows mainly in wet areas, often mixed with mangroves. We might get lucky and spot one from the water. That could save a lot of swamp crawling. You know what it's like inside a mangrove forest."

"I sure do."

We went back home, took Prince for a walk, and then got in my skiff for the short trip over to the Purple Isle. Prince howled as we left the dock, because he loved boat rides better than just about anything, not counting food and naps and getting scratched behind the ears. Katie yelled back that we'd be home in time for a family sunset cruise, but he was still howling as we motored on down the canal.

I parked the boat in one of the two spaces reserved for club deliveries. It was just after 6:30 AM. Katie was wearing a sweater over her tank top even though it was 78^0. Our personal thermometers had always differed. I was already sweating.

Mo Murikami was at the dock when we pulled in. "Hi guys," he said. "What's up?"

Katie told him what was up, because she understood he was privy to our investigation and knew how to keep his mouth shut. She gave him copies of the photographs of manchineel that Tom Wordsburg had printed up for us the day we visited his botanic garden in Miami.

Mo thumbed through the photos. "You think some of these trees might be growing around here?" he asked.

"That's what we came to find out," Katie said. "That and maybe find some fruits lying around in significant places."

"Like where?" he asked.

"Ideally in somebody's refrigerator," she replied with a grin. "But seriously, Mo, this could be the key to our whole investigation. So whatever happens today, keep your own eyes peeled, and let us know if you find anything."

"Of course," he said.

On our way in toward the dock, I'd seen a Purple Isle skiff heading out in the opposite direction. I recognized Norberto Padilla on board, but not the young man driving the boat. "You have a new guide on the payroll?" I asked Mo.

"Yeah, that was Martin Krasuski, Johnny's grandson. He's on summer break from college, and Johnny vouched for him. Seems like a nice kid, and a pretty good fisherman too."

We left Mo to his duties and got back in the boat for a tour around the island. I had binoculars and a pretty decent mental picture of what a manchineel tree might look like mixed in with the red mangroves that dominated the perimeter of the Purple Isle.

We circled the key counterclockwise, motoring at idle speed. I hugged the shoreline so closely that we disturbed brown pelicans, egrets, and frigatebirds roosting in the trees, none of which appeared to be a manchineel.

"Well so much for that plan," Katie said once we were back at the dock. "Guess it's time to take the terrestrial approach."

"Where do you think we should start?" I said. "This is a pretty big place."

"I've thought about that. Someplace close to the cabins would make sense, assuming our bad guy got his fruits from a tree on the island. But as Tom Wordsburg told us, manchineels like it wet, and most of the island interior is pretty dry. Let's start here at the fishponds, and then work our way around the shoreline, or as close as we can get. I'm afraid it's going to be a soggy, buggy mess."

Fortunately, we'd come prepared with knee-high rubber boots, face masks, and plenty of bug spray.

"I've got some high-powered DEET that guides use in the back country," I said to Katie, as I pulled a small bottle out of my shirt pocket. "It'll help keep the mosquitoes and noseeums at bay." I handed her the bottle. "Just be careful with this stuff. It can etch your phone cover or your glasses or anything else plastic."

"Sounds nasty," she said. But she took the bottle, opened it, and spread its contents on her hands, wrists, and those parts of her head not covered by her mask or hat.

And it was a good thing too. As soon as we left the dock and made our way into the mangrove fringe around the island, the noseeums in particular went on the attack.

Over the next three hours we slogged and sweated and swatted our way through the tangled vegetation separating the interior of the Purple Isle from the open waters of Florida Bay, all the time watching for manchineel.

Unfortunately, it all came to nothing. Katie found a couple of rare plants she'd never seen in the Keys, but even that only minimally raised our spirits.

We sat back down on a bench beside one of the fishponds and took off our masks. Katie pulled a red bandana out of her hip pocket and wiped sweat off her face.

"Maybe we should go back home and clean up before we start the rest of our search," she said. "I don't know about you, but I'm feeling pretty stinky."

"Good idea," I said. "We could grab a snack and give Prince a walk."

We were getting into my skiff for the ride home, when I noticed Ralph Weatherbee running toward us, waving his arms in the air. We waited while he came puffing up. "You guys find anything?" he asked between puffs. "Detective Reynard said you'd be searching the island for some sort of a tree or something."

"No luck so far," I said. "But we still need to check the grounds and inside the main lodge and employee quarters."

Weatherbee frowned. "But not the members' cabins, right? That's what Reynard said."

"That's right," I said. "But please understand that we will be searching near those cabins. Perhaps you should alert the members so they won't be surprised?"

"Actually, I have a suggestion. We're having a guest speaker this afternoon. The event will be in the lodge, starting at 5:30. Perhaps you could search the lodge now, and then wait to look around the grounds until after the members have gathered for the meeting."

I didn't much like Ralph Weatherbee, but this actually sounded like a pretty good idea. "We can do that, as long as you don't mind a couple of grubby people poking around inside your office and your restaurant and kitchen."

Weatherbee frowned again. "No. I suppose not. How long do you think this will take?"

"Search warrants are about thoroughness, not speed, Mr. Weatherbee," Katie said. "But we'll do our best to get out of your way as quickly as possible."

As we were walking back toward the lodge, I asked Weatherbee who was speaking that afternoon. I did this more to be sociable than out of any particular interest, but it turned out to be a fortunate coincidence.

"It's State Senator Mack Snodgrass," Weatherbee replied. "He'll be talking about legislators' efforts to promote tourism in the Keys. Should be of interest to our members, especially Mr. Farrelli, who arranged his visit."

Just a coincidence? It didn't seem likely, but then Weatherbee said something puzzling.

"Unfortunately, Mr. Farrelli is unable to be here today. There was an emergency with his cruise line I understand. I'll be handling the introduction and hosting the senator at dinner afterwards."

"That's odd," Katie said after Weatherbee had left.

"Yeah. Makes me wonder if the trouble with his cruise line is even worse than we thought."

We started in the kitchen, which seemed a likely place for somebody to stash manchineel fruits. Jacques Petain was there, chopping things up as we walked in. "Ralph told me you'd be coming," he said, not bothering to look up from his work. "Hope you can make this quick. We've got a big dinner coming up tonight, and I've got a lot to do."

Katie went straight to a big refrigerator standing against the back wall. "I'll start here," she said to me. "Why don't you check out the freezer?"

We rummaged through the drawers and shelves of the two cooling units and then, when that came up empty, started in on the cabinets above and below the counters and beneath the big wood-topped island in the middle of the room. The whole process took maybe a half hour, with Petain getting increasingly agitated as it went along.

"Is there any other place where somebody might keep things cool?" I asked the cook, when it had become clear that the kitchen was another dry hole.

"There's a small refrigerator behind the bar," he said. "You might try there. At least then you'd be annoying George Light instead of me."

We ignored the barb, thanked the cook for his time, and walked over to the bar. Light was there, sitting on a bar stool and reading a *People* magazine. Apparently the big night ahead had not yet come up on his planning horizon.

Light looked up from his magazine and frowned. I wasn't sure he recognized me, and I knew for certain he'd never met Katie, so I introduced the two of us and told him why we were here.

"A search warrant for what?" he asked.

We were under no obligation to tell him specifically what we were looking for, but I was interested to see how he would react when we told him, and couldn't see a downside.

"You probably heard that Mr. Broom had a strange fruit in his stomach when he died. We have now identified that fruit, and we're looking for it in likely places."

"Like in my bar?"

"Mr. Petain said you have a refrigerator back there. We'd like to look inside."

George "Bud" Light cut right to the chase. "And if you find that fruit in my refrigerator then I get to be your prime suspect, right? Just how stupid do you think I am? But go ahead, knock yourself out. I've got nothing to hide."

~ ~ ~

Two and a half hours later, Katie and I were in the Hell's Bay, motoring back home, empty handed and discouraged. Just like in the kitchen and the bar, our search through the rest of the lodge had turned up nothing. Stella had called just as we were getting back into the boat, and we'd given her the bad news.

"But you still haven't looked around the cabins, right?" she said.

"Right. We'll do that part later tonight. Weatherbee thought it would be a good idea to wait until all the club members have gone over to the lodge for a meeting."

"What meeting?"

"He told us Senator Mack Snodgrass would be giving a talk."

"Huh. What about?"

"Something about tourism in the Keys. Anyway, I'll let you know if we find anything."

Prince burst out the door as soon as we opened it, and immediately ran downstairs and jumped into the boat. The message couldn't have been any more obvious: next time you're not going without me. He stayed there until we came out onto the porch for a late lunch. Katie had made tuna salad sandwiches, and Prince never missed a meal: his or ours.

A little before six, we got in my Jeep and drove back to the Purple Isle. Reuben Fletcher was working the guardhouse. He scowled when he saw us, but raised the gate without saying anything. There were dozens of people milling around inside the lodge as we pulled up and parked. Evidently the talk hadn't started yet, but the members had assembled.

I was worried about the coming darkness, and suggested we search the grounds around the cabins first, before looking inside employee quarters.

We walked back up the entrance road, and then began systematically looking around the members' cabins. Weatherbee had given us a map, so we knew which cabin was whose. One of the first ones we checked belonged to Rashaan Liptan, an unlikely suspect to say the least. An impressive variety of garden vegetables grew out back, watered by an automated sprinkler system that happened to come on just as we approached. I recognized Brussels sprouts, okra, green beans,

170

tomatoes, and onions. I wondered if the garden was a project headed by his daughters. Flowerbeds rather than vegetables surrounded most of the other cabins.

Each cabin had a pair of garbage cans in the back. Rashaan's were empty.

Some members had a third can, painted red. We learned the hard way that these were for dog poops.

"Poor Prince," Katie said. "He doesn't have one of those."

"I'm not sure he cares," I said.

As we made our way among the cabins, a booming voice echoed across the grounds, interspersed with laughter and bursts of applause. Senator Snodgrass knew how to entertain a crowd.

It was nearly dark and we were almost finished with our survey when we finally got a break. We were behind Lou Farrelli's cabin. I was poking around in his garbage cans, while Katie was scanning the area with her flashlight.

"Shine your light over here," she said, pointing to a patch of ground next to the cans. "It's stronger than mine."

Katie got down on her knees, and began sifting through the sparse vegetation. "There!" she said. Then she pulled on a pair of rubber gloves, handed me a pair, and pointed to several objects half-buried in the grass. They looked to me like pieces of apple peal, but covered with little bumps.

"That's definitely it!" she said, holding up one of the pieces that she'd already slipped into a plastic bag.

"Manchineel?" I asked.

"Yep. I'm almost certain these are skins from their fruits. We'll double check against Tom's pictures when we get back to the Jeep. But right now let's get some photos of the skins in place, and then make a collection. And we'd better hurry. It sounds like the meeting is breaking up."

~ ~ ~

As soon as we got home I called Stella with the news.

"You're sure about this?" she asked.

"Absolutely. I think Katie knew it as soon as she found them, but when we compared them against the photos her colleague gave us, there wasn't any doubt."

"And you say they were outside Farrelli's cabin?"

"Right."

"Did you see him?"

"No, and that's an odd thing. The club was hosting his friend Senator Snodgrass this evening, but Ralph Weatherbee told us earlier that Farrelli couldn't be there because of some problem with his cruise line."

"We need to interview that guy right away. Did Weatherbee say where he was?"

"No. But his company is based out of Miami, right?"

"Right. And I've got a home number that Weatherbee gave me. I'll give him a call right now."

After getting off the phone with Stella, I joined Katie out on the deck. She was sipping a glass of sweetened iced tea, and she'd poured one for me. We sat for a while, drinking our tea, and listening to the night birds. The air was humid and still. The daytime heat had begun to dissipate. Prince had nuzzled up between Katie's feet and was sound asleep.

"You think Farrelli did it?" she asked.

"From the beginning it seemed like a stretch, especially compared with some of the other club members. I mean, to kill a guy in order to make room in the club for somebody else? Even if that somebody is in a position to trade membership for a favor? I just couldn't see it. But now . . ."

"Now that we found manchineel fruits in his backyard, you're thinking he could be our killer?"

"Maybe, Katie. You gotta wonder how those fruits got there otherwise."

"I am curious what Stella finds out when she gets in touch with the man. How he reacts and all. Whether she decides to bring him in for questioning. I guess we'll just have to wait and see."

"Actually, I have a better idea. Unless you're busy tomorrow."

"I have a morning class, but I'm free all afternoon. What do you have in mind?"

"Let's assume our bad guy heard about manchineel, and decided to use it, but couldn't find one on the Purple Isle. If you were that person, what would you do next?"

"Look someplace else, obviously."

"I know. But where? Where could you find help?"

I let Katie stew on that while I went back into the house to refresh our iced teas. When I came back, she'd figured it out.

"The State Parks. You're absolutely right. They have naturalists on staff who not only would know whether there were manchineel in a particular park, but probably would know exactly where they were."

"What say we pose as a couple of curious visitors to the local parks and see what happens?"

"No need for that, Sam. As a forensic botanist with a faculty position at the college, I have all sorts of legitimate reasons to be looking for manchineel. I think we can be straight up about this and tell them exactly the reason for our visit. It might even get us some extra attention."

Chapter 27

I called Stella first thing the following morning and told her what Katie and I planned to do.

"That sounds like a great idea," she said. "Finding the fruits in Farrelli's backyard is strong circumstantial evidence, but even better would be an eyewitness who saw him actually picking them off a tree."

"You have any luck tracking him down?"

"Nope. Nobody answered his phone. I decided not to leave a message."

"Why not?"

"Thought I should clear any plans with the Sheriff first. He didn't answer his phone either. This time I did leave a message but he hasn't called back. The way he and the State's Attorney carried on when we met about the case last time, I didn't want to go rogue on 'em. Hope you understand."

"I do. But off the record, what do you think should happen?"

"If it were up to me—and this is what I will be suggesting by the way—we should get Farrelli back down here for questioning asap."

"I agree. Let me know how it goes, will you?"

"You bet. And you let me know what you find in those parks, if anything."

While I was waiting for Katie to get home from the college, I went online and typed in Lou Farrelli's name on a search engine, hoping for a decent photograph we might be able to show park personnel. I found one on the website for his cruise line. It wasn't all that good, but I printed it up anyway.

Katie got home a little after 1:30, and we headed out.

Our first stop was at Windley Key State Park. It was the one closest to our house and also one of our favorites. The core of the park included a giant quarry of fossil coral rock that was used in construction

174

of the railroad between Miami and Key West, and for other more modern uses as well. We stopped at their little office at the entrance to the park and encountered a young man in uniform, whose name tag read "Jeremy." We recognized each other, because he'd taken an ornithology course from me a few years back. He knew a great deal about the birds in the park as well as its geological history. Jeremy was intrigued with Katie's pictures and what she told him about manchineel. He said he'd heard of the plant but had never seen it at Windley. He told us park personnel were very aware of their obligation to educate the public about dangerous plants and animals. However, there was little likely habitat for manchineel here because most of the area was relatively dry. Jeremy said he would keep looking for the tree and its fruits and would ask other park staff about it as well.

Our second destination was Long Key State Park, southwest of the small village of Layton, and only a few miles from our house. However, our next actual stop was to go home and pick up Prince. An extensive nature trail at Long Key was one of his favorite places, and it just didn't seem right to leave him at home, even though this was a business trip. Lots of other dogs enjoyed the trail as well, which meant Prince spent a lot of time sniffing and peeing whenever we walked there. For some perverse reason, Katie had kept track. So far, his record was fifteen pees in the first half mile.

We stopped at the kiosk where you paid to enter Long Key, and a young woman dressed in a park uniform came out to greet us. The nametag on her shirt said "Becky."

Becky spotted Prince in the back seat of my Jeep and asked if she could give him a treat.

I said sure.

While Prince was crunching on his dog biscuit, Katie introduced herself and explained the reason for our visit. "We believe somebody might have used manchineel fruits to poison a person, and we're attempting to find out where they could have come from."

Becky had been paying more attention to Prince than to us, but this stopped her. "So you think somebody came here to pick manchineel fruits?"

"Possibly," Katie said. "Do you know of any on the property?"

"There used to be a good number of manchineel bushes inside the park, but most of them were taken out early on by state and federal foresters. You know, because they're so dangerous. That was way before my time. Today there's only one, or at least only one that we know of. We have it fenced-off, with an interpretive sign explaining about the tree. It's part of our education program."

"Would it be alright if we had a look?" I asked.

The ranger hesitated. "Normally, that wouldn't be a problem. But it's in a part of the park that's currently closed to visitors because of road damage caused by Hurricane Irma."

"Would it be possible for us to go in there?" Katie asked. "This could be important to our criminal investigation. Our Jeep shouldn't have any trouble."

"I suppose that would be alright. Let me make a call to my supervisor. What did you say your name was again? And you're a scientist at the college?"

"That's right. My name is Dr. Kathryn Sawyer, and I'm a forensic botanist."

Becky kept repeating the words "forensic botanist" to herself as she went back inside the kiosk to make the call.

She was back in less than five minutes. "My supervisor says it's okay, as long as I go with you. But first, I'll have to get somebody to cover me here." She pointed to a parking area off to our right. "Why don't you wait over there? It shouldn't be long."

We followed Becky in her pickup down the main road leading through the center of the park, to the point where it curved right and followed the Atlantic coastline. A pair of white egrets were wading in the shallows, and out beyond them a half dozen black cormorants were diving in the surf. An assortment of sunbathing tourists almost certainly would have been using the beach if it had been winter. But this was summer, and except for the wildlife we had the place to ourselves.

In about two hundred yards the paved road stopped abruptly at a fence with a locked gate. A sign attached to the gate read "Park Closed Beyond This Point." Becky got out, unlocked the gate, and waved us through. From this point on the road was little more than a sandy track, but clearly passable. We drove on, not more than a quarter mile, when Becky pulled to a stop in a stand of red mangroves bordering the Atlantic. A head-high wire mesh fence surrounded a small clearing in the mangroves, and in the middle of the clearing was a single manchineel tree. It was the only one I'd seen besides the one at the botanic garden in Miami.

"Doesn't seem likely this is our tree, given how hard it was to get in here," Katie said.

"Maybe. Maybe not. We're actually not all that far from the highway, for somebody willing to go on foot."

"Good point," she replied. "Anyhow, let's go take a look."

We got out of the Jeep and joined Becky at the edge of the clearing.

"Well there it is," she said, unnecessarily. "I can unlock the gate if you need to get inside, but please, please, be careful. My supervisor would have my ass if something happened to you."

Becky blushed, and Katie and I both laughed.

"We would like to get inside, thanks," Katie said. "But be assured we know how dangerous this species can be."

The manchineel was about twenty feet tall, with branches that spread nearly to the edge of the enclosure. We ducked under the branches, being careful not to touch any of the foliage. Unfortunately, there were no fruits in the tree or on the ground beneath it. Katie took some photos and we backed out of the enclosure.

"Did you find any of those fruits?" Becky asked.

"No we didn't," Katie replied. "But that could be because somebody took them. Has anybody else been in here recently?"

Becky shook her head. "Not that I know of, and it's not likely because of the closure."

"What about other people who might have come to the park asking about manchineel?" I said.

"Actually, we've had quite a few ever since that television show," Becky replied.

"What television show was that?" Katie asked.

"It was on one of the local news channels in Miami. I didn't see it myself."

"When was that?" Katie asked.

"Must have been a couple of months ago, because that's when people started asking about it."

Katie walked over to the Jeep and came back with a file folder. She opened the folder and took out the photo I'd copied off the Internet of Lou Farrelli. "Was this one of the people who asked you about manchineel?"

Becky looked closely at the photograph. "I don't think so, but I couldn't say for sure. Like I said, we've had a number of folks wanting to know if we had any of those trees, and I wasn't paying all that much attention to what they looked like."

"Would you mind asking the other people who work here?" Katie asked. "You can keep that picture."

We thanked Becky for her time, and then explained that we were going to take Prince for a walk on the nature trail before we left. He'd been waiting next to the Jeep, not all that patiently, and clearly was both puzzled and miffed that whatever we'd been doing up until now hadn't included him.

The nature trail wound through dense hardwood forests, with occasional openings onto the Atlantic. It included boardwalks strategically placed to cross relatively wet places dominated by mangroves. Prince liked all of it except the boardwalks, because he knew he wasn't supposed to pee there.

We were about halfway around the roughly circular route when my cell phone rang. The caller ID said it was Stella. She didn't even wait for me to say hello.

"I've got some weird news. Lou Farrelli's dead. They found his body hanging from a boat dock up in Miami. Looks like he hanged himself."

"Good grief!"

My thoughts turned to Farrelli's granddaughter Rosalie, and to the worry she'd shared with me about his failing business. I'd seen in her a real passion for fly fishing. I hoped it survived this trauma and perhaps even helped her get through it.

"They're sure it was a suicide?"

"Apparently."

"Was this on the news or something?"

"Maybe," Stella said. "But that's not how I found out. I finally got through to the Sheriff to get his permission to track Farrelli down for an interview, and he told me about it. He wants to meet with me and the State's Attorney, and you're invited. You and Katie, that is."

"When?"

"Tomorrow morning, nine o'clock, at headquarters in Key West. Can you make it?"

"Absolutely."

"Good. I'll pick you up a little before seven-thirty."

Chapter 28

The Sheriff and the State's Attorney for Monroe County were a contrast in sizes and shapes. I'd never met either of them, but I'd seen photos in newspapers and on television. The contrast between the two gentlemen was even more striking when they were sitting next to each other, as they were when Stella, Katie, and I met them the next day in an interview room at the Sheriff's office down in Key West. Attorney Del Blains was middle-aged, big and jowly, with a gut suggesting he spent too much time at all-you-can-eat restaurants. Sheriff Michael Spivey was older, at least a foot shorter, and on the skinny side of being lean and fit. Both wore suits and ties. Blains' was rumpled and gray. Spivey's was brown and recently pressed.

Based on their half-empty coffee cups, it was apparent that Blains and Spivey had already been there awhile when we came into the room. We were right on time—nine o'clock sharp. That and the coffee cups suggested their early start had been planned.

Stella made the introductions and we all took seats around a big wooden table that dominated the windowless room. There were bottles of water and a coffee machine on a cart sitting against one wall, but we all declined the refreshments. The room was eerily quiet except for the sound of Blains shuffling some papers from his position at the head of the table. Finally, Blains cleared his throat and began.

"Thank you all for coming today. And let me start by thanking Dr. and Mrs. Sawyer in particular for the help they have provided Detective Reynard in her investigation of the recent unfortunate events at the Purple Isle Sportsman's Club."

I was waiting for Katie to point out that it actually was Dr. and Dr. Sawyer, because she'd done it in the past. But this time she shot me a "don't go there" look, and demurred.

180

Blains shuffled more papers. "When the death of Mr. Arthur Broom first came to our attention, including the evidence provided by Detective Reynard and the Medical Examiner, the Sheriff and I felt that his death most likely was accidental. He had too much to drink, fell into the pond, and suffered a fatal heart attack. But the discovery of a poisonous fruit in his stomach . . ." Blains paused again to look at his notes and then glance at Katie. "A fruit identified by Mrs. Sawyer as, . . . uh, manchineel. And then finding those same fruits outside a cabin owned by Mr. Louis Farrelli, suggest he actually may have been poisoned. For this reason we understood and were prepared to authorize Detective Reynard's request to interview Mr. Farrelli as a possible suspect in Mr. Broom's death. Unfortunately, as you all know, Mr. Farrelli has taken his own life, so that obviously won't be possible."

In my previous dealings with law enforcement in the Florida Keys, mostly with Stella Reynard, things had been businesslike enough, but also decidedly casual. This felt way different. The State's Attorney, at least, was being almost rigidly formal. It made me uncomfortable and suspicious. What were these guys up to?

Next it was the Sheriff's turn. "Detective Reynard, is it your opinion that Mr. Farrelli is, or was, a viable suspect in this case? And may I ask the same of you, Mr. and Mrs. Sawyer?"

So much for everybody getting more relaxed.

Katie and I both looked at Stella. It was her case to pursue.

"Thank you, Sheriff," she said. "Frankly, I'm of two minds on that question. His only known motive for killing Mr. Broom seemed weak from the beginning: to make room in the club for a new member who was in a position to do him a favor in return."

"That would be State Senator Snodgrass?" Blains asked.

"Correct. But after we found those fruits in his backyard, along with a realization that he may have been truly desperate to save his failing cruise line, it became more plausible that he could have been driven to do such a thing."

"But Mack—uh, Senator Snodgrass—denies there was any such relationship," Blains said.

From the look on her face, this clearly was news to Stella.

"Which doesn't rule out the possibility that Mr. Farrelli still had that in mind," Spivey added. "And doesn't the suicide add to your suspicions about the man, Detective Reynard?"

Stella shook her head. "No it doesn't, because there's a timing problem. I never had a chance to question Farrelli about the fruits we found outside his cabin. So, unless somebody tipped him off—and I don't know who that might have been—it couldn't have had anything to do with why he killed himself."

"Then let's leave Farrelli aside for the moment," Blains said. "Are there any other people at the club that you suspect might have killed Broom? For instance, what about his wife, or other family members? We understand Broom was very wealthy."

"Broom had no children. His wife Fiona was in Palm Beach at the time of his death, so she couldn't have done it. At least not by herself. Plus the motive appears weak at best. Broom had no life insurance. Fiona is the major beneficiary in his will, he was in bad health, and—as far as we can determine—he was extremely generous and their marriage was a strong one."

"What about other club members?" Blains asked.

"Arthur Broom was not particularly well-liked by certain other members, because of his passion for saving the Everglades and Florida Bay and his willingness to spend large amounts of capital toward that end."

"Anybody in particular?" Spivey asked.

"Yes," Stella replied. "Besides Lou Farrelli and his docking problems, we have Norberto Padilla and Royal O'Doul. Both men made no secret about their dislike of Broom because of the threat he posed to their economic activities: big sugar in Padilla's case, and golf resorts in O'Doul's."

Did Blains and Spivey tense-up at the mention of those names, or was it my imagination?

"Do you have any evidence either one of them might have done it?" Blains asked.

Stella shook her head. "At this point, not one shred."

Blains and Spivey exhaled simultaneously, and their shoulders seemed to relax.

Blains opened another folder. 'Then I think we should continue to look into Farrelli," he said. "To that end, we have obtained a warrant authorizing you to search his cabin at the Purple Isle club for any additional evidence." He handed Stella the warrant. "And we are arranging to seize his computer and phone from his residence in Miami. We'll keep you posted on that."

Blains started gathering up the various papers and folders in front of him, signaling that the meeting was over. "Thank you again for coming, and please let us know of any further developments in the case."

There were several odd things about the meeting just concluded, but one in particular hit me as we were heading back to Islamorada. Why had there been no mention of the other case on our plate: the murder of Mel Campbell? I asked Stella about it as we drove past Stock Island.

"Yeah, I noticed that too," she said. "And didn't you catch how relieved they were that we didn't have diddly on Padilla or O'Doul?"

So it wasn't just my imagination.

There was plenty of day left, so we decided to drive directly to the club and search Lou Farrelli's cabin. We didn't talk about it, but I'm sure we all had the same thought. If a couple of manchineel fruits turned up in his refrigerator, the case would suddenly get a whole lot stronger.

We stopped at the guardhouse, where Reuben Fletcher waved us through with his usual frown. We got the same treatment from Ralph Weatherbee when we went to his office and asked for the key to Farrelli's cabin.

"Why do you want to go in there?" he asked.

"Routine investigation," Stella replied.

"I suppose it has something to do with that poor man's, . . . uh . . . death," Weatherbee said. "We were all shocked at the news."

He got up from his chair and walked across the spacious room to a cabinet attached to one wall, and opened it up. Inside were several dozen keys on little hooks, each with a name taped above it. He took one out of the cabinet and handed it to Stella, who had followed along behind him.

"Thanks," she said. "We'll return it when we're done."

Weatherbee had a right to be curious as to what was going on, but Stella did nothing more to satisfy that curiosity.

"Don't you need to know which cabin is his?" he asked. "Perhaps I can show you?"

"That won't be necessary, but thank you. The Sawyers here know the way."

The inside of Lou Farrelli's cabin was more luxuriously appointed than the guides' quarters where I'd spent considerable time. The floor plan was much like Rashaan's cabin, but with more expensive looking furniture. There was a great room with separate living, dining, and kitchen areas, three bedrooms, two full baths, and a utility room. One of the bedrooms had been converted into an office, though it still had one single bed opposite the desk and chair. The desktop was empty except for an array of photographs. I recognized Farrelli's grandchildren in most of them, along with two adults I assumed were their parents. There was no computer. When we looked inside the refrigerator it was empty except for a variety of sodas.

"So much for the telltale manchineel,' Stella said. "No big surprise, I suppose. Why would he have left any lying around after feeding some to Art Broom?"

"Yeah," Katie said. "But then why would he have left any in his backyard either?"

"Good point," Stella said. "Anyway, let's check the rest of the place."

"What are we looking for?" I asked.

"Who knows? Maybe some paperwork related to that State Senator?"

And that is exactly what we found. In the top right hand drawer of his desk there was an application for membership in the Purple Isle Sportsman's Club. The space for the applicant's name was filled out as "Mack Snodgrass and family." This was followed by several paragraphs describing the initiation fee and subsequent dues structure, along with the various privileges and obligations. At the bottom of the four-page document there were spaces for the names of three nominating members. Farrelli had put his name on the first line. The other two were blank.

"Looks like this was a work in progress," Katie said.

Death of a Glades Man

Nearly three weeks had passed since the day I'd witnessed Farrelli suggesting Snodgrass as a potential club member to Johnny Krasuski. Farrelli must have had trouble drumming up more support.

Chapter 29

That night after dinner Katie and I went out on the deck to enjoy the air. It was eerily quiet: no night birds calling, no tarpon splashing in the canal, not even the sounds of wind in the mangroves. It was as if the whole world were holding its breath. A flash of lightening lit up the sky. But it was far out in the gulf. The clap of thunder was muffled by distance.

"You think Farrelli did it?" Katie asked.

"Wish I knew. It would solve one problem if he did."

"Yeah, but I still have my doubts."

We went back to listening.

The noise when it came was jarring and loud, and right at my elbow. It was my cell. I didn't recognize the number.

"Hello?"

"Hello Sam? This is Rashaan."

I hadn't talked to him since the day we interviewed his daughter about finding Mel Campbell's body. I hoped the family was doing okay.

"Hey Rashaan. How's it going?"

There was a moment's hesitation. "Good. But there's something we need to talk about, and I'd rather do it in person."

"Uh, sure. Where would you like to meet?"

"Actually, I was thinking we might go fishing together."

"Absolutely. But you know I'm no longer working at the club, don't you?"

"Yeah, I heard that. And I'm not hiring you as a guide. Let's just call this two friends going out to talk and see if we have any luck."

"Fair enough. Can you be at my dock by seven tomorrow morning? And just so I can be thinking about it, did you have anything specific in mind?"

"Actually, I do. I was wondering about tripletail. I've eaten them before—delicious by the way—but never fished for them. Can they be caught on a fly?"

"Yes. But I'll bring some live shrimp as well, just in case. You know where I live?"

"Yup. Found your address online, and last time I checked my GPS was working just fine."

"Great. See you in the morning."

Katie had been listening to my half of the conversation. When it ended she asked the obvious question. "I gather you and Rashaan are going fishing tomorrow?"

"We are. He wants to try for tripletail. And he says he wants to talk about something."

There was enough light coming from inside our house that I could see Katie's right eyebrow go up. "Any idea what?"

"Not specifically. But he knew Art Broom pretty well, and served on the board of his foundation. I asked him once to let me know if he heard anything that might be relevant to our case."

"Here's hoping."

~ ~ ~

Rashaan showed up the next morning at 6:45, dressed all in white and carrying a nine-weight Sage rod and a small suitcase. He said good morning to Katie, and bent down to scratch Prince behind the ears when he came running up.

I pointed at the suitcase. "What's that for?"

"Thought I might want to change clothes before heading back to Miami."

"You aren't staying at the club?"

"No. I quit, Sam. That place just isn't right for me and or my family. Especially now that Art Broom is gone." Rashaan paused and looked out toward the canal. "Anyway, you ready to go fishing?"

"Sure am. I've already got the skiff loaded with gear and liquids. You brought lunch, right?"

"I did," Rashaan said. "I learned the hard way that in the Florida Keys the client is expected to supply food for the trip rather than the guide, which is different from a lot of places. I've got ham sandwiches. Hope that's okay."

"Of course. I like ham. But even if I didn't, the least I would do is be quiet about it. Not all my clients have been aware of this tradition, and sometimes it's made for a long hungry day."

Ten minutes later we were headed down the canal for our trip across Florida Bay. Before we got out into open water, while he could still hear me over the sound of the outboard, I told him about my plans for the day.

"Tripletail are an unusual fish in lots of ways. For one thing, there are only two species in the genus worldwide, and only one genus in the family: the Lobotidae."

"Spoken like a true zoologist, Sam. But can we get on to the unusual parts that have to do with how we're gonna catch 'em?"

"Sure. Tripletail like to feed right near the surface. What works best around here is to check the floats attached to lobster traps. They'll be hunting small fish and crustaceans living in the vegetation and debris that's gotten hung up on the ropes."

"So it's sight fishing?" Rashaan asked.

"Right."

"Sounds like fun."

We rounded the corner at the end of the canal. Florida Bay with its scattered small keys lay before us. So far the day was clear and calm. "You ready for a boat ride?" I asked.

He said he was, so I opened up my Yamaha outboard and headed out. We crossed into the Rabbit Key Basin, then exited into open water through the Iron Pipe Channel and proceeded west beyond Sandy Key. Commercial fishing isn't allowed in Everglades National Park, so there weren't any lobster traps until we got beyond the park boundary. As soon as we came to the first line of colored floats, I slowed my skiff and began following the line. I'd rigged-up his Sage with a shrimp pattern, and had spinning gear ready with bait as a backup.

"What, exactly, are we looking for?" Rashaan asked, as he moved up into the bow. "I mean I know it's tripletail, but what do they look like?"

"They'll be right up under the trailing vegetation, and—here's the weird thing—they're usually on their sides."

"You mean like a flounder or a halibut?"

"No, not like that. They have body symmetry just like an ordinary fish. They're just swimming on their sides."

"Huh. What about color?"

"Usually they're pretty dark: gray or chocolate brown."

"Is there a size limit?"

"Yep. They have to be at least 18 inches, and you can only keep two a day."

"That sounds pretty strict."

"It is. Because they're so conspicuous compared to other fish, they get hit pretty hard. If this ends up like most days, we'll see plenty of tripletails, but not many over 18 inches."

We passed eight lobster floats before we had our first hit. A good-sized tripletail was working a red and white float. I cut the throttle and circled back around, pulling in even with the float but staying off about twenty feet.

"I didn't even see that," Rashaan said.

"Takes a while to get the search image," I replied. "By the end of the day you'll be an expert, assuming we get lucky. You want to throw a fly or try a live shrimp?"

"Let's go with the fly. Just tell me what to do."

"Try to drop it just beyond and a little up-current from the float. Then make a slow retrieve and let the tide carry the fly right in next to the float. You'll be able to see the fish make a move when it happens."

Rashaan missed on his first cast because the fly landed behind the float and the fish was looking in the wrong direction. But it hadn't spooked. It just kept finning in place, about two feet under the water, which gave him a second chance. This time the cast was just right. As the fly drifted into the fish's line of vision, it rose up and ate it.

Rashaan fought the fish well, and we soon had it in the net. I laid it against the ruler taped to my transom: sixteen inches. Not a keeper, but still a good fish. We both admired the catch, took some photos, and released it.

"That was great!" Rashaan said. "I really don't care if we get one 18 inches. That fish was plenty strong enough for a fly rod."

We motored on, following several lines of floats, until eventually we approached the park boundary near Cape Sable. Rashaan had shots at six more tripletails, landing two on a fly and one on a shrimp. The last one topped 19 inches, and we opted to keep it.

"Since you brought a change of clothes, what say you spend the night at our place, and we'll have tripletail for dinner? I know Katie'd be thrilled."

"You know that sounds pretty good. Julie has taken the kids off to summer camp, and she won't be coming back for a couple of days." Rashaan grinned and pointed to my live well. "And that fish is way too big for just one person, don't you think?" Then he looked at his watch. "But speaking of food, let's find some shade and eat. I'm hungry."

I drove the boat up into the East Cape Canal and found a spot under a mangrove canopy. The bugs weren't that bad, and it was good to get out of the sun.

I was hoping this would be the time when Rashaan got around to whatever it was he wanted to tell me.

Rashaan drank some water, took a bite out of his sandwich, and got down to business. "Last time we talked, or maybe it was the next to last time, you asked if I would keep my eyes and ears open for anything related to Art Broom. To start with, let me be clear I have no idea who actually might have killed him. But I've been looking into his Everglades Rescue Foundation, of which I am a member, and something interesting turned up."

Rashaan paused for another bite of sandwich, and I couldn't help myself.

"And?"

"At a recent meeting, John Belknap—he's the board treasurer— told us that Art was planning to dramatically increase his funding for the foundation. That he intended to make sizable regular contributions, as suited his tax situation."

"More than he already was making?"

"Way more, apparently. To the point where nearly all his fortune would be doled out before he died."

"Leaving the widow Fiona out in the cold?"

"Not by our standards I suppose, but close enough. She'd still be getting millions, but not the billion plus she might have been expecting."

"Wow. Talk about a motive for murder."

"Yeah. But wasn't she somewhere else the night he died?" Rashaan asked. "That sounds like a pretty good alibi."

"She was, and it is. But that leaves another possibility."

"That she had an accomplice?"

"Yep."

"Any idea who that might be?"

I remembered the first night I met Fiona Broom. It was in the club bar, and George Light the bartender had been real attentive, including walking her home. It was tempting to mention this to Rashaan, but I thought better of it. We were friends, and I trusted him, but pointing the finger at somebody without any real proof didn't seem prudent.

"No," I said.

"Well I might just have one. Or maybe two."

"You'd better explain that."

"I intend to. And that's the main reason I asked to go out with you today." Rashaan grinned. "That and the tripletail, of course." Then he got serious. "This is way out of school, and I need your word you'll pretend you learned this from somebody else. But another thing Belknap told us was that before Broom died several people were poking around trying to find out what his long-term plans were about funding the foundation."

"Did he say who they were?" I asked.

"Uh huh. One was Fiona Broom. The other two were Norberto Padilla and Royal O'Doul."

Right at that moment a huge tarpon did a noisy belly flop a hundred yards up the canal. Normally I would have gotten all excited. This time I barely even heard it.

Chapter 30

It was all I could do not to call Stella right then and there, and tell her what Rashaan had learned. But I'd given him my word, and even if I left his name out of our conversation, it just didn't feel appropriate with him sitting right there in my skiff. So I put it on hold, and we went back to fishing.

Over the next two hours we found three more fish and Rashaan caught two of them on a fly. After landing the second one—a nice fifteen incher with unusually dark coloration—he pronounced himself a tripletail veteran and suggested we head home.

We'd just passed the Peterson Keys when my cell phone pinged. I pulled it out of my pocket and looked at the message. It was from Stella. "Call me as soon as you get this," it said. "Things are happening."

I decided to wait until we got back, when I could hand Rashaan off to Katie if she was home. Then I would take Prince for a walk and make the call somewhere down the road. That way we could discuss not only the items on her plate but on mine as well.

It worked out well. Katie had taught a late afternoon lab, and while she was home she hadn't yet had time to walk Prince. I leashed him up and we headed down the road together. I called Stella, and she answered on the second ring. It sounded like there was road noise in the background, and maybe some radio chatter.

"Got your message," I said. "What's up?"

"Your plan was a good one, Sam. We got DNA off those beer glasses from the Safari Lounge, and there's a match to the blood on Mel Campbell's shirt."

"I had a hunch about that guy Reuben Fletcher. I reckon Mel caught him poaching and they got into it, huh?"

"Nope. Wrong hunch. The match is with Chet Avery, the guy with the fish market on Conch Key. We're on our way right now to pick him up on suspicion of homicide."

And I thought mine was going to be the big news of the day.

"You're sure it was Chet and not Reuben?"

"Dead certain, Sam. Unless you got those beer glasses mixed up."

"We didn't. We were real careful about that."

"I'm sure you were."

"But what about Reuben?" I asked. "Maybe he was there too."

"As soon as we're done here, I'm gonna track him down," Stella replied.

"Got time for another juicy item?"

"Yeah, but make it quick. We're almost there."

I told Stella what I'd learned about Art Broom and the Everglades Rescue Foundation, but I left Rashaan's name out of it.

"That's great work, Sam. How did you figure it out?"

"I didn't. It was somebody else."

The phone went silent, doubtless because Stella was waiting for me to reveal my source.

"Aren't you gonna tell me who?" she finally asked.

"There's a confidence involved, Stella. I need to think about it."

"But you're sure about all this?"

"Yes."

"Then we should interview Fiona Broom asap, along with Padilla and O'Doul."

"I'd like to be in on those interviews. Maybe I could—"

"Sorry, Sam. Gotta go. We're just pulling up to the fish market. Talk to you soon."

~ ~ ~

I later learned from Stella that the arrest of Chet Avery had gone off without incident. They booked him into the detention center in Marathon that night. Stella attempted a quick interview, but he clammed up except to demand a lawyer. Apparently the guy was basically broke, because it ended up being a public defender, and he couldn't make the arraignment until late the following afternoon.

The Assistant State's Attorney assigned to the case was Walter Stone. I'd met him before, and liked him. Compared to his boss, Del Blains, Walt was an absolute charmer.

Stone and Stella arranged a formal interview of Chet Avery for the next day, in the company of his lawyer. Stella invited me to witness the interview.

I wouldn't have missed it.

~ ~ ~

They stashed me in a booth next to the room at the Marathon Detention Center where suspects are interviewed. It was wired for sound and had one-way glass. Stella and Walt Stone were seated on the prosecution side of the little wooden table in the middle of the room, but the defendant and his attorney hadn't yet shown up. In a little while Sheriff Spivey came into the booth and took a chair next to mine.

"Morning," he said. "You're Mr. Sawyer, right? Good to see you again."

We shook.

"Looks like we've got the goods on the fella' killed that employee at the Purple Isle club."

"Looks like it."

"From what Detective Reynard tells me, you were the one who got hold of some DNA that's gonna make this case. I thank you for that."

"No problem. But actually there were three of us involved, including my wife Katie and an old friend who tends bar at the Safari Lounge. It was his beer glasses that caught the evidence, so to speak."

Spivey laughed, and I started to like him better. Maybe.

Just then Chet Avery came shuffling into the interview room, along with a prison guard and a mousy middle-aged man in a brown suit that I assumed was Chet's attorney. Avery wore an orange jumpsuit and he was cuffed at the wrists and ankles. Presumably this was protocol for a murder suspect.

The guard sat Avery down in one of the chairs opposite Stella and Walt Stone. Stella asked the guard to remove his cuffs, which she did before leaving the room. Stella then looked up at the one-way glass and lifted a finger, which was my signal to start the recorder in the booth.

Walt Stone began by stating the time and date and the identities of the four people in the room. I learned the public defender's name was Alden Jones. Stone opened a file folder in front of him, and started reading from it.

"Mr. Avery, you are charged with the murder of Mr. Mel Campbell, the fisheries manager at the Purple Isle Sportsman's Club. Yesterday at the arraignment you entered a plea of not guilty to this charge. Is that still your position?"

Avery's response was immediate, without even a glance at his attorney. "It is. I had nothing to do with that. I don't even know why I'm here."

"Then how do you explain the fact that blood on the victim's body contained DNA identical to yours?" Stone said.

Chet Avery hesitated and squirmed in his chair. "I can't. There must be some mistake. Maybe it was Reuben's. Yeah, that's it. It must have been Reuben's and you've got things mixed up. You analyzed the wrong beer glass."

Stella's eyebrows shot up. Whether he realized it or not, Chet Avery had just revealed two things. First, he knew where and how we'd gotten his DNA. And second, he was more than willing to throw Reuben Fletcher under the bus to save his own skin.

"We're virtually certain about the DNA, Mr. Avery," Stone said.

"And besides," Stella added. "You remember we swabbed the inside of your mouth when we booked you into jail? Even if a jury could be persuaded we mixed things up before, we'll pull your DNA off that swab, and it's gonna match the blood on Campbell's body."

"Are you sure you don't want to change your story, Chet?" Stone asked.

Public Defender Jones leaned over and whispered something in Avery's ear. Avery nodded once.

"I need a word with my client," Jones said. Then he glanced up at the one-way glass. "In private."

Stone nodded and pushed back in his chair. "Of course," he said. "You have my word we'll turn off the sound."

While Avery and his attorney huddled together, Stone and Stella came up and joined the Sheriff and me in the booth.

"What do you think?" the Sheriff asked.

"I think he's gonna cave," Stella replied. "He knows we've got him."

"But what about Reuben Fletcher?" I asked. "Did you get a chance to talk to him after Avery's arrest?"

"I did. He was on duty at the guardhouse when I drove up there yesterday. He claimed to know nothing about it, which wasn't surprising."

"But you have no evidence proving otherwise."

"That's right. But we know they're drinking buddies, so I have my suspicions."

"Let's get back to Avery," Stone said. "It looks like he and Jones may be finishing up their little chat. I'm guessing he's gonna change his story and say it was an accident. Since there were no witnesses, except possibly Fletcher, we need a plan if that's what happens."

"You mean like a plea?" Stella asked. "I wouldn't be in favor of that unless he gives us something super valuable in return."

"Like what?" the Sheriff asked.

"Like fingering Fletcher as an accomplice?" Stone said. "I'm not sure that would be enough."

I'd been waiting for this opportunity. "There is one other thing we could ask him about," I said.

"What's that?" Stone asked.

"We know that Chet Avery sold live lionfish to somebody at the club, and those fish likely played a role in the death of Arthur Broom. I'd sure like to know who that person was. Both Stella and I asked Avery about it, but he claims he doesn't remember."

"Isn't that a little off the subject?" the Sheriff asked.

I recalled the wariness and unease both the Sheriff and State's Attorney Blain had exhibited when we'd discussed possible suspects in Broom's death two days ago. The Sheriff had exhibited no such behavior yet today. But had I just seen it come back?

Alden Jones walked up to the one-way glass waving his hand before I had a chance to be sure. It was time to get back to the interview.

Jones began by reading something off a yellow legal pad. "After further reflection, my client is prepared to admit that he caused the death of Mr. Campbell, but that it was not his intention. Instead, he and Mr. Campbell became involved in a physical altercation and at one point

Mr. Campbell fell backwards, hitting his head on a block of coral next to one of the fishing ponds. Mr. Avery panicked and fled the scene, without knowing whether Mr. Campbell was dead or alive."

"Then how does Mr. Avery explain the fact that we found Campbell's body some distance away from where he was killed?" Stella asked.

Jones and Avery exchanged looks. "Uh, that's right," Jones said. "Mr. Avery's first instinct was to hide the victim. He panicked afterwards."

Stella raised a skeptical eyebrow. "And what, exactly, were they supposedly fighting about?"

"Mr. Avery had—ah—an arrangement where he would collect fish from some of the ponds to sell in his market. Mr. Campbell was unaware of that arrangement, and accosted my client when he discovered him doing that."

"So Mr. Avery admits to poaching," Stone said. "And this so-called 'arrangement.' Who was that with?"

"Reuben helped me out with that," Avery blurted out. "We were buddies. It all seemed okay. After all, those rich bastards at the Purple Isle, they could afford to get more fish for their precious ponds, right?"

Stone shook his head. "That's beside the point, Mr. Avery. But tell me. Did you pay Mr. Fletcher for helping you with this scheme? And just what was his role, anyway? Did he help you with the poaching?"

"No. He only let me through the gate. And he knew how to switch off the security cameras. I paid him a couple hundred each time."

"I see. And for the record, was he there the night you killed Campbell?"

There was just a moment's hesitation. "No. And I didn't tell him about it afterwards, either."

"But he must have suspected."

"Maybe," Avery replied. "You'd have to ask him about that."

"Oh we intend to," Stella said. "But now I have another question. On two occasions, once by me and once by Dr. Sam Sawyer, you were asked to identify the person who bought live lionfish from your market. Both times you denied knowing who that person was. I'm wondering if now you might be willing to tell us his name?"

"And why would I want to do that?" Avery asked. "Even if I could, that is."

Stella looked at Walter Stone, because it was his decision and not hers.

"If you can help us out here, it's possible that might influence our decision about what punishment we recommend to the judge for your killing Mr. Campbell."

Once again, Alden Jones leaned over and whispered in Chet Avery's ear. This time it went on longer than before. Finally, Avery sat back up and looked at Stone.

"It was George Light, the bartender at the Purple Isle club. He never identified himself, but I recognized him from one time when I went into the building looking for Reuben."

"In light of this valuable new information provided by Mr. Avery, what sort of a deal are you proposing for my client?" Jones asked. "It had better be substantial, or we're more than ready to take this to trial. After all, Mr. Campbell's death clearly was accidental."

"Give us a minute on that," Stone replied. Then he pointed to the door and motioned for Stella to follow him outside. Shortly after that they joined the Sheriff and me in the observation booth.

"I'm thinking he pleads to voluntary manslaughter, with a recommendation to the judge of nine years minimum," Stone said. "What do you all think of that?"

Stella wasn't completely happy, and neither was I, but in the end we agreed. We had no way to disprove Avery's story that the death was accidental.

Back in the interview room, Avery and Jones groused and grumbled when they heard our offer. But in the end, they too agreed to the plea.

Sheriff Spivey, Walter Stone, Stella, and I met after the interview in a conference room at the detention center. The Avery case almost certainly was settled, but that left the matter of George Light. It seemed likely—almost certain in my opinion—that he was involved with the death of Arthur Broom. Stella agreed, and argued that we should arrest him right away and bring him in for questioning.

But the Sheriff demurred. "Maybe he was just buying those fish to serve in their restaurant or something. You're gonna need more than this to justify an arrest."

Chapter 31

Stella and I got back in her cruiser for the ride up to Islamorada. We'd gotten beyond Duck Key, and she wasn't saying anything. She just stared straight ahead and drove, occasionally drumming her fingers on the steering wheel.

"Why so glum?" I asked. "You just cracked the Campbell case and got a big clue on the Broom killing."

"I'm used to being stonewalled by suspects. I'm not used to getting it from my own boss."

"You really wanted to arrest George Light, didn't you?"

"Damn straight. I want to bust his ass and get him in the same chair that Chet Avery was in when he spilled his guts. But the Sheriff nixed it. Why was that?"

"Sheriffs are elected officials, Stella. They're political animals."

"You think I don't know that? It's just disappointing is all."

We came to a passing lane, where Stella sped up and passed a big dump truck filled with concrete slabs that was lumbering along at about 25 miles an hour. She shook her head. "No, I'm not disappointed. I'm pissed as hell. Somebody with clout wants the Broom case to go away." She slammed her hand down on the steering wheel. "Well, it's not gonna happen!"

"You don't think Lou Farrelli killed Arthur Broom?" I asked.

"No, I don't. And neither do you."

"Then who was it?" I asked.

"The mysterious person with clout? It sure as hell wasn't George Light."

I could see where Stella was going with this, because I'd come to the same conclusion. "Light was in on it with Mr. or Ms. Clout, and there are three obvious possibilities."

"Uh huh. Fiona Broom, Norberto Padilla, and Royal O'Doul. The question is, why would Light help any of them commit a murder?"

"Maybe we'll find out when we interview them. My money's on the grieving widow."

"Because she stood to lose the most if her husband gave away all his riches before he died?"

"Yeah that, plus one other thing. I don't know if I ever told you, Stella, but the night I met Fiona in the bar, I got the clear sense she and George were involved."

"You mean *that* kind of involved?"

"Uh huh."

We'd passed Layton and were getting close to my neighborhood. It was nearly six o'clock. "You need to get home, Sam?" Stella asked.

"Probably should stop off and walk the dog. Katie has a seminar today that usually runs late. But afterwards, I'm available. Why?"

"The Sheriff said I couldn't arrest George Light, but he didn't say I needed to stay away from him."

"Which you wouldn't have done even if he had, right?"

Stella just grinned.

Prince was thrilled when Stella and I both took him for a walk. But he got all morose and wouldn't make eye contact when he figured out we were leaving again.

We found George Light behind the bar, wiping things down with a white towel. The place was empty, but there was loud chatter coming from the restaurant, so that must have been where everybody had gone. In other words, our timing was perfect.

Light looked up as we walked in, bar towel suspended in space. "Detective? Mr. Sawyer? How can I help you?"

"Is there someplace we could talk?" Stella asked.

"Is it important? I'm supposed to say open for a couple more hours."

"We can wait. But why don't I shut the door, and we can talk right here, right now? If anybody knocks, you can let them in. This shouldn't take too long."

"Okay, I guess. What's this about anyway?"

Stella closed the door behind her and we took stools at the bar. "We'd like to ask you about lionfish," she said.

It was hard to read the expression on George Light's face. A mixture of fear and surprise, perhaps?

"What about 'em?" he asked.

"We understand you recently purchased a number of those fish from a market down on Conch Key. Why was that?"

Light didn't miss a beat. "I bought them for our restaurant. Jacques Petain—he's our cook—likes to serve 'em from time to time. He usually has me go down there and get 'em."

"But our source says you bought them live. Why would you do that? What would Mr. Petain do with live lionfish before he was ready to cook them?"

"You'd have to ask him."

"We have," I said. "He confirms your story, that somebody—he wasn't sure who—brings him lionfish to put on the menu. But he didn't say they were alive."

"Well they were, I can assure you."

"You know we can ask Mr. Petain about this, George," I said. "You think he'll confirm your story?"

The bartender shrugged, and pretended to go back to wiping off the bar.

"Let me suggest something else," Stella said. "We think you bought live lionfish deliberately to put in one of the fishing ponds. Then you pushed Arthur Broom into that pond and the lionfish stung him to death. Do you deny that?"

I expected this would elicit a one-word denial, but George Light had something else in mind.

" I knew the minute you started talking about lionfish where you were headed with this! And I uh, . . . okay, I did buy some live lionfish that weren't for the cook. But they weren't for what you think. We had a guest in here the other day who said he wanted some for his aquarium. Said he'd pay me $50 apiece. I knew that man on Conch Key could get lionfish, so I asked him to keep some alive for me. And that's the truth."

It struck me as ironic that I'd used the same bullshit line about wanting lionfish for a friend's aquarium when I'd first confronted Chet Avery in his fish market.

"We're gonna need the name of that guest," Stella said.

"He never said."

"Is he still here at the club?"

"I don't think so."

"Whose guest was he?"

"I can't remember."

"You know Mr. Light," Stella said, "you could be in a lot less trouble if you told us the truth about this lionfish business. You had no reason to kill Arthur Broom. Wasn't it in fact Mrs. Broom who put you up to it?"

For the first time since we'd walked into his bar, George "Bud" Light looked genuinely puzzled.

"What does Fiona have to do with any of this?" he asked.

Chapter 32

"What do you think?" I asked.

"I think the guy's completely full of it," Stella replied. "Does he think we're stupid or something?"

Stella was giving me a ride home. We'd just made the turnoff from the Overseas Highway onto my street. "There was only one time in our whole conversation when I thought he was being real."

"When we asked him if his partner in the crime was Fiona Broom? He looked puzzled, didn't he?"

"Exactly. Makes me wonder if she really is the one we're looking for."

"Maybe we'll get somewhere when we interview her."

We pulled up in front of my house. Katie's Prius was in the driveway and the living room lights were on. Stella kept the motor running, but she put her hand on my shoulder when I started to get out.

"I've been thinking about those interviews we talked about having with Fiona and Padilla and O'Doul."

"What about them?" I asked.

"I'm thinking they'll be a complete waste of time. We ask Fiona *'Did you conspire with George Light to kill your husband?'* She says "No, of course not. What a silly question,' or something like that. End of discussion. And it would go just like that for the other two until we have some actual evidence to bring into the conversation."

"What do you think we should we be doing instead?" I asked.

"We keep after Light until he breaks. He's our only solid lead in this case."

"Then what are our next steps, Stella?"

She hesitated. "I'll get back to you on that. Good night, Sam. And thanks for your help today."

Neither of us knew it, but our next big break in the case was only minutes away.

~ ~ ~

Katie and I had eaten and given Prince his pre-bedtime walk, when I got a call on my cell phone. The number had an unfamiliar 530 area code.

"Probably another spam," I said to Katie. "Somebody wanting to sell me an extended maintenance contract on the Jeep. They must not know how old it is. But I guess I should find out."

I pushed a key, accepting the call.

"Hello Sam? This is Mo Murikami."

"Oh hi, Mo. What's up?"

"I found something out here at the club you'll want to see. I was moving some boats around just before dark, when I spotted what I think is one of those trees you've been looking for."

"A manchineel?"

Katie's head came up from the magazine she'd been reading.

"It's hard to see from the water. But yeah, I think so."

"And it's on club property?"

"Uh huh."

"Will you be around tomorrow?"

"Sure."

"Good. Katie and I will meet you at the cabin about seven, okay?"

"Okay."

~ ~ ~

Max Welty, their head of security, was at the Purple Isle guardhouse when Katie and I arrived the next morning. There was no sign of Reuben Fletcher, which didn't surprise me. Welty waved us on through. We proceeded to the main lodge and walked over to Mo's cabin. He came outside as we approached, carrying a big yellow mug.

"Got time for a coffee?" he said, lifting up the mug.

"No, we're good, thanks," Katie replied.

"Alright, then. You want to try this on land, or in my boat?"

"By land if possible," Katie said, "because we'll want to look for sign somebody's already been there. You think you can find your way in?"

"Pretty sure, but it could be buggy. You got DEET?"

"Always," I said, patting my shirt pocket.

"Then let's go. Let me dump the rest of this coffee and grab my hat."

The route we took to the manchineel wasn't that far and it wasn't that hard. I wondered how we'd missed it the first time. There was even a hint of a trail winding through the mangroves leading to the spot.

It wasn't a very big tree—less than fifteen feet tall—but Katie got all excited as soon as we got close. "Look!" she said, pointing up into the branches. "It's got fruits!"

The more we looked, the better things got. There were fruits on the ground as well as in the tree.

"I need to check something," Katie said. "But you guys stay back. Even touching this thing can be dangerous." She put on a pair of gloves she'd stuck in her hip pocket before leaving the house. Then she moved right in next to the trunk, reached up and pulled down one of the branches, and inspected it with a small magnifying lens that hung on a chain around her neck. I'd learned a long time ago that these hand lenses, as they are called, are an essential piece of equipment for a field botanist, just as binoculars are for ornithologists.

After a couple of minutes, Katie let go of the branch and backed away from the tree. "Not only do we have fruits, gentlemen, but I can see where somebody has pulled some off the tree. This is great news!"

While Katie had been inspecting the manchineel, I'd been using those binoculars bird people always carry to scan the area, including back in the direction from which we'd come.

"There may be even better news," I said.

"What's that?" Katie said, perhaps just a bit miffed at my attempted coup.

"Unless I'm mistaken, Mo, isn't that a security camera back there?"

Mo looked where I was pointing. "I think you're right, Sam. It's the one we have on a light pole next to the last fishpond."

"Do they rotate?" I asked.

"I think so," he said.

"Do they have night vision capability?" I asked.

"I don't know, but it seems likely. You'd have to ask security."

"That's just what I intend to do. Plus, I wonder how long they keep the footage."

Katie collected some of the fruits, took multiple photos of the tree, and then we made our way back to Mo's cabin.

"Are you going to talk to security now?" she asked me.

"No. I think it's time to call in the cavalry. We don't have the authority to make somebody do something they don't want to do. But a friend of ours does."

"You mean Stella?"

I pulled out my cell and punched in her number. "Yep."

Stella was down in Marathon doing some wrapping up on the Campbell murder when she got my call. It took her close to two hours to get to the Purple Isle club, during which time Katie and I had nothing to do but sit on a bench in the shade outside Mo's cabin.

Katie began sorting through the fruits she'd collected off the manchineel. "If it turns out to be important, we can compare the DNA between these and the ones we collected outside Mr. Farrelli's cabin to see if they came from the same tree."

"Not that it would prove Farrelli was our guy," I said.

"No, but it sure would suggest the killer—whoever he or she was—lived here at the club. Are you thinking it probably wasn't Farrelli?"

"No solid proof either way, Katie, but neither Stella nor I have him as our number one suspect. His motive just seems too far-fetched."

At this point Mo came back from the direction of the dock and plunked down on the bench beside us.

"How are you liking your new job?" I asked.

"It's okay I guess."

"Just okay?"

"That Ralph Weatherbee is kind of a prick. He's always on my case about something. Yesterday it was about the fishing boats. Somebody complained that I wasn't keeping them tidy enough."

"Wouldn't that be the guides' responsibility?"

"It should be, I suppose, but all we've got is Johnny Krasuski's grandson, which means I'm having to do some guiding in addition to everything else. Fortunately it's the middle of summer and we're not all that busy. Otherwise, there's no way I could handle it." Mo stopped and stared off toward the fishing ponds. "Say, you wouldn't be interested in working here again, would you? I sure could use the help."

"No, I don't think so. And even if I were interested, I doubt Weatherbee would approve it. I'm definitely not his favorite guy at the moment."

"Why's that?"

"Mostly because he sees me as giving the cook a hard time. He and Jacques Petain—or whatever his name is—they're pretty tight."

"Is the cook one of your suspects in what happened to Mr. Broom?"

"Who knows, Mo. We don't have any hard evidence."

"Maybe you're about to get some, depending on what you find on those security tapes."

"Yeah, maybe."

As if on cue, right then Stella Reynard came walking up. She knew what had happened from my call, and she'd already gotten down to business. "Hi guys. I had a word with Max Welty at the guardhouse. He'll be meeting us in the security room in twenty minutes. If that gives us enough time, I sure would like to have a look at that tree. And Mo, thanks for your help on this. It could be the break we've been waiting for."

Mo scuffed a toe on the ground, and almost blushed. "I grew up on a farm, ma'am. Looking for plants is in my background."

"It's buggy and kinda wet, Stella," Katie said. "I could show you the pictures I took instead."

Stella, who was in full uniform, looked down at herself and grinned. "You know, I'm not all that into buggy and wet. Maybe the pictures will do. But what about the security camera? Can I have a look at that?"

We took Stella down to the end of the bank of fishing ponds and showed her the camera. She spent some time walking around underneath it. "And where from here is the tree?" she asked.

I pointed in the direction. "You can't actually see the tree from here, but we could see the camera when we were next to it, probably because it's high up on that pole."

"I know this brand," she said. "It's a good one, and we may be in luck. They rotate and they include night vision. Let's just hope they keep the footage long enough."

"Yeah, and that our perp didn't turn the thing off when he went down there to get the fruits," I said.

"Or she," Katie added.

By the time we got back to the lodge, Max Welty was waiting for us in the room where they kept the security monitors and recording equipment. Stella introduced him to Katie, and explained what we were after.

"So it's that camera down at the end of the fishing ponds?" he asked.

"That's right," Stella said. "From what I could see, it scans a wide area and has night vision, is that right?"

"That's right."

"How long do you keep footage?" she asked.

"Sixty days," Welty replied. "What particular time period are you interested in?"

"We can't be certain about that, Mr. Welty. But it had to have been before we found Arthur Broom's body in one of the fishing ponds." Stella pulled out her cell phone and looked at a calendar app. "Which was twenty-five days ago, right Sam?"

I was less tech-savvy than Stella, and had no such app. "That sounds about right."

"Any particular time of day?" Welty asked.

"No. It more likely would have been at night, but we can't be sure of that."

"Alrighty then," Welty said. "This could take some time." He turned to the computer console on the desk in front of him, and began tapping keys. "The camera you're interested in is number seventeen. I've selected that, and scrolled back twenty-five days. Now we just start watching. You want to do this? I really should get back to the guardhouse. There's nobody else around today."

"That's fine," Stella said. "But you're gonna have to give me a lesson."

"You bet."

Stella proved to be a quick study, and in no time she was scrolling through the recordings on her own. Welty left and she continued, with Katie and I watching over her shoulder. The setup had a fast-forward option, so she could move quickly through portions of the recordings where nothing happened. There was considerable activity, however, mostly at and near the ponds. Mel Campbell came nearly every day to feed the fish. Assorted club members fished, mostly with their kids and often accompanied by Mo. But for the first twenty days we checked, there was no activity out in the direction of the manchineel tree.

I was beginning to get discouraged, when something showed up on the night of the fifth day before Broom died. The recording was grainy, but the image showed somebody coming on screen from the left, walking toward the shore of the island. The person's back was to us, and he quickly disappeared into the trees. No identification was possible, except we all agreed that it looked like a man. I realized then it was unlikely we would get an image of the man at the tree itself because he was obscured by surrounding vegetation. But then, perhaps five minutes later in real time, he came walking back out, carrying something in his left hand that looked like a bucket. Once he cleared the trees and walked into the relatively open area leading toward the members' cabins, we got a good image. The bur haircut, the goatee, and the powerful build left no doubt. It was George Light.

Stella and I both recognized him at once. "Hot damn!" she said. "We got him!" She pushed back in her chair and swiveled to look out the door and across the lobby toward the bar.

"You gonna call the Sheriff now?" I asked. "This time I don't see how he could refuse your request to arrest the guy."

"You know what" she said. "I'm not giving him the chance." Then she stood up and headed for the bar. I followed along, as did Katie.

The double doors to the bar were open, and I could see a handful of patrons sitting on stools as we approached. One of them was Norberto Padilla. Another was Jacques Petain. But the man behind the bar wasn't George Light. Instead it was Ralph Weatherbee.

Weatherbee had been chatting with Padilla. He looked up when he saw us coming.

"Is George Light around?" Stella asked.

Weatherbee shook his head. "No. He didn't show up today."

"Do you have any idea where he might be?"

"I know where he *should* be," Weatherbee replied. "And that's right here doing his job."

"So this isn't his day off or anything?"

"It certainly is not."

"Did you try his cell?"

"Of course I did. But he didn't answer. I left a message telling him to get the hell in here."

"Could I trouble you for his address and his phone number?" Stella asked.

Weatherbee sighed conspicuously. "They're over in my office. Is this really important? I'm kinda busy here covering George's ass."

"I wouldn't be asking you if it weren't important, Mr. Weatherbee."

"You mind telling me what this is about?" he replied.

"Routine sheriff's business. Now please go get me that information on Mr. Light. Oh, and while you're at it, tell Mr. Welty we're going to need a copy of your security footage from camera seventeen."

Chapter 33

George Light lived in mobile home at an RV resort on the south end of Marathon, bay side. Because the place catered mostly to snowbirds from places like Ohio and Quebec, it was nearly empty in the middle of summer. Stella had called ahead for backup, just in case, and Deputy Oscar Wilson already was there talking to the manager when we arrived. Stella must have liked Wilson, and maybe it was mutual, because he always seemed to be the one coming around when she needed help.

Wilson came huffing over when he saw us pull in, bald dome beaded with sweat on a hot cloudless afternoon. He pointed toward the back of the resort. "It's that green and white job under the coconut palm."

Wilson got in his cruiser and followed us to the spot.

Light's living quarters looked modest at best, at least from the outside. Paint was peeling off the sides and the roof, one of the window screens was torn, and the two wooden steps leading up to his front door were warped and saggy.

Stella got out, walked over to the door, and knocked. When no one came, she called his name and knocked again. Three lots down from us a dog came out from behind a big Winnebago RV and started barking and growling. It looked like it might have come after us if it hadn't been chained-up. Perhaps because she'd heard the dog, a middle-aged woman in a yellow sleeveless t-shirt came to the door of the Winnebago and looked out in our direction, shielding her eyes against the sun.

"You looking for George?" she asked.

"Yes, ma'am," Stella said.

"Well he isn't here," the woman replied.

"When did you last see him?"

"Uh, I think it was yesterday morning. What is it you need?"

"Sheriff's business ma'am. Just routine. Do you have any idea where he might be?"

"Not really. I know he works at some fancy resort up in Islamorada. Maybe he's there."

"You guys wait here," Stella said to Wilson and me. "I'm gonna go talk to that woman. Seems like they might be more than just neighbors. Oh, and Oscar, did you find out what kind of a vehicle Light drives like I asked you?"

"Yep. He drives a 2003 Toyota Corolla, silver, with Florida plates. I have the ID if you need it."

"Later," Stella said as she started walking away.

"Did you get a search warrant?" Wilson asked.

"Not yet. But I'm thinking we suspect foul play here, don't you?"

"Which means we're going in anyway, right?"

"Soon as I get back, Oscar. Just sit tight and keep an eye out for that Toyota."

Stella came back in less than five minutes. "Mrs. Sattley lives there with her husband, who works at a local marina. They don't know Light very well, pretty much just to say hello. She did tell me something interesting though. Apparently somebody came by here late last night. The dog barked and woke her up. She looked out the window and saw what she thinks was a SUV parked out in front, probably black. Two men came out of the home and drove off while she was watching."

"Any ID on the two men?" I asked.

Stella shook her head. "I guess it was too dark. Oscar, have you tried the door?"

"Yeah. It's locked," Wilson replied. "But it shouldn't be much trouble to—"

"Then have at it," she said.

The inside of George Light's trailer was stuffy and hot: just one room with a bath walled-off at the opposite end from the door. There was an old-fashioned swamp cooler built into one of the windows, but it wasn't running.

It was obvious we were alone. Thinking that Light might have fled after we quizzed him about the lionfish, we checked his bathroom, along with a closet and a bank of drawers built into one wall. Since we had no inventory of Light's possessions, it was difficult to say if anything was missing, but our unanimous opinion was that wherever Light had gone, and for how long, he hadn't taken much with him. Our best clue came from the bathroom, which was stocked with the usual personal items, including a razor, shaving cream, deodorant, toothbrush, and toothpaste. There also was a big bottle of AXE body spray for men. Apparently George liked to smell good.

The only thing that seemed odd about the place was a small desk in one corner of the living room: odd not for its contents, but because of the lack of them. There was nothing sitting on top except a blue computer mouse along with its pad. We took a peek and all three drawers were completely empty.

"What do you make of that?" Stella asked me.

"If I had to guess, either Light took everything with him, or somebody else did. I mean this trailer is small enough, why cram in a desk if you aren't gonna' use it?"

"My thinking exactly," Stella replied. "I bet it was those two guys last night in the SUV, and they took his computer."

"What do we do next?" Wilson asked.

"First thing is to try his phone. But Sam, why don't you make the call? Then if he answers just make up a story so he won't get suspicious that the law is after him."

"A story about what?"

"Oh, I don't know. Maybe you're at the bar with Mo Murikami having an argument about a drink recipe?"

"That could work, I suppose."

Stella gave me the number and I punched it in, but it only rang once before going to message.

"Nothing," I said.

"Alright Oscar, let's get a BOLO out on that Toyota. The guy's gotta be someplace. And we'll want a stakeout here. Hope I can persuade the boss to spring for the personnel."

"I can stay here tonight, Stella, if that would help," Wilson said.

"Thanks, Oscar, you're a prince. Be sure and keep me in the loop if anything happens."

"What about family?" I asked.

"Good question," Stella said. "We really don't know anything about this guy's background. Guess I need to go talk with Weatherbee again." She stopped and sighed. "He's such a charmer I can't wait."

~ ~ ~

For the next two days pretty much nothing happened. Then on the third day I got fired. Sort of.

Stella called early, said something important had come up, and we should meet in her office as soon as possible. It took me twenty minutes. She was at her desk when I walked in, and I could tell from the look on her face that something was wrong. She pointed to an empty chair and invited me to sit. There was no offer of coffee, which was unusual.

"Last night word came down from the Sheriff." She looked down at a notepad lying on the desk, and began to read off it. "Since your investigations at the Purple Isle seem to be coming to an end, and they no longer have anything to do with fish or fishing in any event, the services of Mr. Sam Sawyer are no longer needed and are an unnecessary expense."

"Yeah, I can see how that $500 a week might break the county."

I regretted it the minute I said it. "Sorry, Stella. I know this wasn't your idea."

"No it wasn't, Sam. But it is what it is."

I thought about what had happened, and wondered about the actual reason. Was I close to something? Did I know something about the Broom case that was making somebody uncomfortable? If so, what was it?

"This doesn't mean I really have to quit, does it?" I asked Stella.

"You're a free man, Sam. Free to do as you please. I can't tell you where to go or what to do. And god knows I could use your help, despite what the Sheriff thinks. But if you do decide to continue your—investigations—there is one favor I need to ask."

"Sure. What?"

"Don't go near Fiona Broom, or Norb Padilla, or Royal O'Doul. I've pretty much come to the conclusion that one of them—probably whoever worked with George Light to murder Arthur Broom—is tight with the Sheriff. If you bother that person, the word is sure to get back to him, and that could mean trouble for both of us. Big trouble."

"Okay, but what about you? Will you be talking to those three? I thought you'd decided it would be a waste of time."

"That was before George Light disappeared. I've already had a chat with Padilla, and I'm tracking down the other two."

"What did Padilla have to say?"

"Just what you'd expect. He denied having anything to do with Broom's death. Said he barely knew George Light. Which was hard to believe, since I know he drinks at the bar. But like I said before, we've got nothing on any of these people in terms of actual evidence."

"Except motive."

"The key to this whole case is George Light. We've gotta find that guy, Sam."

"Were you able to learn anything about his family or his background?"

"I did. He grew up on a truck farm west of Homestead. His parents still live there along with his brother. But when I called they hadn't heard from him in over a week, and they had no idea where he might have gone. They sounded pretty worried when I told them he wasn't showing up for work."

"What would you like me to be doing?"

"Oh hell, Sam, I'm not even sure what I should be doing, let alone you. Help us look for Light, I guess." She wrote something a notepad and handed me the slip of paper. "Here's a description of his car, along with the plates. Just keep an eye out as you go about your other business."

"Which is back to guiding I suppose. What about the stakeout on his trailer? Maybe I could help with that."

"No, we've got that covered. And before you ask, so far nothing. No sign of Light and not even that mysterious black SUV."

"Do you have a BOLO on Light?"

"Of course. We've sent it out to all law enforcement agencies in the Keys, as well as the rest of Monroe County and Miami-Dade. We got a photo off his driver's license, plus a description of the car. So far, nothing."

Death of a Glades Man

~ ~ ~

A patrol deputy found George Light's Toyota three days later. It was in the parking lot next to the Publix supermarket in Islamorada. There was nothing inside it besides the usual registration papers and a receipt from Jiffy Lube dated six months earlier. There was no sign of the man himself.

Chapter 34

A week went by and still nobody had found George Light or heard from him. In between fishing trips I made intermittent contact with Stella, just to keep abreast of things. She told me she was becoming increasingly discouraged. Without Light, she said, the Broom case was stuck. She'd managed to talk with all three of our remaining suspects, assuming Lou Farrelli was off the list. Fiona Broom, Norb Padilla, and Royal O'Doul all denied having anything to do with Arthur Broom falling into the fishpond at the Purple Isle club. Anthony Hernandez had long since released Broom's body to Fiona, and she'd taken his remains back to New York for burial in the family plot. The Sheriff—Stella said—was pushing her to find Light, convict him of the murder, and be done with it.

I'd been having trouble with my Yamaha outboard. Because Snooks was way better than me at dealing with the idiosyncrasies of internal combustion engines, I asked him to come over to see if he could figure out what was going on. After tinkering for the better part of an hour, while I stood on the dock watching and listening to him mutter things I didn't understand, he announced that he'd come up with a diagnosis.

"It's your fuel pump," he said. "It's not quite dead yet. But if I were you I wouldn't wait for that to happen somewhere out in the bay."

"Would they have a new one at the West Marine store?" I asked.

"Maybe. Maybe not. But I know a guy down in Marathon who repairs 'em. Shall I yank yours out, and maybe we can go down there together?"

"That would be great, thanks."

Thirty minutes later we were on the road, heading for Marathon. Snooks' friend was expecting us.

Just beyond the small village of Layton, there's a big county landfill. Locals call it Mount Trashmore. The mound stands taller than anything else in our part of the Florida Keys. It's visible for miles out in the bay, which is testimony to the lack of other topographic features, and also to the increasing numbers of people in the area making garbage.

An ornithological feature of Mount Trashmore is the large numbers of vultures that hang out there, attracted as they are to odors of decay. As expected, there were perhaps a dozen of those big black birds circling around the landfill as we drove past it on the way to Marathon.

What I didn't expect was an even larger concentration of vultures just a short ways farther on. They were on the bay side, but there wasn't any way to see what might have attracted them to this particular spot, because a dense stand of mangroves grew between the road and the gulf.

"That's odd," I said.

"What's odd?" Snooks asked.

"Didn't you see all those vultures back there?"

"Yeah. So?"

"So I'm used to seeing vultures back by the landfill, but not down here. Or at least not that many. I think we should take a look."

Snooks remained skeptical. "What for?" he asked, not unreasonably.

"Just a hunch."

I found a place where we could pull off to the side of the highway, where the beach was close enough you could see it through the mangroves. The circling vultures were no more than a couple hundred yards back up the road. I pulled a bottle of DEET out of the glove box and lathered up.

"You going through there?" Snooks asked.

"Yeah. I'll be right back. Shouldn't take too long."

Snooks sighed as he exited the passenger side of the Jeep. "I probably should go along, even though I have no idea why we're doing this. If you get eaten by a crocodile, somebody should know about it."

We set off, slogging and splashing our way through the mangroves. It took us better than fifteen minutes to move no more than twenty yards. As soon as we broke out of the mangroves, I looked north, back up along the beach. Something big was up there, lying on the shore.

When we got close enough I could tell it wasn't a crocodile. Instead it was a dead human. Five vultures were standing on it, pecking away, while twenty or thirty more were in the air overhead.

The body was face down in the sand. It was wearing a white t-shirt and green Bermudas but no shoes. There was a hole in the back of the head that looked like it might have come from a bullet. I bent down, grabbed the body by one shoulder, and rolled it over. There was another hole where its left eye once had been.

"Jesus," Snooks said, as he backed away from the body. "What gave you the idea this is what those birds were after?"

"Just a hunch, like I said."

"You and your hunches."

The hole in the eye could have been from a second bullet, or perhaps it was the work of the vultures. I knew that eye sockets were among the first places where scavengers gained access to a carcass. But even in its present decayed and half-eaten condition, I knew who we were looking at.

I pulled out my phone and dialed Stella Reynard.

"We just found George Light," I said. "Or what's left of him."

Chapter 35

Two weeks went by after we'd found George Light's body, without any significant developments. Somebody obviously had killed the man, but there had been no progress on figuring out who. As to why he'd been murdered, there was general agreement. Somebody wanted to shut him up, and that somebody had to be our prime suspect, not only for Light's murder but for Arthur Broom's as well. The Sheriff could hardly ignore the fact that somebody had killed George Light, so he'd backed off Stella and was letting her do her job. But so far she'd hadn't come up with anything solid. They'd recovered two slugs in George Light's skull, both from the same 0.38 caliber pistol. The working hypothesis was that the killer or killers had dumped Light's body somewhere out in the bay, but—as Stella put it—"they must have forgotten the cement shoes."

I went back to guiding and Katie resumed teaching her class in basic forensic science. We learned that Fiona Broom had resigned from the Purple Isle, probably just before they kicked her out anyway because she wasn't a fisherperson. State Senator Snodgrass had been asked to join, even though Lou Farrelli was no longer around to promote him. But perhaps the most surprising development was that Royal O'Doul also had quit the club. In fact, he'd moved his whole operation out of Florida and over to the Gulf Coast of Texas. Apparently he'd given up on tarpon and set himself a new goal: to catch the world's record redfish on a fly. At the same time he was going to develop a new suite of fancy golf courses. Or that was the story Stella got from Ralph Weatherbee when she asked him about it.

~ ~ ~

Katie and I were at the Safari Lounge one afternoon, enjoying sweet tea and Flo's special nachos. Prince was downstairs entertaining the cats when I got a call from Stella. I hoped it was good news, or at least some sort of news.

"I'm gonna be out of town for a while," she said. "Thought you'd want to know."

"What's up?"

"I went to the funeral for George Light a couple of days ago up in Homestead. You know, just to see who was there."

"Like maybe his killer? I've heard that cop rumor about murderers showing up at their victims' funerals, but I didn't know there was any truth to it."

"Yeah well, there wasn't in this case. Or at least not that I could tell."

"No club members? None of our usual suspects?"

"Nope. The only people I recognized at the service were Ralph Weatherbee and Jacques Petain."

"Huh."

"But something interesting did happen. Light's service was at a Baptist Church in Homestead, with burial afterwards in the family plot on their farm west of town. After that was over, I went up to Light's family to express my condolences and to promise we were doing all we could to find his killer. You know, the usual spiel."

"Who were his family?" I asked.

"His parents, a brother and a sister. I got the impression the brother manages the farm, but they all live there except the sister, who's away at college. Anyway, I was about ready to leave, when the brother—his name is Paul—said 'You probably don't know it, but we're standing on what was supposed to be the 18th green. But now that's all gone, along with George. We were gonna be rich—*really* rich—and now all we have left is this crummy piece of land.' Or something to that effect."

"Their farm was going to be a golf course?"

"Yeah, apparently. But Paul told me his dad refused to sell to the developer, among other reasons because his sister was studying agriculture at Arizona State, and she wanted to come home and run the farm. The golf course guy kept pushing, but Paul's dad refused to budge. Finally the guy gave up and actually left Florida."

Stella stopped, probably to let that sink in. "Which is why Sheriff Spivey has authorized my trip to Kleberg County, Texas, to meet with the sheriff down there. I'll be taking Oscar Wilson with me, in case I need backup."

"Kleberg County. That's on the Gulf, right?"

"Right."

"Good luck with that one," I said.

"Thanks," she said. "I think I'm gonna need it. Buy here's something you might want to consider. The Sheriff has authorized three plane tickets. Want to come along?"

I thought hard about that, for maybe five seconds. "Wouldn't miss it."

"What was that all about?" Katie asked after the call had ended.

"That was Stella, chasing a suspect. And it looks like I'm gonna be in on it."

THE END

ACKNOWLEDGMENTS

Our thanks to Captains Steve Friedman, Eddie Yarbrough, and Billy Dahlberg for sharing their passion and deep understanding of Florida Bay and the Everglades backcountry. We are grateful to John Helzer for keeping the boat running so we could get out there, and for being the best sort of fishing companion. Thanks to our family for all their support, and especially to our daughter Laura, a loyal reader and booster. Fellow members of the Red Herrings writers' group, Milt Mays, Jean McBride, and Beth Eikenbary, provided critical feedback on both content and style. Thanks to Beth Steele and Brandon Fies, who have made our stays in the Keys more comfortable than we have a right to expect. Finally, we thank John T. Colby Jr. and his colleages of Absolutely Amazing eBooks for their editorial assistance.

ABOUT THE AUTHORS

Carl and Jane Bock are retired Professors of Biology from the University of Colorado at Boulder. Carl received his Ph.D. in Zoology from the University of California at Berkeley, while Jane holds three degrees in Botany, a B.A. from Duke, an M.A. from the University of Indiana, and a Ph.D. from Berkeley. Carl is an ornithologist and conservation biologist. Jane is a plant ecologist and an expert in the use of plant evidence in criminal investigations. She is co-author with David Norris of *Forensic Plant Science* (Elsevier-Academic Press, 2016). The Bocks have co-authored numerous articles and two books based on their fieldwork in the Southwest: *The View from Bald Hill* (University of California Press, 2000), and *Sonoita Plain: Views from a Southwestern Grassland* (with photographs by Stephen Strom; University of Arizona Press, 2005).

Now largely retired from academic life, the Bocks have turned their creative efforts toward fiction writing, and are co-authors of two ongoing mystery series, the Arizona Borderlands Mysteries and the Florida Keys Mysteries, both published by Absolutely Amazing eBooks and J. T. Colby & Company, Inc., New York.

The Arizona mysteries include *Coronado's Trail* (2016), *Death Rattle* (2017), *Grace Fully* (2021), and *Day of the Jaguar (2021)*. The Florida Keys mysteries include *The Swamp Guide* (2018), *The White Heron* (2019), and the present volume.

Today the Bocks divide their time between Colorado, Arizona, and Florida, mostly fly fishing (Carl), fighting crime (Jane), and writing.

Thank you for reading.
Please review this book. Reviews help others find
Absolutely Amazing eBooks and inspire us to keep
providing these marvelous tales.
If you would like to be put on our email list to receive
updates on new releases, contests, and promotions, please
go to AbsolutelyAmazingEbooks.com and sign up.

AbsolutelyAmazingEbooks.com

or AA-eBooks.com

For sales, editorial information, subsidiary rights information
or a catalog, please write or phone or e-mail
AbsolutelyAmazingEbooks
Manhanset House
Shelter Island Hts., New York 11965-0342, US
Tel: 212-427-7139
www.AbsolutelyAmazingEbooks.com
bricktower@aol.com
www.IngramContent.com

For sales in the UK and Europe please contact our distributor,
Gazelle Book Services
White Cross Mills
Lancaster, LA1 4XS, UK
Tel: (01524) 68765 Fax: (01524) 63232
email: jacky@gazellebooks.co.uk

Printed in the USA
CPSIA information can be obtained
at www.ICGtesting.com
LVHW081746031123
762986LV00046B/1045